EVERY NOBLE KNIGHT

Recent Titles by Maggie Bennett from Severn House

THE TAILOR'S DAUGHTER
THE UNCHANGING HEART
STRANGERS AND PILGRIMS
EVERY NOBLE KNIGHT

EVERY NOBLE KNIGHT

Maggie Bennett

severn House

This first world edition published 2012
in Great Britain and in the USA by
SEVERN HOUSE PUBLISHERS LTD of
9–15 High Street, Sutton, Surrey, England, SM1 1DF.
Trade paperback edition first published
in Great Britain and the USA 2012 by
SEVERN HOUSE PUBLISHERS LTD.

British Library Cataloguing in Publication Data

Bennett, Maggie.
  Every noble knight.
  1. Great Britain – History – Edward III, 1327–1377 –
  Fiction. 2. Knights and knighthood – Fiction. 3. Historical
  fiction.
  I. Title
  823.9'2-dc23

ISBN-13: 978-0-7278-8166-3 (cased)
ISBN-13: 978-1-84751-429-5 (trade paper)

Dedicated to the members of the Halesworth Branch of the Women's Institute.

All Severn House titles are printed on acid-free paper.

Severn House Publishers support The Forest Stewardship Council [FSC],
the leading international forest certification organisation. All our titles that
are printed on Greenpeace-approved FSC-certified paper carry the FSC logo.

Typeset by Palimpsest Book Production Ltd.,
Falkirk, Stirlingshire, Scotland.
Printed and bound in Great Britain by
MPG Books Ltd., Bodmin, Cornwall.

One

'Make way for a Wynstede!' roared the young horseman, urging his chestnut stallion to a gallop. 'Let's show them, Troilus, show 'em who's master of the field!' And to gasps and rather uncertain cheers Wulfstan's lance knocked that of his opponent from his grasp, unseating him as Troilus thundered on; the horse was in no mood to be reined in, now that his master had scored yet again.

The other competitors ran forward to attend to their fallen friend, though Wulfstan had already swung himself down and was ahead of them.

'My God, Eric, are you hurt?' he asked. 'Say not so!' He held out his hand, and Eric got himself up to grasp it and grin ruefully.

'No broken bones, Sir Galahad, only bruises to remind me for a week to come. The day is yours.'

The youthful horsemen were as impressed by Wulfstan's victory as they were relieved to find Eric not badly injured. It had only been a casual practice session in the tournament field to celebrate the completion of their training at Monseigneur Duclair's military academy.

'Come on, let's broach a cask of wine,' said Jean-Pierre, 'and drink to our noble winner!'

'And ease the pain of the vanquished,' muttered Eric Berowne, straightening up and giving no sign of the impact that had unhorsed him. If there was no obvious injury the Monseigneur discouraged any complaints as unmanly.

The three friends led their horses to the stables, and Wulfstan patted Troilus's neck.

'We've done well, old fellow,' he murmured to the six-year-old chestnut stallion he had brought with him from England five years ago when he had been but a boy of twelve. His

home, Ebbasterne Hall in the Hampshire hundred of Hyam
St Ebba, had not seemed the same to him since his widowed
mother's death and the marriage of his elder brother Sir Oswald
Wynstede; seeing the new Lady Wynstede in his mother's place
had caused resentment between them both. Thanks to Count
de Lusignan, whose wife had been a friend of the Wynstedes,
Wulfstan had been recommended to Monseigneur Duclair's
military school at Lisieux in Normandy, and now here he was,
proficient at horsemanship, swordplay and archery – and
learning something more than the arts of warfare: they had to
study chivalry, correct conduct and good manners, and courtesy
to ladies of all rank as the mark of a true knight, which Wulfstan
hoped one day to become through his prowess as a soldier of
King Edward III, who reigned over large tracts of France in
Normandy, Gascony and Aquitaine.

At seventeen with youthful good looks, broadening shoulders, strong calves and enough hair on his face to warrant
shaving once a week, Wulfstan was a perfect product of the
Maison Duclair, and the youngest among its fully trained
members. He was also a favourite of Madame Duclair who
was English, buxom and motherly, and who sometimes invited
him to sit at table with the family and share their conversation.
Although shy about joining in, he was always happy to answer
a direct question, sometimes from Madame Duclair, or from
one of the ladies like her cousin Madame la Gouvernante who
resembled her, except that whereas Madame Duclair's soft blue
eyes beamed upon the company, la Gouvernante's sharp, intel-
ligent glances missed nothing. The two sometimes whispered
to each other and smiled, giving Wulfstan the uncomfortable
suspicion that they were talking about him, which brought
colour to his cheeks. Though he excelled in the tiltyard and
could wield a sword with confidence, he did not yet understand
the unsettling changes in his young body, the unnamed desires
and dissatisfactions that came over him at times. He had less
knowledge than others of his age about the mysteries of womankind, like Jean-Pierre Fourrier whose talk of conquests among
local girls embarrassed him, the more so since the others had
begun to tease him about his ignorance.

As they made their way across the sunlit cobbled yard and

under the trellised archway covered with June roses, they saw two maidservants at the kitchen door, whispering to each other and giggling.

'That saucy Fifi seems to think I belong to her,' said Jean-Pierre. 'She needn't hope so, for 'twas but the whim of a moment when she lay on the newly cut hay, pretending to be an untouched virgin!' He laughed and waved casually in Fifi's direction. 'What of you, Eric? Have you not yet tasted her honey?'

Eric grunted. 'Not her, but . . .' He hesitated.

'Then who?'

'One of the dairymaids, and too young.'

'Too young? Did you or didn't you?' asked Jean-Pierre, much amused.

'There are some things best not talked over,' Eric muttered, for his one and only experience of coupling with a woman had brought consequences: Ange, a fifteen-year-old dairymaid was carrying a child she said was his, and such things could not be concealed for very long. He confessed as much to his companions, and Jean-Pierre laughed derisively.

'What *you* have to do now is get away from the Maison Duclair before the girl's belly starts to swell,' he said, 'because she'll accuse you to the Duclairs, and then woe betide you! The Monseigneur could force you into marriage, a life sentence, unless *Père* Berowne can pay her off. Get away from here, boy!'

'Wouldn't it be cowardly, to forsake her like that?' asked Eric, and Wulfstan silently agreed, though with no experience in the matter.

'My good fellow, Ange could probably name half a dozen who might be the father, but she's chosen you because you're such a greenhorn!' said Jean-Pierre with a grin. 'The sooner you put the Narrow Sea between you and the Maison Duclair, the better!'

Another peal of female laughter rose in the air, and Jean-Pierre turned to Wulfstan.

'Tell us, Sir Galahad, when did *you* last enjoy a choice little morsel?'

'Never,' retorted the boy. 'And if I had I wouldn't crow about it for all to hear.'

He led Troilus into his stable, wondering why his honest words should make *him* feel a fool rather than Jean-Pierre.

The question now for Wulfstan was what should happen next. Jean-Pierre, Eric and the others were returning to their parents' homes for the rest of the summer, to plan their futures as military men. King Edward was known to be preparing for another invasion of France, and his eldest son Edward, the Prince of Wales, had been appointed as King's Lieutenant of Gascony, which meant that he might arrive in that province at any time. All sorts of stories of the Prince's valour were told, and he was universally worshipped as the young hero of England, only eight years older than Wulfstan, who could dream of nothing better or more exciting than to fight at his side under the flag of St George.

But meanwhile he had to decide on his next move; he knew that he ought to return to the Hampshire hundred of Hyam St Ebba and see his brother Oswald and sister Ethelreda, both married and with families; but his much-loved sister Cecily was dead, drowned in a shipwreck on her way home from escorting him to Lisieux and handing him over into the care of Monseigneur and Madame Duclair. If Cecily had still lived, he would not have hesitated to return to England, at least for a few weeks, but now everything was changed; Cecily's second husband still lived with his widowed daughter Maud, bringing up Cecily's son and daughter who might not know their Uncle Wulfstan if he were to visit them. No matter how he thought about it and pondered what to do, his conscience told him he should return to Hyam St Ebba, while the voice of inclination, equally insistent, advised him to stay in Normandy if he could find a reason for doing so. In the end the Monseigneur solved his problem.

'So, Master Wynstede, your companions have flown home to their nests,' said the stocky, dark-browed man with a short pointed beard. He motioned Wulfstan to walk with him in the tree-lined alley that stretched the length of the grounds of the Maison Duclair. Wulfstan obediently fell into step beside him.

'It is five years since your good sister brought you here,

Master Wynstede, and we know that she was sadly drowned in a shipwreck on her return, a tragedy for her husband and children. Her husband still lives, I believe?'

'Yes, sir. My sister Mistress Blagge was dear to us all,' said Wulfstan, sadly.

'And you blame yourself for her tragic death,' said the Monseigneur with a bluntness that Wulfstan appreciated.

'Yes, sir, I cannot help but think so.' His voice was very low.

'And do you have no wish to see her children, your nephews and nieces?'

'One nephew and one niece, sir, now growing up,' replied Wulfstan, a little embarrassed by this untypical probing into his family history. 'They have been cared for by my sister's . . . by Cecily's sister-in-law and friend, a widow.'

The Monseigneur nodded. 'And do you not wish to see your brother and your other sister, both married and blessed with children, I believe?' he went on, having been discussing the subject with Madame Duclair. 'Have you no wish to visit either household?' He gave Wulfstan a sidelong glance from under heavy-lidded eyes. 'You fear that Master Blagge would blame you for his wife's death?'

'I . . . I fear he might, sir,' answered Wulfstan, his face flaming. What in God's name was this man driving at? They walked on a little way in silence, then Duclair spoke again.

'You appear to be a squire with no knight to serve, and it happens that I am at present without a squire – a manservant, since my last one has been called to Gascony.' He smiled, and turned to look straight at Wulfstan. 'Would you care to fill his place, just over the summer months?'

Wulfstan's jaw dropped, but he quickly recovered. 'Oh . . . er . . . yes, I will – I'd be glad to stay, Monseigneur, to serve you as squire – I mean, I thank you for the honour, sir!' The words tumbled out breathlessly, for he was unable to believe such good fortune. 'Thank you, sir, thank you!'

'Good.' The Monseigneur's mouth curved into a smile. 'Madame Duclair will be pleased, for it is on her recommendation that I offer this position to you. So we shall be in each other's debt, young Wynstede!'

★ ★ ★

As squire to the Monseigneur, Wulfstan's duties involved far greater responsibility than he had known while in training. Not only did he wait upon his lord, grooming his horse and riding at his side through the rich farmlands of Normandy, it was also his duty to act as messenger and receive messages to be conveyed in absolute confidence to the Monseigneur. He prided himself on being so well trusted, for his place in the household was now several degrees higher; he took his turn at helping the new arrivals through their practice of horseman-ship, swordplay, wrestling and archery, all essential skills for a man embarking on a military career, and learning by practice the essential arts of chivalry. Sometimes he was required to oversee their early efforts as horsemen, showing them how to control a trotting horse, then cantering, and how to keep their seat on a steed at full gallop. They had to learn, as he had learned, how to calm a frightened horse, how to keep control of the animal while carrying a lance and shield; and on foot, how to use a dagger and a battleaxe when fighting hand-to-hand in the service of their leader, be he king, prince or duke of the realm appointed to lead an army. The new young candidates deferred to him with gratifying respect, calling him Monsieur Wynstede and not Sir Galahad, as his former friends had done in jest.

His skills at instructing pleased the Monseigneur who compli-mented him openly, and must have confided his satisfaction to his wife again. Wulfstan was aware of the two ladies talking and smiling as at some private joke, and his face flamed, for it seemed that these mature matrons behaved little better than a couple of giggling maidservants; and yet for some reason they made him think of the mysterious sensations which suddenly overcame him at any hour of the day or night, when his most private member seemed to have a mind of its own, and would erect and discharge itself, bringing a certain unex-plained physical release.

It was on a clear evening in August that the Monseigneur beckoned to Wulfstan and asked him to join himself and the ladies, his wife and her cousin, on a steep walk above Lisieux, a well-worn pathway that was stony and overgrown in places. Wulfstan instantly obeyed, and enjoyed the view across the town and surrounding countryside. When the light began to fail, the Monseigneur took his wife's arm, and told Wulfstan to support Madame la Gouvernante while they descended in the growing dusk. The air was warm, and moths fluttered in the light of a half-moon; the Duclairs went on ahead, but Wulfstan had to guide la Gouvernante's hesitant feet along the uneven path. She lightly held his arm, and he could feel the curve of her left breast, soft and ample against his elbow. When out of respect he drew himself a little apart from her, she held on to his arm more tightly, and begged him not to let her fall; he was overwhelmingly aware of her warmth, her perfume, the brush of her body against his.

'It's a lovely evening,' she said softly, but he could scarcely answer; his tongue seemed stuck to the roof of his mouth, while his breathlessness could hardly be accounted for by an unhurried downhill walk. The other couple had disappeared when they reached the back entrance of the Maison Duclair, and the lady no longer hesitated.

'Follow me,' she said, holding his right hand and leading him through a door into a passage in pitch darkness, and along it to a short flight of stairs up to a landing on which there were three doors. She opened one of these and beckoned him in, closing the door behind them and drawing a bolt across it. The last of the daylight showed through the curtains of an open window, and Wulfstan saw a low couch against the opposite wall. He stood uncertainly in the middle of the room, his head in a whirl, half-afraid, half-excited; he did not know what was about to happen, and yet in a way he did know. It was as if he were two people, two Wulfstans, one embarking on the adventure of a new experience, the other standing aside and regarding him with trepidation. What was now expected of him? What, as a man, should he do? Would he be shown up as totally inadequate to satisfy a lady's wish for – or would she denounce him to the Monseigneur for attempting to ravish her, a respectable woman twice his age – and how could he defend himself against such accusations?

While he stood and debated with himself in the half-light, he felt a light touch on his thigh; he put out a hand to touch her in return, and gasped as he encountered warm naked flesh;

while he had stood there wondering, she had removed her gown and headdress. Her dark hair fell tumbling down over her shoulders, and hung down her back. And here she was putting her smooth arms around his neck and whispering, close to his face.

'Kiss me,' she said, and what could he do but obey? He returned her embrace, putting his arms around her and pressing his lips to hers. The sensation was overwhelming; she opened her mouth to kiss him in return, a kiss that left him breathless.

'Touch me,' she murmured as her hands travelled down his body, pulling at the loose tunic and the gipon that covered his nether parts, down to his knees. With a curiously practised hand she unlaced the strings that attached to eyelet holes in his hose.

'Kiss me.' And as they kissed, his garments fell to the floor.

'Let me touch you *here*,' she said, and he drew in a sharp breath. 'And you must touch me *there*, like that, so . . . aaah!'

Her body was pressed against his manhood, which he knew had doubled to twice its size, and was hard and swollen.

'And *here* . . . oh, but you're ready, and we must be quick, *mon chéri*,' she said with sudden urgency, and swiftly led him to the couch, pushing him down to lie on his back on a feather-filled quilt. She put a cushion behind his head, and then with surprising agility for a woman of her build, she stretched herself on top of him, separating her legs so that she sat astride him; he felt her fingers expertly guiding his erection to the secret place between her thighs, warm and moist to receive him. He was breathing deeply and rapidly, as if he had been running. She pulled him more closely inside her – and suddenly there was no couch, no room, no night, no past or future, only an incredible present as he sank into her softness and a stream of life poured out into her, unstoppable, totally beyond his control. He groaned as if in pain, and she too sounded breathless. He had known in theory how a man's body joined to a woman's, but he had never dreamed that it would be like this!

'Madame la Gouvernante,' he said as his breathing calmed; she kissed him lightly, then slid off him and went over to a wash-bowl on a stand below the window. He watched her dip a cloth into it and come over to him, wiping between his legs and the now diminished part of him that had stood to do its duty. She then took a clean towel to dry him. He looked at her shadow, silhouetted against the wall, and tried to seize the hand that held the towel.

'Kiss me again, Madame la Gouvernante!'

'No, the time for kissing is past. Put on your clothes,' she ordered in a firm voice which he hastened to obey while she resumed her silken gown and mantle; her hair still hung loosely down her back.

'Follow me, Monsieur Wulfstan,' she said, taking him by the hand and leading him out of the room, down the uncarpeted stairs, along the pitch-dark passage and out into the warm, velvety night. They were in the kitchen garden of the Maison Duclair.

'Take that path you see there, and go round to the side door,' she whispered. '*Bonne nuit, chéri.*'

But he seized her around the waist, and drew her close to him. 'Madame – Madame la Gouvernante – kiss me, kiss me one more time!'

'No, no, get back to your room, and say nothing of what you have seen of mine.' Her voice held authority, and she did not offer her lips for a final kiss. 'Go on, be quick!'

He had to obey, but first he took hold of her right hand and pressed it to his lips.

'*Merci, Madame la Gouvernante. Merci beaucoup.*'

'*Bonne nuit, Monsieur* Wynstede.' And she turned away, seemingly like a moth to disappear into the night.

The day following his initiation into manhood, Wulfstan lived in a changed world. Every person, every object, everything his eyes lighted upon, every sound that fell upon his ears was different, bathed in a summer glow as he relived that unbelievable interlude with Madame la Gouvernante, which had lasted less than half an hour, but was now recalled as a moment out of time, infinite, endless. Surely it could never have happened, and yet it had; it couldn't be true, and yet it was: no dream could be as real. Facing his students as he put them through their paces of learning the arts of warfare, he wondered whether he looked any different today than yesterday, but they behaved with their usual deference to an instructor. Would his peers, Jean-Pierre and Eric have noticed a change in their virtuous Wulfstan — their *Sir Galahad*? The bolder maidservants flashed him their usual saucy smiles, and the more modest ones averted their eyes as they had usually done since he'd become the Monseigneur's squire.

The question now, of course, was how *she* would respond when they met in the course of the day. Suppose Madame Duclair invited him to join the family table? He went hot and cold at the thought of meeting la Gouvernante's eyes. Would she send him a secret signal, a glance that would acknowledge what had taken place? If so, what should be his response? A brief answering nod? To smile would be disrespectful, considering the difference in their status — but a mere nod might look cold, and he felt nothing but a deep and passionate gratitude for her condescension. And would she honour him again at another time? How soon? Did *she* relive that moment of incredible pleasure over and over again, as *he* did? Surely she must be thinking about him — for surely she couldn't possibly regret it — could she? Part of him longed to see her, yet at the same time he was nervous, almost dreading their next meeting.

At around midday, a butler called to him from the kitchen to run an errand. The man was a senior member of the staff who had charge of the menservants, and he asked Wulfstan to take a couple of wineskins down to the tiltyard to refresh the men who were practising jousting in full armour, helmets down, shields and lances ready to strike an opponent down.

'They must be sweating under all that metal on a day like this,' he said. 'The Monseigneur keeps his men ready for war!'

Wulfstan took the two bulging wineskins and set off for the terrace from which a flight of steps ran down to the tiltyard. Rounding the corner of the house, he came face to face with Madame Duclair and Madame la Gouvernante sitting on a cushioned bench in the sunshine, at work on their embroidery. He stopped short in his tracks: they looked up at him.

'Ah, I hope you're taking those to the tiltyard, Master Wynstede,' said the lady of the house with a smile. 'It is surely cruel of my husband to make them practise in this heat!'

He stood and stared at the two ladies, unable to move or speak, and almost dropped the wineskins.

'Are you not well, Wulfstan?' asked Madame Duclair in some concern. 'Are you feeling the heat?'

Still he stood before them, like a man paralysed. Madame la Gouvernante looked up and stared straight into his eyes as she drew her needle up through the length of fabric on her lap, placing another stitch. Her dark eyes were those of a stranger, cold and authoritative, as was her voice.

'Be on your way, Master Wynstede, don't keep them waiting,' she said, and lowered her head over her work. It was like a douse of cold water in his face, and he recovered his wits, bowing briefly to them both and walking on. She had spoken to him like a servant, as if she had chastised him for his thoughts. He must abide by her wishes, though he burned with humiliation; she clearly *did* regret last night's encounter, and out of respect for her he too must pretend that it had never happened – though he could not possibly forget it.

That afternoon Monseigneur Duclair beckoned his young squire to walk with him in the tree-lined *allée* in the grounds, an ideal venue for quiet, out-of-earshot talks.

'I've been thinking about our young newcomers, Wulfstan,' he said. 'We have French, English, Flemish and a couple of Milanese, all planning to be soldiers on the side of one king or another; we cannot be certain with such diversity.'

Wulfstan nodded, thankful to discuss a subject he understood.

'As you know, Madame Duclair is English, and I have no quarrel with your English King Edward who has Norman blood in his veins. It has come to my ears that Edward's son, much praised for his courage and skill, is planning to invade Gascony with an army. We must never ignore the movements of the military at any time or in any place.'

Wulfstan nodded again, following his lord's reasoning. 'And the newcomers here may be called to serve their leaders sooner than they thought, sire.'

'Exactly so, Wulfstan, you understand me well. So far, our beardless boys seem promising, but they should know the nature of the terrain where they may one day be fighting. I propose to send a few of them, five in fact, on a *chevauchée*, an exploration of Normandy, to learn the geography, the places where a battle may be fought – hills, valleys, forests, points of the compass, the best positions to take up in a battle. It's nine years since the English overcame the French at Crécy, and the French may be ready to exact vengeance. So, young Wulfstan,' he said with a sidelong glance from under heavy-lidded eyes, 'am I right to choose *you* to lead them on this expedition, and share your knowledge, as early as Thursday next?'

To get away from the Maison Duclair was a welcome proposition, and Wulfstan replied eagerly, 'Yes, I would be glad to take charge of them, sire, and I thank you for choosing me!'

'Just as I expected,' smiled the Monseigneur. 'Now that you're an accomplished product of the academy, skilled in the arts of warfare – and of chivalry, for you are skilled at *that* art too, are you not?' His mouth took on a quizzical expression. 'You know how to please a woman, and your standing at the Maison Duclair is much enhanced thereby!'

There was a dreadful silence. Wulfstan could have wished the ground to open up beneath him, for there was no doubt of the meaning of these words, at which the Monseigneur was laughing softly and not unkindly, as if he actually approved of his squire's new status.

In a flash Wulfstan understood everything. The Monseigneur *knew,* and so, no doubt did Madame Duclair. It had all been planned and arranged between them – and Madame la Gouvernante. *La Gouvernante* – the governess, the teacher of children! He burned with humiliation, and for a moment he thought his only course would be to leave the Maison Duclair forthwith and return to England; but meanwhile the Monseigneur was waiting for a response, so summoning up all the dignity he still possessed, he answered coldly, 'I am at your command, sire.'

'Well,' said Wulfstan, 'the youngsters look up to you, and I can safely commit them to your care. Demoins and Lemaitre are high-spirited, and inclined to mock Van Brunt because of his nose – but he's not such a fool as they may think. Eldrige and Merand have their heads well screwed on, and shouldn't give you any trouble. You will ride out with them on Thursday, and I shall have to do without my squire for a short while.'

Wulfstan thought he almost detected an unspoken apology, as if he had acquitted himself well by his reaction. He therefore changed his mind, and resolved to keep to his arrangement to stay at the academy over the remaining summer months.

Even so, he could hardly wait for Thursday.

Two

A shaft of golden September sunlight streamed through a high window of the Cathédrale St-Pierre, and rested on the bowed heads of the six young men kneeling in a group waiting to receive the Sacrament at the first Mass of the day. Young Master Wynstede gave hearty thanks for the privilege of taking charge of them on this expedition into Normandy, and the trust that Monseigneur Duclair had placed in him; he was also thankful in equal measure for the escape it provided from the Maison Duclair. After the revelation that his rite of passage into manhood had been planned by the Duclairs and executed by Madame la Gouvernante, he had avoided contact with them as far as was possible, especially the two women. Madame Duclair, buxom and motherly, had shaken his hand in farewell early this morning, and wished him safe travelling, but his unsmiling response had restrained her from embracing him as she sometimes did, and her cousin had avoided him altogether. When he had met la Gouvernante accidentally in the Maison, indoors or out, the coldness of his glance had equalled her own. She had cheated and humiliated him by her businesslike seduction, and how she must despise him, he thought bitterly – but now I despise her in return.

Kneeling on the marbled floor of the nave, Wulfstan shook his head to dispel such unseemly thoughts while the celebrant priest was consecrating the Bread and Wine, and resolutely set his mind on the adventure ahead. The five young men in his charge were a good mixture, three recruited from families of the aristocracy who could pay the academy's fees, but not the other two. Léon Merand from Paris had inherited a legacy from a godfather, and young Theobald Eldrige from an English shire had won a valuable prize in an archery contest which had needed only another fifty marks from his carpenter father to pay the Monseigneur's annual fee. Léon was twenty, a handsome youth three years older than Wulfstan, and sported a short pointed beard which proclaimed his seniority, while the rest were all younger by two or three years.

'Treat them all the same – have no favourites,' the Monseigneur had advised. 'You have my written instructions as to what landmarks to look out for, and I have supplied you with money enough to buy plain food and perhaps a bed overnight in some farmhouse or manor, and this you will keep in a purse worn under your tunic. There can be no luxuries. Don't choose comfort – be prepared to sleep in a byre or barn – or even under the stars, as soldiers in battle have to do. Speak in Norman French to all that you meet, and remember that you hold the honour of the Maison Duclair in what you say or do. You alone have a sword, which I hope you will not need to use, and the boys may keep a dagger in their belt, but it is *not* to be used for anything but to slice bread or meat. Don't take any nonsense from them, but settle disputes immediately, and don't allow any quarrelling – and keep an eye on the Flemish Van Brunt; the others are inclined to taunt him because of his nose, but he has borne it throughout his life so far, and it has served him as well as a Roman one. This will be a test of your leadership, Wulfstan, and though I cannot foresee who or what you may meet on the way, I trust in your common sense. Now, set forth with my blessing, and come back safe and sound by Sunday!'

So they were off, each sitting astride his horse; young André Demoins riding beside Charles Lemaitre who was bouncing up and down in his saddle for sheer exuberance. These two, like Wulfstan, had their own horses, while the other three rode horses from the Maison Duclair's stables. Wulfstan's stallion Troilus had faithfully carried his young master without mishap.

It was a fine early autumn day, and they made good progress through the lush Pays d'Auge countryside of fruitful farmland and scattered villages with their churches and manor houses, orchards and meadows where brown and white cattle grazed. They met the occasional peasant with a cart drawn by an ox or a cow in horses' harness, and all was a picture of peace and plenty. Wulfstan recalled how his elder brother, now Sir Oswald Wynstede, had gone to fight in the king's army some nine years ago, when the English had defeated the French king's army at the Battle of Crécy, and had looted and ravaged the land. It was never referred to now, because of the sorry figure Oswald had cut, often drunk and incapable, having to be brought home to Ebbasterne Hall by his groom, to be nursed back to health by his widowed mother. Wulfstan had been but a child then, but had heard Oswald shouting and cursing, drinking to blot out the memory of what he had seen and heard. And hadn't there been a Franciscan friar, a friend of the Wynstede family, who had also gone with the army to Crécy, but rarely spoke of his memories of Normandy at war. Was that the same green and peaceful countryside as this, the Pays d'Auge? Surely not! Wulfstan saw himself as a defender rather than an attacker, a knight who would fulfil all the aims of chivalry and be hailed as a hero. Five years at the Maison Duclair had strengthened his determination to reach those heights.

At midday the little band was ready for a rest and some refreshment; Wulfstan reined in Troilus, and suggested that they approach a prosperous-looking farmhouse and ask to buy bread and cheese and whatever was on offer, and to refill their leather water-bottles.

'I will go first,' he told them, 'and be warned that I have only a little money, so we must eat sparingly, for everything has to be paid for. We are not beggars.'

The farmer's wife met them in the yard where geese and chickens scattered at their approach. She smiled at the fresh-faced youths, and dropped a curtsey.

Wulfstan's French was fluent after five years at the Maison Duclair, and he asked courteously if there were any suitable victuals on sale for him and his companions.

'You are most welcome, messieurs. There is good fare to be had at this time of harvest, roast pig and ripe cheese, wheaten loaves, fruit—'

'We ask only for a small repast, good dame,' Wulfstan broke in quickly. 'Bread and cheese will suit us all, and water for our bottles. Our horses also need watering, so if you will direct us to your well . . .'

'As you wish, sire,' she said, dropping another curtsey, and disappeared through the kitchen door. Presently a bearded, thickset man in a short, unbleached shirt and knee-length braies, came out carrying a wooden bucket like a wine cask cut in half.

'There y'are, ye can fetch it y'selves and give the beasts to drink,' he said in a surly tone. 'And I'll see yer money first,' he added, standing before Wulfstan with a belligerent air, casting dark eyes over the group. Demoins and Lemaitre had sat themselves down on a wooden form in the yard, which irritated Wulfstan who had remained standing. He gestured to the two youths to rise, and nodded towards the bucket.

'Take that and go to fetch water for the horses,' he ordered, and turning to the man, asked him to show them the way to the well. Theobald Eldrige grinned at their mutinous faces, but the Flemish Claus Van Brunt joined them, asking if there was another bucket, and one was produced.

'Oh, *him,* he'd as likely bring it back in a sieve,' muttered Demoins, as the three of them followed the man to an orchard, on the edge of which was a covered well. Wulfstan was distinctly annoyed; the Monseigneur had told him to be firm with these boys, and so far there had been no trouble, but only a few hours into their *chevauchée*, he sensed a defiance in Demoins' manner, as if he were testing him out, to see how far he could go with his young leader. Wulfstan knew he should stop trouble before it started, and when the three of them returned with full buckets, he ordered André Demoins and Charles Lemaitre to attend to the six horses before they sat down to eat the crusty bread and creamy cheese set before them on a trestled table. He motioned the others to be seated, and noticed that Van Brunt thanked the dame and a pretty serving wench who came to wait on them, and got a smile in return from the girl, at which he blushed deeply. Wulfstan noticed the amused glance that passed between Léon Merand and Theobald; Van Brunt had a pleasingly open face, and though his large, freckled nose frequently caused mirth, he seemed to be quite indifferent to the jokes.

When Demoins and Lemaitre returned they sat down to the repast and added to it some sweet, rosy apples they had gathered from the orchard.

'One for each of us,' said Lemaitre, 'including our esteemed leader! The branch was near to breaking under their weight, so we've done them a favour. Don't you agree, Monsieur Wynstede?'

Wulfstan frowned. 'You had no right to pick apples without permission,' he said sharply. 'Now I shall have to pay for them out of the allowance I've been given.'

'Oh, is that a problem, Monsieur?' asked Lemaitre. 'Happily, *I'm* not limited to a meagre allowance!' And he drew from beneath his tunic a purse out of which he tipped a handful of silver coins. 'Will that cover the cost?' he asked with feigned politeness, for the money would pay for much more than half a dozen apples.

Wulfstan's mouth set in a hard, straight line. 'You had no right to bring money with you, Lemaitre. This *chevauchée* is to test our initiative and self-denial. I've a good mind to order you to take it back, but your companions are already eating the fruit, so just put your purse away. This is not to happen again, do you understand?'

'If you say so, Monsieur.' The youth's eyes were insolent, and he did not conceal his amusement when the dame reappeared and exclaimed at seeing the money on the table.

'Oh, but this is far too much, messieurs! I can give you newly smoked ham with eggs and a game pie for such largesse!'

Wulfstan could hardly forbid her to supply more food, nor stop the young men from eating it with enthusiasm, but he smarted inwardly, and refused to eat any of the appetising extra fare. Theobald Eldrige and Van Brunt looked at him questioningly for a moment, clearly wondering if they should follow his example, but their stomachs overcame their scruples, and they rather sheepishly helped themselves to it.

'I see you're enjoying the game pie, Monsieur Eldrige,' said Demoins with a grin round the table. 'Would you like another slice? Can I tempt you to take one?'

Poor Theobald felt like guilty Adam when Eve offered him a bite of the forbidden apple. He shook his head and wiped the crumbs from his tunic.

'The sun's past its zenith, and we must move on,' said Wulfstan shortly. He remounted Troilus, and beckoned them to follow him out on to the dusty road. The incident had spoiled the sense of adventure he'd had on the morning ride, and he blamed himself as much as Lemaitre; to report the matter to the Monseigneur when they returned would sound unbelievably petty, like a falling-out between silly girls rather than soldiers in training. He had been outwitted, and there was nothing to be done but press forward. The written instructions told him to go due south on a path that climbed upward through a stony and sparsely populated terrain, which would eventually descend into a wooded valley where there was a large Cistercian monastery; possibly they could stay overnight there. Ordering his charges to follow closely behind him, he urged Troilus forward, hoping that they would reach some kind of stopping place, some habitation, be it a humble cottage or wayside inn, where he could purchase food before nightfall, however plain. The others, well refreshed after their feast at the farmhouse, were content to traverse an increasingly bare landscape, where the view to their right was of thick forest, darkening almost to black in the fading light.

Having surmounted a small rise, they were suddenly confronted by a fork in the road. There were no signposts to point the way before or behind, and the Monseigneur's instructions said nothing of a fork at this point. Wulfstan had therefore to decide which way to take. To go to the right, proceeding due south led directly towards the forest, while to their left the road appeared to turn eastwards and continue uphill. Wulfstan dared not hesitate, and chose to turn right, assuming that the path would skirt the edge of the forest and then lead down to the valley.

'This way, messieurs!' he called, aware of murmurings being made about the purpose of this expedition, and of his ability to lead it. He ignored them, though was somewhat taken aback when the path entered the forest and continued along a track just broad enough to accommodate horses. He rode boldly straight ahead in the half-dark, tired and hungry, trying to quieten a nagging suspicion at the back of his mind that this was not the right way. Monseigneur's directions had mentioned woodlands, but these trees were dark and dense. Their way became narrower, and thorny bushes had closed in on either side. The horses seemed reluctant to pursue it, and there was a shout behind Wulfstan when Léon Merand's horse stumbled over a tree root and almost shook his rider off; fortunately there was no harm done apart from thoroughly disconcerting the horse, but Merand dismounted and spoke quietly to the beast. Wulfstan then gave the order for them all to dismount and lead their horses, proceeding in single file.

The density of the forest shut out the darkening sky, and they had to feel their way forward; progress became slower and slower, until Wulfstan unsheathed his sword and used it to hack away at the undergrowth which now impeded every step they took. The darkness was complete, but there was no silence; the woods were full of scufflings and rustlings as the creatures of the night went about their foraging. An owl hooted, making Van Brunt jump and tighten his grip on his horse's bridle. There were croakings and mysterious whisperings among the trees, and Wulfstan thought of the outlaws that lurked in the forests of England, coming forth at night to steal and plunder and then disappearing before dawn. Were there such bands of robbers in the forests of France? He felt increasingly unsure of himself and his judgement.

The path then seemed to peter out altogether, overgrown with bushes, and they came to a standstill. The mutterings of the company were getting louder, and Wulfstan now seriously doubted that they had come the right way. It was pitch dark, the tops of the trees cutting out moon and stars, and he did not know what he should do. Not generally of a religious nature, he now prayed silently that he was not leading these young men into danger, and when he heard Claus Van Brunt whispering in his own Flemish language, he knew that the boy was also praying for their protection; after all, except for himself and Merand they were hardly more than boys.

Every one of them cried out when there was a sudden horrible screeching quite close to them, like a man in unbearable pain. It was followed by a furious bellowing, and more agonized screaming. Wulfstan crossed himself. Was it a killing, a strangling or a knifing of some unlucky traveller? Was it, heaven forbid, a spirit of the forest, a howling demon – or was it the ghost of one who had perished at this spot? Or a messenger from hell, come to seize their unshriven souls? The hairs on the back of his neck prickled, and the cold, creeping fingers of fear seized him. His heart was pounding, so that he could hardly draw breath, but when more grunts and screams followed, Léon Merand shouted, 'Pigs! It's a wild boar having his way with a female!' Wulfstan heard the shaky laughter of the others, and thought he would faint from sheer relief. Of course, there were boars a-plenty in the forests of France, as in England, but even as he breathed a shuddering sigh of thanks, he knew that the time had come for him to make a decision, either to admit his mistake and turn back, or to struggle on towards whatever lay ahead. These five souls were in his care; on his decision might hang their fates, whether or not they would see their mothers and fathers again. And yet he could not decide, though he prayed desperately to be shown the way, to be granted a sign . . .

And then there came upon his ears from a long way off, the sweetest sound imaginable: far below them he heard the faint distant chiming of a church bell, marking the hours of the night. One – two – was that three? Or four? He could not be sure of the hour, but heaven be blessed, they were within reach of human habitation! The thought gave him the strength to forge ahead, thankful that he had not shown his terror. After a short while the ground began to descend, the path reappeared and broadened into a track. Wulfstan remounted Troilus, and triumphantly called to them all.

'Follow me, boys!' he roared. 'Get on your horses and follow me out of the forest!'

There was a cheer as they obeyed, but they soon encountered another obstruction. The sound of a great snuffling and snorting turned out to be a large herd of pigs being driven up the track by a surly swineherd, to forage among the trees for acorns and suchlike delicacies. Wulfstan's 'Good morning, friend!' was hardly out of his mouth before their horses began to shy and rear in fright among the heavy, noisy creatures. Wulfstan managed to stay in the saddle, but Theobald slithered off his steed, and Lemaitre and Merand dismounted and led their horses through the herd. Demoins shouted, 'Look out, it's the Gadarene swine!' and the swineherd glared at them for upsetting his animals. Once they were past, the track ran straight down to a village, where they found no monastery, just a country church, its bell marking the passing hours. It stood at the centre of a small group of wooden and stone houses arranged around three sides of a cobbled square with the church on the fourth side. A handsome stone house faced the church, taller than the rest, and with a balcony around its upper storey. A plump woman wearing a brown kirtle and laced-up bodice stared in amazement and alarm at the six young horsemen who had cantered into the square.

Wulfstan dismounted and greeted her politely. 'Good day to you, Mistress! We are soldiers of—' He got no further, for the woman recoiled in fear, and began to run towards the tall house.

'It's the English, they're here, they've come!' she shrieked. 'Help, good *Père* Bonnat, they've come for us!'

A man appeared on the balcony. 'What's the matter, Claudine? Who—oh, I see,' he said as his eyes took in the strangers. If Wulfstan and his little band had hoped for hospitality, they were soon disappointed, for they were definitely unwelcome here.

'Who are you, and what are you after?' the man shouted down to them. 'How have you got here?'

'We have come over the hill yonder, sire,' Wulfstan answered, 'through the forest.'

'Liar! One man might cut his way through the trackless forest, but not six men on horseback! Where have you come from?'

'We are from Lisieux, sire, and are on *chevauchée*,' replied Wulfstan, somewhat disconcerted in the face of such hostile questioning. He was about to ask the name of the village and whether they could purchase food here, but the man cut him short.

'You look English to me! English soldiers, come to spoil our land and turn us into slaves of that accursed island! Tell me at once, are you enemies of France?'

Wulfstan was at a loss as to how to answer the question, and hesitated for a moment. He was standing in front of his company, and did not see Léon Merand creep silently up behind him; in a flash he had pulled Wulfstan's sword from its sheath on his belt, pushed Wulfstan aside and stepped forward, holding up the sword in a gesture of truce.

'*He* is an English enemy of France, *mon Père*, and is our prisoner under escort. I am Capitaine Léon Merand of Paris, and we have indeed come over the hill and through the forest. It took us all night, and I have had to cut a way through with my sword. We will pass through your village with peaceful intent, and ask for nothing but to buy a little refreshment and water for ourselves and our horses.'

Wulfstan was thunderstruck, and so were the others, judging by their incredulous gasps. Léon's well-bred Parisian French had clearly impressed the man who then turned away from the balcony to come down to the square. While they waited, Léon muttered furiously to the rest, 'Keep your mouths shut. Don't deny what I've said. Leave him to me.'

The man appeared at the door, and came towards them. He was tall, with an air of authority, and wore the long black cassock of a priest.

'I am *Père* Bonnat, priest and notary of Sailly,' he said, unknowingly giving the name of the village to Léon, who bowed. 'We seldom see military men here. And where are you bound for?'

'We are on our way back to the military academy at Lisieux, *Père* Bonnat, to which place I am returning these boys. They are mainly French and Flemish. We have been on *chevauchée* in Normandy as part of their training.'

'Lisieux is a fair way off, surely? And who is this prisoner, and where are you taking *him*? And why did you make him your spokesman?'

'I have to be careful, *Père* Bonnat,' answered Léon promptly. 'I needed to find out the allegiances of your village, whether you would welcome us or our prisoner. Is it possible to detain this fellow here?'

'Indeed, Capitaine! I have a cellar, a prison cell beneath my house, securely locked. I seldom have to use it, but you may leave this fellow here while you go on to Lisieux without the encumbrance of him.'

'Ah, that is a most gracious offer, *Père* Bonnat,' said Léon with another bow, 'but what we truly beg for is some refreshment after our ordeal. There are five of us and six horses. I . . . We will pay you well,' he added, thinking of Lemaitre's purse of silver coins.

'Good! I shall give you breakfast, and your horses may drink from the trough in the square. And your prisoner will stay with me, to save you the trouble of guarding him.'

Léon hesitated. He suspected that Wynstede would in fact be a hostage, to ensure that 'Capitaine' Merand and his youthful band would behave themselves and leave Sailly without causing any trouble. He decided to accept the offer for the time being, and ordered Wynstede forward.

'I thank you, good *Père* Bonnat, and ask that this man too may be given breakfast; he has had very little to eat for the past day and night.'

'Huh! He'll get bread and water, and be thankful. We don't fatten up our enemies. So, Capitaine, I will see that you and your young charges are given hospitality in Sailly – and I'll call my guard to escort *him* to the cellar. You are welcome!'

Wulfstan felt as if he were in the grip of a nightmare, so soon after their deliverance from the forest. Why had Léon taken his sword and told such a string of lies? While waiting for Bonnat to call for a guard, he turned his head and looked straight into Léon Merand's eyes in a silent question. The self-styled 'Capitaine' did not flinch from his gaze, but closed his left eye in a deliberate wink of reassurance.

As he was led away to the cellar, *Père* Bonnat invited the others to partake of bread, bacon, cheese and a light wine set out by Claudine on a table in the square. They were utterly mystified by Merand's behaviour, not having seen the wink he had given Wulfstan, but dared not ask questions. The priest stood over them, and when they had finished, showed them the way out of Sailly on the road that ran north-east towards upper Normandy. They had no choice but to be on their way, though Troilus absolutely refused to leave without his master.

'See that you smile and wave farewell to the man,' Merand ordered, for any reluctance to leave on their part would arouse suspicion. They rode for about three miles, passing the empty and odorous piggery on their way, until they came upon a shady bank on the edge of a wood. Merand halted, and told them that here they would stay and rest, out of sight of the road. They dismounted and stretched out on the grass, but did not rest, for they now had the opportunity to challenge Merand.

'Why in God's name did you step in, and why did you snatch his sword?' they demanded. 'Why did you lie to that priest? Why have you left him there, a prisoner?' And the most urgent question of all, 'What are you going to do about him now? How is he to be rescued?'

Merand answered that he cared about Monsieur Wynstede as much as they, but he had feared that they might all be taken prisoner because of Wynstede's uncertain replies. By posing as a French capitaine, he had got the five of them out of danger and secured a good breakfast. They continued to accuse him.

'Yes, *we're* free, but our leader's in a miserable cellar, under lock and key,' said Eldrige. 'I for one will go no further until he's out of it.'

Merand tried to reassure them. 'And *I* shall go no further. Please believe me, and let us rest a few hours in this place – and tonight under cover of darkness we will go back to Sailly where I have a plan to release our leader. Take it on my word, friends, I have a plan.'

'How can we believe you?' asked Eldrige. 'You have already told so many lies, and can tell a whole lot more. You had better tell us about this plan.'

'Yes, let us hear it,' said Claus Van Brunt, 'and see if we all agree upon it.'

When he told them, they readily agreed to accompany him back to Sailly that evening, each one having his own special part to play.

Wulfstan had never lived through a worse experience than the one he now endured. In the dark of the windowless cellar, he could not rest on the narrow straw mattress against a wall, weary though he was. The guard had come in with a loud clanking of keys, to leave him a crust of bread and a cup of water, and pointed to an earthenware pot in one corner for him to relieve himself. Confusion and bewilderment filled his head, and he relived the speed with which Merand had snatched his sword and taken over the leadership of the *chevauchée,* denouncing Wulfstan and leaving him a prisoner in the priest's cellar. He had been somewhat relieved by the wink Merand had given him, but began to doubt that it had any meaning, other than to give him a sense of false security. He had heard the sound of horses' hooves as his charges rode away, and a distant voice had called out, 'Come on, Troilus, you stupid creature, you're coming with us!' followed by another voice, 'No, leave the stubborn beast here.'

Wulfstan's uncertainty about Léon Merand was his greatest burden: had the man betrayed him? And what would happen to the four other young soldiers under his leadership? Would they ever see the Maison Duclair again? And would the Monseigneur be told a cock-and-bull story about Wynstede's treachery, and Merand's bid to save them? The thought of the Maison Duclair brought back the memory of Madame la Gouvernante, she who had initiated him to manhood: what would *she* be told about his alleged misconduct, and would she care? No, she would be more contemptuous than ever. He groaned aloud, and was almost inclined to give way to despair, but he thought of his mother and his sister Cecily, God rest their souls: what would they say to him if they could see his wretched condition? He knew that they would tell him to put his trust in God and pray.

He fell to his knees, and tried to remember the words he heard every week at the Mass, but to which he often paid little attention, his thoughts straying to more adventurous matters like horsemanship, jousting and his dream of one day fighting alongside the Prince of Wales, his hero in black armour who would one day be King Edward the IV of England.

'*Pater noster, qui es in caelis, sancti − sanctificetur nomen tuum. Adveniat regnum tuum . . .*' What came next? If only Cecily were here to pray with him! She would tell him that God gives ear to all prayers, whether offered up from a great cathedral or a miserable prison cell like this; and that he makes no distinction between rich or poor, young or old, just so long as the words come from the heart. So he began to pray in English, asking Cecily to look down from heaven and intercede for him.

'Listen to my cry, O Father in heaven, and look after those boys; save them from all dangers and bring them safely home.' He paused, and wondered what else she would have told him to pray for. He knew in his heart what he should ask, but was reluctant at first to say the words. Tears filled his eyes as he continued, 'And if Léon Merand has really betrayed me, give me the grace to forgive him as I ask for my own sins to be . . . to be f-forgiven.' The words faded on his lips, but he felt calmer, and a measure of peace came over him, even in this dismal place. He lay down on the mattress, and the sleep that had been denied him for a day and a night now enfolded him in merciful oblivion.

The sun had not risen, but a few pale streaks had appeared in the eastern sky. *Père* Bonnat in his bare white chamber on the second floor had recited the Office of Matins in the dark hour after midnight, for which he needed no candle, for he knew the words by heart. When he'd finished, he crossed himself and settled on his narrow bed to the peaceful sleep of a clear conscience. In her rather more comfortable chamber on the floor below, his housekeeper Claudine had lain awake for some time after retiring, unable to forget the face of the young prisoner as Udo the guard had marched him down to the cellar and locked the door with a clanking of heavy keys. The boy's eyes had been full of fear, and held a question, as if he could not believe what was happening to him, or why. Claudine would never disagree with anything the good priest said or did, but hoped that when he came to question the prisoner, he would discover him to be at least partly innocent of the charges laid against him. Late that evening she had taken a bowl of soup and a hunk of bread downstairs to the cellar, and when Udo had unlocked the door, they found the youth on his knees. His courteous thanks to her for his supper had touched her heart. When he hesitantly asked if *Père* Bonnat would be coming to question him, the guard had shaken his shaggy head.

'Not today, he ain't,' he said, and when the boy raised pleading eyes to Claudine, she had smiled and told him that the priest would probably come to see him in the morning.

Now she curled up on her goose-feather bed and fell asleep, snoring gently.

Udo the guard too was fast asleep on his straw-filled pallet on the landing at the top of the steep stone steps leading down to the cellar. None of them heard at first the menacing sounds approaching from the eastward road: a noise of many pattering steps, of horses' hooves, men's voices shouting – and a grunting and a snorting as if a pack of wild beasts were on their way to Sailly. One by one the villagers awoke and trembled. *Père* Bonnat sat up with a start, and Claudine clutched her sheets around her. Udo remained asleep until the invaders came pouring into the village square; heavy bodies were blundering around squealing in terror, horses were neighing, men were shouting.

'This is war! You're all captured!' the villagers heard as they ran to their windows to look out at the heaving confusion below.

'Holy Mother of God!' cried Claudine, leaping from her bed. '*Mon Père! Mon Père* Bonnat, our enemies have come to kill us all! Help! God have mercy on us!'

The priest shook his head to clear away the nightmare he thought had seized him. Throwing on the long black hooded cote-hardie over his nightshirt, he dashed out on to the landing, and saw Claudine on the floor below, in her nightgown, wringing her hands as a great knocking at the front door reverberated through the whole house.

'Open up! Open this door in the name of King John!' a man shouted as Claudine looked up to see the priest.

'Oh, *Père* Bonnat, bid the angels and saints come to our aid!' she cried.

Bonnat was not without courage, and saying a quick prayer under his breath, he descended the stairs at speed. 'Calm your-self, Claudine,' he whispered, then raising his voice, he addressed the would-be intruder.

'Who are you, and what do you want with us?'

'Open this door or it will be the worse for you!' roared the reply.

Gently easing Claudine aside, the priest drew back the bolts, whereupon a tall man at once rushed in, followed by another, and *Père* Bonnat caught a brief, chaotic glimpse of stampeding pigs, horses, and what he took to be soldiers, all creating a deafening noise. It was too dark to see the face of the man confronting him, but he held up his hands in truce.

'I am *Père* Bonnat, and I'll do what you ask, as long as you do not harm my servants,' he said, just as the second man grabbed him from behind, locking his arms across his back.

'Your keys, priest – your keys, where are they?' demanded the first intruder. 'Give me the keys to the cellar *now*, this minute!'

'Udo! Come and give this man the keys!' called Bonnat, and the guard came lumbering on to the scene, his bunch of keys dangling from his belt. He glared at the man who held Bonnat in a vice-like grip, and lunged towards him.

'Let go o' that man o' God, or I'll throttle yer,' he began, but *Père* Bonnat bid him be quiet as the first man suddenly produced a sword. There was a moment of fearful silence, and then Claudine found her voice and spoke shakily to the bewildered guard.

'Give him the keys, Udo; let him unlock the cellar and free the prisoner, who's but a boy. Give him the keys, and save us all.'

'Yes, go in front of me down the stairs, and unlock the cellar,' said the tall man, giving him a push towards the stairs. Udo muttered but did as he was told, and unhooked the bunch of keys from his belt, handing them to the man who shook his head.

'No, *you* know which one unlocks the door,' he replied, and those waiting above held their breath as they heard the scrape of the huge key turning in the lock. The man slowly drew the door back, and out of the blackness within, Wulfstan's pale face appeared. His eyes lit up with joy at what he saw.

'*Merand!* Oh, Léon Merand, praise be to God, you've come!'

'Quick, up the stairs and your horse is tied outside,' gasped his rescuer, 'and here's Lemaitre to help you get away and join the others on the eastward road while I—fly like the wind, Wulfstan!'

Lemaitre and Wulfstan rushed from the house, soon followed by Merand, leaving the priest and his servants open-mouthed but unharmed.

By now the sun was rising, and the villagers were realizing that their invaders were the five young soldiers from the day before, and the herd of pigs belonging to the swineherd who took them up to the forest each day; the man was speechless with fury, attempting to round them up and promising death to whoever had released them at such an hour and driven the poor beasts into the village square. But the culprits and their horses were already well on the road, and Wulfstan's sword was back in its scabbard.

They rode for a good hour, urging their steeds to a gallop in case they were pursued. Wulfstan noticed that there were flecks of foam around Troilus's mouth, and he called a halt when they came to a junction where a path turned off at a sharp right-angle, down a steep track to where a stream tumbled over glittering stones. Wulfstan hoped that any pursuers had been thrown off the scent, and ordered them to dismount and rest both themselves and their horses beside the stream, cupping the clear water up to their mouths, while the horses also quenched their thirst.

No sooner had they arrived at this refuge than deep regrets, explanations and confessions were expressed, especially by Léon Merand who accepted all blame and responsibility for what had happened to Wulfstan.

'I feared we might all be arrested as enemies of France, Monsieur Wynstede, as you had difficulty with speaking, and I humbly beg your forgiveness for putting you . . . and—'

'You did right, and we may all owe our lives to you, Léon,' said Wulfstan, interrupting him. 'We will say no more about our adventures in Sailly, but let me thank *you*, Léon, and all the rest of you for your daring plan to rescue me from the priest's cellar. Now let's give thanks for our freedom, and make our way due north-east across country to Lisieux!'

The *chevauchée* was pronounced a success when Monsieur Wynstede and his five charges arrived at the Maison Duclair on that Saturday evening. The Monseigneur praised Wulfstan, both openly and privately, for the way he had managed the exercise, and the five newcomers loudly agreed that they had learned a great deal during those three days away, and established a close bond with their leader and with each other.

Wulfstan had less to say; he was thankful to return with no casualties, and considered that he had learned even more than his charges about the courage and loyalty, not forgetting the cunning, that turns an armed man into a soldier and a knight. One day, he thought, I shall put myself and all my knowledge of warfare at the service of Prince Edward when I ride into battle at his side!

Three

Monseigneur Duclair spoke as if to an equal, and his voice was grave.

'Yes, Wulfstan, there are rumours that King Edward is preparing to renew the war and gathering forces together, possibly to invade before the close of this year.' He stopped speaking, seeing Wulfstan's eyes brighten. 'Whether France's present King John is as eager to resume hostilities again, nine years after the bloody Battle of Crécy, is something that cannot be known outside of his court, but he will no doubt have spies on the lookout in danger spots. Rumours may swarm in town and country, but there is no definite evidence that he is stirring up anti-English feeling, not yet.'

'But Monseigneur,' Wulfstan interposed, 'surely I – we – saw evidence enough in Sailly, when half a dozen young fellows, scarcely out of boyhood, were accused of being enemies of France before we even had time to announce that we came in peace. If it had not been for the quick thinking of Léon Merand—'

'Yes, yes, I gather what happened, and I've pondered on the danger I put you in,' said Duclair, a little impatient at being interrupted, and making a dismissive gesture with his hands. 'To me it sounds as if Sailly is one of those remote pockets of human habitation ruled over by a priest, notary, mayor and physician all in one man whose word is law because the unlettered villagers have no other ruler, and such men become bigots and tyrants. No, Wulfstan, if you have ideas of offering your service – and in time of war that could well mean offering your life – to King Edward of England, my advice is for you to wait and see what actually happens, and not give ear to every bit of gossip and speculation that travels across our fair Pays d'Auges. I do not wish for you to go charging around looking for armies that may not even exist.' He paused for a moment, seeing Wulfstan's disappointed look, and continued in an almost fatherly tone, 'You have proved your courage, my boy, and I don't want to see it wasted on inconclusive skirmishes.'

'Thank you, Monseigneur, but . . . well, having learned all I can here in the past five years, it is my greatest ambition to be a soldier in the army of the King of England, and also his son, Prince Edward of Wales, Duke of Cornwall, Earl of—'

'Chester and King's Lieutenant of Gascony, already under English rule,' Duclair finished for him, 'a much exalted and ambitious youngster, scarcely older than yourself.'

'He's eight years older than I, Monseigneur, and by all accounts a sure defender of his father's realm,' replied Wulfstan with some spirit, 'and if the rumours of an English invasion prove to be correct, I have no intention of being left behind.'

'A pretty speech indeed, Wulfstan, and likely to strike fear into the Prince's enemies,' said Duclair with more than a touch of sarcasm, though he spoke good-humouredly. Seeing Wulfstan's flushed face and the determined set of his mouth, the Monseigneur softened his approach and played his next card with no little amusement.

'I think there are other matters with which you should be concerning yourself, Wulfstan, but perhaps good counsel would come better from a woman. You will therefore attend on Madame Duclair in her private chamber this evening before supper.'

'But Monseigneur—'

'Enough. You are dismissed into Madame Duclair's care.'

Wulfstan was thrown into a state of angry humiliation. What on earth would Madame Duclair have to say to him? Was it about Madame la Gouvernante? Would *she* be there? Interviews in the private chamber of master or mistress were usually of a highly confidential nature, so probably not – but if la Gouvernante *was* to be present, Wulfstan cringed at the thought of the embarrassment he would suffer. What a disaster! And yet he had to obey.

'Ah, Wulfstan, how pleasant to see you! We have had little opportunity to converse since you returned from the *chevauchée*, and I haven't yet congratulated you on its happy outcome after the dangers you went through, the courage and tenacity you showed. My husband has scarcely stopped singing your praises!'

Deep-bosomed and motherly, Madame Duclair smiled and beckoned Wulfstan to be seated on a carved wooden chair opposite her own as she plied her needle at embroidering a silky sky-blue shirt; to his enormous relief they were alone. He bowed, thanked her for her kind words, and sat down.

'Will you take wine?' she asked. 'I find that a little drop or two of a red claret is good for the appetite, and we shall be taking supper within the hour.' As she spoke, she poured out a generous measure for him and about half the amount for herself. He took the silver cup from her, annoyed to find himself blushing as he thanked her.

'Now we come to the matter of how you will best use the arts you've learned here at the Maison Duclair,' she went on. 'I've no doubt that you have plans to join the military, and it may be the case that King Edward – or his son, that excellent young man – may be preparing to invade these shores again, or so my husband informs me.'

'Yes, indeed, Madame, it is widely rumoured that . . . er . . . that King Edward may intend to lead an army to subdue any rebels in his French dominions, Aquitaine and Gascony,' answered Wulfstan. 'And I would want to be a part of it.'

'As young as you are, Wulfstan? And knowing how much Monseigneur Duclair and I would like to keep you here as his squire and instructor of new young men desirous of becoming soldiers?'

'Er . . . yes, Madame, but if the King were to assemble such an army, I would . . . er . . . want to join it as a swordsman or an archer, as a cavalryman or as a foot soldier,' he replied a little more firmly, because he thought he could see that she was attempting to dissuade him.

'I can see how determined you are to be a military man,' she said with a smile, 'and I shall not waste time trying to change your mind! No, the reason I'd like you to put off your military career for a while is to do with the family you have left behind in England. I am an Englishwoman, as you know, and I feel sympathy for them.'

'Madame?' Wulfstan said uncertainly, not understanding her drift.

'Your family, my boy,' she said in her soft maternal way, looking up from her embroidering and fixing her large blue eyes on his. 'You have no parents, but should you not visit your brother and sister, and make yourself known to your nephews and nieces – especially the girl and boy born to your sister Cecily who brought you here five years ago?'

Now he saw what was coming: her husband had clearly been discussing the matter with her. He shook his head.

'My brother and sister are both married, and any children they've had were born since I've been here, so I don't know them, Madame.'

'Ah, but your brother Sir Oswald Wynstede would surely like to settle family matters before you go to war, Wulfstan – and forgive me for being blunt, I'm talking of money, of course. Arrangements should be made about your portion of the inheritance that would be due to you in the event of . . . of your brother's death, or your own. You should see him and talk such matters over, don't you agree?'

Wulfstan took another sip of wine. 'My brother would surely see that I got my fair portion of the Ebbasterne estate, Madame.'

'Hm.' She made a doubtful little sound. 'So often these things are not recorded in writing by an attorney, and then later there are family feuds which are very regrettable.

'And that isn't all, Wulfstan. What of Cecily's children? They are a boy and a girl, I believe, getting towards ten years old. Do you not feel any responsibility towards *them*, seeing that they have no mother?' She glanced at him shrewdly, and he lowered his eyes.

'Katrine and Aelfric have a kind aunt, a widow and sister-in-law of their mother's,' he said. 'They live with her and their grandfather, Master Blagge.'

'Grandfather? Not their father?' She sounded surprised.

'No, Madame, my sister Cecily was married twice, first to Blagge's son, the father of Katrine and Aelfric – until he died of the black plague, and she married his father who'd lost his first wife.' He hesitated. 'Old Master Blagge is a . . . a disagreeable man, and I was very sorry that Cecily was forced into marriage with him because the family finances were at a low ebb, and he was a wealthy cloth merchant.' At this point, Wulfstan could scarcely hide his true feelings. 'Oh, Madame, I hated that man, and I've no wish to see him again!' He lowered his head between his hands, hardly able to stifle a sob. Madame Duclair put down her embroidery, rose and came to stand beside him, putting a soft, plump arm around his shoulders. For a moment he remembered his motherless state, and was tempted to lay his head upon her maternal bosom, but recollected himself in time to listen to her.

'Thank you, my dear boy, for telling me, and I'm sorry I've stirred up bad memories,' she said quietly. 'I shall say no more about your duties towards your family, but will leave the matter in your own hands, to do as you think best. Now then, finish your wine, and we'll go to supper – you'll be wanting to jest with your young companions!'

By which the tactful lady meant that she would not ask him to join the family table where he would have to face Madame la Gouvernante.

Wulfstan told the Monseigneur that he had decided to visit his relatives at Hyam St Ebba before making any decision about his future as a soldier.

'Well done, you're showing yourself to be as wise as you are brave!' said Duclair approvingly, and added, 'Remember that you're going to see Cecily's children, not old Master Blagge who may accuse you of causing his wife's death. Hold your head up high – and give my salutations to the Count and Countess de Lusignan – you're related to them, aren't you?'

'Yes, sir, my sister Ethelreda married their second son. I'll certainly be seeing them.'

'Very well. Will you take Troilus with you?'

'Yes, sir, though I'm sorry to subject the old fellow to a sea crossing. I shall leave next week from Honfleur, and sail for Southampton.'

'May God go with you, my boy. Madame Duclair and I will pray for you and await your return as for a son.'

After a crowded, stomach-churning crossing of the Narrow Sea on a cog carrying two other horses on their way back to England, Wulfstan was thankful to reach the busy English port. There seemed to be an expectancy in the air, with crowds everywhere, mariners and militia alike swarming around its inns and brothels. Wulfstan decided to take a meal at one of the pie-shops before setting off up through Hampshire to where the hundred of Hyam St Ebba lay on its border with Surrey. A crowd of laughing soldiers gave a roar as he entered a shop where pies were sold to eat straightway, and he felt conscious of his youth. Having bought his dinner, he went outside to where Troilus was tied to an iron ring in the wall, and ate standing up, wondering why the town seemed so busy.

'It can't be – it *is*! Sir Galahad himself!' he heard an eager voice declare, and turned to look into a familiar face – his friend who had trained with him at the Maison Duclair, Eric Berowne! They gave each other a rough embrace, and Wulfstan offered to share his pie.

'No, thanks, I've dined already – but tell me about yourself, old chap! Will you be sailing on this tide, or do you wait for tomorrow? Splendid if we can go together!'

Seeing Wulfstan's puzzled expression, Eric quickly explained that Edward, the Prince of Wales, was about to take a small army over to France, with the intention of putting down an incipient rebellion in Gascony.

'Just what we've been waiting for, Wulfstan! This is what all our training was about, to make us true professionals in the service of the King. Have you not heard of it?'

Wulfstan replied that there had been rumours, but no definite news. 'But Eric, this is a great misfortune for me, for I can't come with you!'

'Why in God's name can you not?'

Explanations followed, but Wulfstan's duties towards his family did not convince Eric. 'But *of course* you must come with us! Are you not a loyal subject of the King and his son? This is what we've been waiting for, all that time at the Maison Duclair!'

Wulfstan was sorely tempted to believe that his primary duty
was to follow the Prince to Gascony, but here he was, a devoted
admirer of the young prince, going in the opposite direction,
to visit a place he no longer looked upon as home. He was
about to change his mind when he remembered Madame
Duclair and her motherly advice, so gently given: and he could
not go back on his word.

'When I've got through the visits I have to make at Hyam
St Ebba, and settled my business there, I shall return to France
and join the Prince's army as soon as I can, wherever it is. I
can say no more than that, Eric.'

'I can only say I'm surprised, but it's your decision,' said
Berowne with a shrug, and Wulfstan thought he heard a certain
contempt in the words.

'Is Jean-Pierre Fourrier with you?' he asked.

'He'll be joining the army at Bordeaux. So, I wish you joy
of your business with your relations, *Sir Galahad* – to get your
legal affairs settled and be sure of your portion.'

He remounted his horse and turned away. Wulfstan watched
him go, and suddenly wondered what had happened to Ange
the dairymaid, whether or not she had carried Eric's child;
he had not asked Eric about her, nor had he told him about
the *chevauchée;* how would Eric have judged him if he knew?
It made no difference now, he had made up his mind, and
turned Troilus's head towards the road north.

The sun was westering down to the horizon when Troilus
raised his handsome head and sniffed the air: did *he* remember
Hyam St Ebba after five years away? Wulfstan wondered. There
was the valley again, and the demesne of Ebbasterne Hall, the
harvested cornfields, the orchards bearing ripe fruit, and beneath
the trees the pigs foraging; the cows and sheep grazing in
meadowland, the great field divided into strips belonging to
the tenants who farmed them for their own families' sustenance.
Here lived Sir Oswald Wynstede, knight and landowner, married
to Janet Blagge, sister-in-law to Wulfstan's beloved sister Cecily,
and there, down in the town stood Blagge House where Cecily's
children lived with their widowed Aunt Maud and grandfather,
old Master Blagge. Some ten miles further up the valley, perched

on a rocky outcrop stood the Castle de Lusignan, home of the Count and Countess whose elder son had fallen at Crécy, and whose younger son's marriage to Ethelreda Wynstede now united the two families. The Count kept a home-trained army ready to depart at any time to fight the king's battles, and put down insurrections at home and in Scotland.

And there, on the opposite side of the valley, its stonework bathed in the rosy glow of evening, stood the Abbey of St Ebba where the holy monks prayed for the world outside its walls. The brotherhood had almost been wiped out by the plague, now being referred to as the Black Death, some seven years ago, but the community had built up again under a new Abbot. He remembered that his sister Cecily had nursed the stricken monks in the Abbey, where no women were usually allowed, and that there had been a monk, a Franciscan friar who had toiled alongside her, both miraculously untouched by the dreaded plague which claimed lives all around them.

And now Wulfstan rode down towards Ebbasterne Hall, his childhood home where his brother Oswald was now the master, and elevated to Lady Wynstede was Mistress Janet Blagge, whom Wulfstan had not been able to bear seeing in his mother's place. Dear Cecily had used her influence with the de Lusignans to obtain a place for him at the Maison Duclair – and had insisted on accompanying him there. It was on her return journey across the Narrow Sea that she had drowned in a shipwreck; and this was the reason that Wulfstan had never been back to visit Hyam St Ebba.

Until now, as he contemplated going to fight in France with Edward, Prince of Wales. He patted Troilus's side. 'Come on, old fellow, take me down to face them all!'

Everybody remarked on the change in Wulfstan, from a rather sulky boy of twelve to this fine, strong, tall young man – though he observed with a smile that it would have been strange if he had *not* grown in five years.

Oswald greeted him with a brotherly embrace, and Janet held out a cool cheek for him to kiss. It was strange to see Ebbasterne Hall and its estate again, somehow not as grand as he remembered it from his childhood.

'The bailiff acts as go-between with the tenant farmers,' Oswald told him. 'They grumble at having to pay tithes to the Abbey, and I have to take rent for their houses, but they know when they're well off, and there aren't many protests.'

Remembering how their mother, Lady Katrine Wynstede, had visited the homes of their tenants with food, kindling and other comforts, and allowed the old and infirm to live in the great hall, to sleep near to the glowing embers of the fire and be fed from the kitchen, Wulfstan innocently asked if this still happened. Lady Janet was quickly on the defensive.

'What time have *I* got, with four young children to bring up?' she demanded. 'The twins are delicate, and the others very young. I certainly don't allow riff-raff to make a bed here for themselves overnight, nor do I take in the old and crazy, making messes in the straw – there's no telling what fleas and fevers they'd bring into the Hall!'

The twins were girls, six years old, with a brother aged three and another not yet a year old. Janet soon made it clear that he was a stranger to them, and not to frighten them by attempting to play the familiar uncle. Feeling constrained and unwelcome indoors, he chose to walk with Oswald and the two dogs on the estate.

'It must seem strange to you after being away for so long, Wulfstan,' his brother began. 'The unfortunate circumstances of my . . . of our sister's death was a bitter blow to us all, and of course there are those who said, and still say, that had she not accompanied you to Lisieux, she would be alive today, a happy mother to little Kitty and Aelfric. Her loss was felt keenly by the Wynstedes and the Blagges . . .' He spread his hands and sighed.

'Do *you* blame me for leaving Hyam St Ebba and going to learn the art of warfare in France?' asked Wulfstan bluntly. 'And does Lady Wynstede blame me?'

'Oh, no, not at all,' said Oswald quickly, for his wife had been extremely thankful to be rid of her young brother-in-law. 'But perhaps you'd better avoid speaking about the past, comparing how it was in our parents' time from how it is now,' he added apologetically.

'You don't mind, do you?'

'Of course not,' Wulfstan replied, in fact feeling sorry for his brother.

'I just like to keep my head down and avoid upsets,' said Oswald, and to change the subject spoke of the management of the demesne of Ebbasterne Hall, and how he relied on his excellent bailiff, Dan Widget.

'Dan Widget? Is *he* your bailiff now? Dear old Dan, the best groom we ever had – and he came with Cecily and me on that journey to Lisieux. How did *he* escape the shipwreck?'

'Sheer good luck, it seems. He was the only survivor, and found himself floating among the wreckage – managed to climb on to part of the ship's timbers, and used it as a raft, until he got picked up by a fishing-smack. He had to come and tell us all that Cecily had drowned. He wasn't thanked for it.'

'I didn't know all this,' said Wulfstan thoughtfully.

'No, and we thought it strange that you sent no word of condolence when you heard what had happened and . . . er . . . there were those who blamed Dan for saving his own skin and letting Cecily drown.'

There seemed to be no answer to this, and Wulfstan was silent for a minute. Eventually he asked where he could find Dan.

'He'll be on the demesne somewhere, but his wife's about to give birth to their third child, so he may be at their cottage on the estate.'

Wulfstan could not imagine Dan as a husband and father; he remembered him as a good-humoured young groom, a favourite with all the family, and devoted to Cecily. He had accompanied Oswald to France at the time of the Battle of Crécy, and had brought his master back, half out of his mind with terror, and drunk more often than sober. Another memory that had to be conveniently forgotten now, thought Wulfstan wryly.

'I'd like to see Dan when it's convenient,' he said, 'and at some time I must go to Blagge house and see my niece and nephew there.'

'Hm, you'll get a cold reception from old Jack Blagge,' said Oswald, turning down the corners of his mouth. 'He's become more of a tyrant since he's grown older, and we don't know how Mistress Keepence puts up with him, but they say he's devoted to the children.'

'I'll go to see Kitty and Aelfric this afternoon,' resolved Wulfstan. 'I am their uncle, after all, just as much as you are, Brother.'

'Janet and I don't see much of them', confessed Oswald. 'We have our own family to consider, and all the business of managing the estate, and . . . well, it's awkward for Janet, being his daughter, just as much as Mistress Keepence is, but he resents her marriage to me, and can be quite offensive. By all means visit them, but steel yourself against his ill temper.'

The warm September sunshine made even the forbidding stone face of Blagge House look mellow as Wulfstan approached the front door, flanked by heavy columns on either side. A serving maid answered his knock, and nodded when he asked for Mistress Keepence.

'If you be young Master Wynstede from up at the Hall, I'll show you into the waiting room,' she said with a conspiratorial look, and he followed her into a small parlour. 'Sit there, sire, and I'll fetch the mistress.'

A pleasant-faced woman came into the room and held out her hand. 'Master Wulfstan! What joy to see you again after all this time – and grown so tall! Kitty and Aelfric are playing out in the field beyond. Come, let's go to them!'

It was the warmest welcome he had received so far. Maud Keepence shared the same birth year as Cecily, and her twin brother, Cecily's husband, had died of the black plague, as had her own husband. Childless herself, she had willingly devoted her life to caring for Cecily's children, and as soon as Wulfstan saw them he felt an affinity he had not felt towards his nieces and nephews at Ebbasterne Hall. Now aged ten and nine, Kitty and Aelfric clearly felt similarly drawn to this tall young man; their Aunt Maud had prepared them for his visit, and they ran towards him with cries of 'Uncle Wulfstan!' He opened his arms to gather them close to himself, and caught his breath at seeing Cecily in Aelfric's bright eyes, and the sweet curve of Kitty's mouth. He went down on one knee to be level with them, and at first was unable to speak; his reluctant home-coming now seemed worthwhile for this moment alone.

Touched as she was by their meeting, Maud felt duty-bound

to warn him of their grandfather's rejection of everybody connected with the Wynstede family.

'If he sees you with the children, he *may* invite you into Blagge House to dine with us, but on the other hand, Wulfstan . . .' She shrugged apologetically.

Jack Blagge, grey-bearded and hard-eyed, was waiting at the kitchen door when the four of them returned, Wulfstan holding Kitty's hand and laughing at Aelfric's attempts to turn a somersault. At the sight of him, little Kitty said, 'He's our Uncle Wulfstan, Grandsire!'

Blagge looked at his daughter Maud. 'What kind of foolery is this? Who let *him* in? Kitty! Aelfric! Come to your grandsire this minute!'

The children obeyed, but with a backward glance at Wulfstan. Blagge sent them indoors, and indicated to Maud that she should follow them. Then he turned on Wulfstan.

'What makes ye think ye can come here *now*, ye bare-faced, unbreeched son o' Wynstedes? Don't ye *dare* look at Cecily's children and make them call ye uncle when if it wasn't for *you*, their mother would be alive today. Go back to that brother o' yours, him who took away my daughter and gave her Wynstede airs and graces! And that wily groom Widget who left Cecily to drown, and then came back and bedded my best serving wench. Ye'll not take away my grandchildren, damn your eyes!'

Wulfstan coloured angrily, and his heart pounded. 'It was not my intention to cause my sister's death, sire, nor did I ask her to—'

'Shut your mouth and get out o' my sight!'

There was no choice for Wulfstan but to obey, and he left the house, resolving never to call there again. Yet it was not anger that consumed him now, but only sorrow for Cecily's death. There was no longer a place for him in Hyam St Ebba, he concluded, and the sooner he returned to France as a soldier of the King, the better.

On his return to Ebbasterne Hall, he found his brother and sister-in-law talking about the Widgets; Dan's wife Mab was in travail with their third child, and Oswald was restless, wanting to know how she was progressing, and being told by Janet in no uncertain terms that a birthchamber was no place for menfolk.

'The midwife and a sensible neighbour will be attending, and Dan will be pacing up and down, annoying them,' she said. 'He'll send us word when they've got the baby, whatever time of night it may be to disturb us. It's her third, so it shouldn't take too long – and now for heaven's sake, come to supper.'

It crossed Wulfstan's mind that if this had been in his mother's time, she would have been down at the Widget cottage, giving what encouragement she could to the mother. Times had changed, and he had learned to stay silent – well, almost.

'How did you get on this afternoon at Blagge House?' Oswald asked somewhat diffidently, and Wulfstan remembered that Lady Janet was Blagge's daughter.

'Katrine and Aelfric are very sweet children, and we got on well for the short time that I was there,' he answered, 'but Master Blagge was not so pleased to see me. He blames me for the loss of his wife – our sister Cecily.'

Oswald and Janet made no reply, and he continued in a matter-of-fact tone, 'And he also blames Dan Widget for surviving the shipwreck when Cecily drowned, and then for bedding his best serving wench.'

'And he *wedded* her soon after, she who is now in travail,' said Oswald quickly. 'And their marriage has been happy.'

Lady Janet said nothing, but pursed her lips, clearly annoyed by this unflattering talk of her father, and at the same time ashamed of him. Wulfstan remembered that old Blagge had said Oswald had taken her away and given her 'Wynstede airs and graces'.

At nine o'clock that evening, Dan Widget came up to the Hall to announce the good news of a little daughter, Grace, and that both mother and child were well. As soon as he caught sight of Wulfstan, he stepped forward to shake his hand vigorously, a move which Lady Janet clearly considered a liberty, coming from a bailiff, though she said nothing.

'Blessings on ye, Master Wulfstan, I heard ye've come home, and at just the right time!' Dan said happily. 'I hope ye'll come with Master Oswald some time to see our little girl – she's going to be pretty, like her mama!'

Wulfstan smiled his congratulations and promised to do so, remembering his friends Jean-Pierre Fourrier and Eric Berowne, only too eager to get away from the girls they had so carelessly deflowered.

The next day was fine and sunny, and he decided to ride over to the Castle de Lusignan to see his sister Ethelreda, married to their second son, Charles; the eldest, Piers, had fallen at Crécy, nine years previously. It had been thanks to Count Robert de Lusignan that Wulfstan had been recommended to Monseigneur Duclair. Lady Hélène, the Countess, had been a friend to the Wynstedes, especially after the tragic death of her son, and when asked by Cecily to use her influence with the Count, had willingly done so. Now Wulfstan knew that he must show how well he had used the past five years at the Maison Duclair. The Count and Countess gave him a cordial welcome.

'You'll want to see Ethelreda and the children, I know,' said Lady Hélène, smiling. 'She can scarcely wait to see *you* after all this time!'

Wulfstan's first impression on seeing his younger sister was surprise at how she had matured from the young, lively girl of scarcely sixteen who had married Charles de Lusignan and produced a son six months later, named Piers for his lost uncle. There was also a younger brother and sister.

'*Wulfstan!*' she cried at the sight of him, and they clung together in a tearful embrace. He shook hands with Charles and allowed himself to be introduced to Piers, Norval and little Sofia, barely two years old. Ethelreda's body was swelling with another child, and she looked tired; she confided her anxieties to her brother as soon as they were tactfully left alone.

'Charles and his father are planning to join the Prince's army when he sets sail for Gascony,' she said, 'and Lady Hélène and I will be fretting every day and night. Oh, Wulfstan, why does this enmity with France go on and on?'

Trained as he was in the art of warfare, Wulfstan assured her that it was an honour and privilege to fight under the king's flag and add lustre to the family name.

'Spoken like a young, unmarried fool,' she retorted. 'Charles has no wish to go, but his father expects him to fight beside him. Dan Widget won't be leaving, he's much too useful as Oswald's bailiff.'

Wulfstan gave her the news of Mab Widget's safe delivery of a daughter, and she clapped her hands. 'Praise God! I must ride over to visit Oswald and Janet before the winter sets in, and call on Dan and Mab. Do you know if Friar Valerian was called to baptize the baby?'

Wulfstan did not know, and she told him of how the Friar, now infirmarian at the Abbey, was skilled both as a physician and a spiritual counsellor. 'I always call on him if any of the children are ailing,' she said.

Memories stirred in Wulfstan's head. 'Didn't he attend to Oswald at a tournament years ago when we were but children?'

'Yes, and he was with Oswald at the time of Crécy, though we don't talk about that now,' she said, lowering her voice as they remembered Oswald's poor showing at Crécy. 'He and Cecily cared for the monks at the Abbey when so many of them died of the plague,' she continued. 'They both escaped it by some miracle – yet we lost her in the shipwreck, coming back from—oh, Wulfstan, what sorrow for you, knowing she drowned after leaving you at Lisieux.' She took hold of his hand, and he shook his head helplessly.

'Yes, Ethelreda, she died because of me. It's a burden I have to bear, and for that reason I must leave Hyam St Ebba for good. It's no longer home to me. I shall go to fight in the Prince's army.'

Her face clouded over. 'Perhaps you'll find yourself alongside Charles and the Count. Heaven save you all!'

Wulfstan did in fact find time to visit the bailiff's cottage on the day before he left for Southampton. Having congratulated Mab and admired the tiny, squirming new arrival, he had a brief exchange with the happy father outside the bailiff's cottage.

'I hear ye're not stayin' long, Master Wulfstan, and I'm sorry for it, 'cause Sir Oswald could do with help at managing the estate. What d'ye think o' Hyam St Ebba now?'

'The place seems much the same, Dan, it's the people who've changed,' Wulfstan confessed to this family servant he had known all his life. 'I don't fit in anywhere now, and I'm reminded all the time that Cecily would be alive today if she hadn't come with me to Lisieux.'

Dan was silent, and gave him a curious look which made Wulfstan add quickly, 'I'm sorry, Dan, I should have remembered, you must feel the same. I . . . I've even heard that you were blamed for surviving the shipwreck that took her. I'm sorry if that's what people say about you, too.' He felt his face blush crimson as the words left his mouth.

Dan continued to regard him silently for a long minute, as if making up his mind about something, and at last he spoke.

'Whatever people say don't bother me, Master Wulfstan, and ye shouldn't let it bother you neither, seein' as our consciences be clear. We know that we wished no harm to your dear sister – and I can tell you, she died as she'd wanted.'

Wulfstan stared. 'What exactly do you mean by that, Dan? Why should she want to die?'

'Ah, Master Wulfstan, I don't know whether I should say. I've always kept it quiet.'

'For heaven's sake, tell me, Dan, tell me; you can't keep it from me now, whatever it is you know,' Wulfstan insisted. 'Why did my sister want to die?'

'The fact is, Master Wulfstan, it wasn't just 'cause o' *you* that she went to France. I could've gone with ye just as well without her, and she knew that. No, she went to look for somebody else, somebody she'd loved and who loved her. She was unhappy being married to that old—to Jack Blagge, and after she left ye at the military school, I went with her to find this man. And we found him, just as we were about to sail back to England. He came aboard with us and she was happy again, more happy than I'd ever known her before.' Dan's eyes filled with tears at the memory.

'Good God, Dan, what are you saying?' demanded Wulfstan. 'My sister was always a faithful and loyal wife, both to Master Edgar Blagge and then to his father. Are you telling me that she had a—that there was somebody else – a *lover*?' He stumbled with embarrassment on saying the word.

'No, never, she was a virtuous woman, and when they met again on the boat, they thought they'd have to part again when they reached Southampton – but the boat we were on, one o' them flat-bottomed cogs, carryin' wine casks too heavy for it, sank in the Narrow Sea, and took the crew with it. There was only me survived by the skin o' me teeth, and I—,' Dan's voice broke as he said the words, 'I was happy for her, Master Wulfstan. They didn't have to part again, and she never had to go back to that old tyrant.'

Wulfstan could hardly believe his ears. 'And you were the only survivor, Dan?'

There was a long hesitation before Dan replied, 'No. She drowned and he wanted to drown with her, but he came up to the surface and I got him breathing again. I've told ye now, Master Wulfstan, and let it rest between us, for Cecily's sake. But don't blame yeself, whatever they may say.'

'Thank you, Dan. You've been the best friend our family ever had,' Wulfstan replied, awkwardly holding out his hand. 'And for Cecily's sake I shall never repeat what you've said. Only . . .' He hesitated, and then asked, 'Can you tell me the name of him she went to find?'

'No, Master Wulfstan, nor where he went, for *his* sake. God bless ye, master, and give ye a safe crossing!'

Dan's strange story gave Wulfstan much cause for thought, and he pondered on it as he rode the faithful Troilus to Southampton. He had clearly not been told the whole of it, and he respected Dan's reticence, without wanting to know more. Even so, he felt that a burden had been lifted from his shoulders, and there would be no need ever to visit Hyam St Ebba again. His aim now was to take part in military service under Prince Edward, along with Count de Lusignan and Charles, Eric Berowne and Jean-Pierre Fourrier. The young, untrained boys he had taken on *chevauchée* would have to stay at the Maison Duclair – except perhaps for Léon Merand who at twenty would be old enough to fight if he chose to forego his training. Wulfstan smiled happily to himself: this would be the adventure of a lifetime!

Four

1355–1356

Delays due to shortage of available ships and trained soldiers
hampered the Prince's plan to invade Gascony that autumn;
troopships carrying men, horses and weaponry left Southampton
and Plymouth on different dates in September, and Wulfstan
was among the last to embark, with Troilus. He had to wait
for tides and weather before boarding a large, double-sailed
cog crammed with men of the rougher sort on the voyage
along the Narrow Sea, out into the Atlantic ocean and round
the Bay of Biscay, to Bordeaux. He heard more foul oaths and
blasphemies than at any time in his life, and tried to keep
himself apart from his fellow passengers, but found it difficult
to be dignified while retching miserably with sea-sickness. He
felt pity for Troilus and the other luckless horses, gasping for
water and standing in their own excrement.

The sight of the long quays lining Bordeaux's inland harbour
raised a cheer from all on board after a debilitating journey on
the meagre rations of dry bread and brackish water, over which
the men were actually fighting by the time they disembarked.
They were met by a couple of officers who directed them to
different locations: the majority went to tents and temporary
wooden huts in a bare field beyond the city, while Wulfstan
was beckoned up to the archbishop's palace just above the main
square, where the Prince was lodging. Troilus was taken to a
stable with half a dozen other horses, and Wulfstan was
summoned to appear before the Prince, who had heard that
he had been trained at the Maison Duclair.

Rapidly gaining confidence, he bowed low before the tall,
handsome man who more than lived up to the legends that
were already circulating about his strength and manly beauty.
He had been only sixteen at the Battle of Crécy where he had
acquitted himself well, and now, a decade later, he was his

father's dearest hope, the future King Edward IV, and England's glory. He sat at a long table, flanked by the Earls of Warwick and Salisbury. Wulfstan confirmed his name, family and age, and while the earls raised their eyebrows at his youth, the Prince said that his five years at the military academy stood him in good stead. His ability to read and write in French and English, as well as being an accomplished archer and swordsman earned him a smile and nod of approval from the Prince, who welcomed him as an officer in spite of his tender years, and told him that he would stay in the palace until suitable billets had been found in Bordeaux for men such as himself. Wulfstan's heart swelled and his eyes shone as he vowed to live or die in the service of King and country, under the flag of St George.

He was shown to a dormitory in the palace, furnished with four wooden beds with horsehair mattresses and one wooden chest between the occupants for storing clothes. For Wulfstan it was an honour to sleep under the same roof as the Prince and his earls, but two days later he and another young Englishman, Robert Poulter, were directed to a house in the town, occupied by a widow, Madame Merlette, where they would stay until called upon to join the Prince in an exploratory *chevauchée* through Gascony and the adjoining duchy of Aquitaine. Wulfstan smiled at hearing that word again, and began telling Robert something of his own experience of 'a ride on horseback' in Normandy, but Robert seemed more interested in Madame's daughter, Dorine, a fresh-faced girl of not more than fifteen years. With her mother and a serving wench she waited at table, bringing the young men freshly baked bread from her mother's kitchen, with cheese, bacon and good bean soup.

'Do you not think her pretty, Wulfstan?'

'She's very young,' replied Wulfstan dubiously, thinking her hardly more than a child.

'Ah, but her smiles are sweet, and cause me to daydream,' Robert replied, touching the girl's fingers as she collected their trenchers after dinner. When she retreated to the kitchen, his gaze followed her dainty figure in frank appraisal.

'Let's look at her in another year or two,' suggested Wulfstan, not wanting to appear a greenhorn.

'But who knows where we will be then?' Robert speculatively narrowed his eyes. At twenty he considered himself quite the man-about-town, a connoisseur with no doubts about his own attractiveness to women. It was therefore a surprise when they found that Dorine's smiles and blushes were directed towards Wulfstan rather than Robert, and when he realized this, Wulfstan too began to daydream. Unbidden memories of Madame la Gouvernante came back to him, though there was little resemblance between the woman and the girl, only that they were both female and had the power to stir a man's imagination. Whether Dorine knew of her own powers they did not have time to discover, for on the fifth of October they set out with the Prince of Wales and his noble earls on the *chevauchée*.

When all the officers left their billets to assemble before the palace, Wulfstan heard a boisterous greeting, a shout of, 'Look, comrades, if it isn't Sir Galahad! So you got here after all!' And there to his delight were his former fellow trainees, Jean-Pierre Fourrier and Eric Berowne. With Robert Poulter the four set off in high spirits. It was a cold but clear autumnal morning with a freshening breeze that sent the gold and crimson leaves whirling down from the trees. There was much speculation about the Prince's intentions as the march processed peacefully along the Garonne valley, the river on which Bordeaux stood. They entered land held by the French king's lieutenant, the Count d'Armagnac, and marched through villages and farms; the Prince allowed the men to help themselves to whatever food they needed, but not to harm the people in any way. Even so, Wulfstan saw some excessive plundering of dairies, and thefts of hens and ducks from farmhouses they passed, eventually toiling up a steep path through woodland that came out on to a wide area of scrubland where they paused while the Prince held council with his earls; his idea had been to march deep into d'Armagnac territory, but after consultation he settled his army on the open plain, and sent out scouts to find out the Count's whereabouts. A whole day passed before the scouts returned to say that the Count d'Armagnac was sheltering behind the walls of Toulouse with a large army to prevent the Prince from venturing beyond that city. The Prince

cursed roundly, and was for going ahead to attack d'Armagnac
head-on and scatter his army, and would have done so, had
not his earls urged him against this course at a time when
winter was drawing on with its cold and darkness; at length
he was persuaded to return to Bordeaux and wait for spring.
He felt humiliated, and his mood changed; he gave his troops
leave to loot and plunder wherever they chose. Heavy rains
soaked them and the ground became muddy, adding to their
discomforts, and when they reached the town of Rejaumont
the Prince ordered the people to turn out of their houses to
let his troops luxuriate in dry lodgings, drink their fill of wine
and eat whatever food they could find. Wulfstan was horrified
to see women and children forced to stand outside in the
pouring rain, but Robert said it was exactly what d'Armagnac
would do if *he* invaded enemy territory, that is to say England.

They were back in Bordeaux by the second week of
December; the trees were now bare and their colours replaced
by winter's black and white, merging into a ghostly grey. Dorine
welcomed Wulfstan with unconcealed delight – so much so
that Madame Merlette ordered her to stay in the kitchen, to
be replaced by a snub-nosed, button-eyed serving wench.

'Our gracious lord and master is said to be spitting out
more flames and smoke than St George's dragon,' said Jean-Pierre
Fourrier with a grin. 'I'm not sorry to be lodging outside the
palace right now.'

'Well, it *was* a weak ending to the *chevauchée*, you must
admit,' replied Robert. 'And it means we'll be holed up here
until the New Year.'

'With precious little cheer over the Feast of the Nativity,'
added Eric, turning down the corners of his mouth.

Wulfstan said nothing. He was thinking of pretty Dorine,
who threw a smiling glance in his direction on the few occasions when their paths crossed at Madame's.

The four friends were seated in a tavern near the centre of
Bordeaux, and around them sat other young officers in the
Prince's army. The topic of conversation was general: the late
start to the Prince's invasion of Gascony via the seaport of
Bordeaux made the *chevauchée* too close to winter, and some

of the Bordelais were calling it a failure, a virtual defeat by the Count d'Armagnac, causing the Prince's men to retreat (or to be chased?) back to their starting point in that fair city.

'We've got the worst of winter to get through before setting out on a *chevauchée* again,' observed Eric. 'It's not so bad for *us*, quartered in Bordeaux, but God help the poor devils in tents and wooden huts! I've heard the Prince has spread them out to towns forty miles from here. If we get a few hard frosts and snowfalls, they'll be dying of cold.'

'Yeah, their cocks'll drop off when they unbutton,' grinned Robert, tossing back a large beaker of red wine, and reaching for the flagon to refill it. His face was flushed, and Wulfstan foresaw another evening of guiding his uncertain footsteps back to the lodgings they shared. 'The Prince will see them taken care of,' continued Robert. 'They'll have blazing braziers to keep them warm and for cooking – and they'll be drunk half the time on the wine casks he'll have sent up to them. Ha! The locals of Sainte-Émilion will have to lock up their daughters, but *we* shall have to behave ourselves here in Bordeaux. Don't go swaggering around getting wenches with child and pissing in the archbishop's gateway, or you'll be sent to join our brothers-in-arms forty miles away!'

Wulfstan nodded at the warning; anything would be better than being sent to join the kind of riff-raff he had sailed with, now kicking up their heels in rough winter quarters.

As it turned out, the Feast of the Nativity passed very pleasantly for Wulfstan. The Prince and his senior commanders attended High Mass at midnight in the Cathédrale Saint-André, a huge, looming building close to the archbishop's palace. All militia stationed in Bordeaux were ordered to attend, and the four young officers were there to receive the Sacrament. Wulfstan dutifully remembered his family and friends at Hyam St Ebba, though he had no desire to be with them. On the contrary, he suddenly espied Madame Merlette and Dorine sitting among their neighbours, and when the Mass had ended and he was invited to the palace to take wine with the Prince and his officials, he whispered to Robert that he was going back to their lodgings because he felt a fever coming on. Declining

Robert's reluctant offer to come with him, he vanished into
the crowd surging out of the great doors, keeping Madame
and Dorine in sight. When he caught up with them, he
expressed surprise that they were alone, and offered to escort
them safely home.

'With all these people milling around in the dark, Madame,
it would be an honour if you will allow me to accompany
you and your daughter,' he said with a bow.

The lady hesitated. 'A neighbour and her husband said they
would see us home, sire,' she said, looking round uncertainly
at the unfamiliar faces. Suddenly a man lurched against her
heavily, and Wulfstan put out an arm to steady her. She held
on to him, and Dorine held her other arm.

'Our neighbours don't seem to be anywhere around, Mother,'
said the girl. 'Pray, let us accept Monsieur Wynstede's offer.'

So Madame agreed, hanging on to them both in the seething
midnight crowd, Dorine on her left side, Wulfstan on her
right. He would rather have walked between them, but
Madame, grateful as she was, clearly wanted to keep him apart
from Dorine who was able to flash him a grateful smile before
lowering her eyes modestly. When they left the cobbled stones
of the main street, they made better progress amid the thinning
crowds.

'This is most kind of you, sire,' murmured the lady, and
Dorine gave a shy, almost inaudible assent.

'It is my pleasure to protect you, Madame,' he answered
truthfully, for he was enjoying every minute of his self-imposed
task; the air was cold and sharp with frost, and the night sky
glittered with stars. All too soon, it seemed, they reached
Madame's door, and she withdrew her arm from his to take a
key from a pocket she wore under her cloak, and insert it into
the lock.

She pushed the door open, and looked up at Wulfstan who
quickly withdrew his eyes from Dorine.

'I believe that the Blessed Virgin must have sent you to us,
sire,' she said. 'And you'll be wanting to go back to your friends
now.'

'Thank you, Madame, but after receiving the blessed
Sacrament, I think I would rather be . . . er . . . quiet, and

go to bed – to pray,' he added hastily. 'So I wish you goodnight, Madame – and Mademoiselle.'

'As you wish, sire.' The front door opened straight into the room where the patrons were served; it was pitch dark, but Madame quickly slipped through to the kitchen and lit a candle from the glowing embers of the fire beside the bake-oven.

'Here is a light for you, sire – but first can I offer you some refreshment and a hot drink after your kindness?'

How could he refuse? He saw Dorine's pretty little face light up, and followed them through to the kitchen where Dorine lit two more candles, and invited him to sit on a bench before a well-scrubbed table. Madame instructed her to heat blackcurrant cordial in a pan over the fire, while she cut slices from a cottage loaf, and spread them with drippings of fat and meat juices from the tray below the roasting-spit. They then sat down on either side of him, and he was conscious of Dorine's narrow hips against his thigh.

'You are welcome at our table, Monsieur Wynstede,' the lady said simply as they ate and drank the plain, sustaining fare. Wulfstan gave himself up to enjoying this unexpected interlude between the eve and the day of the Feast. Memories of la Gouvernante inevitably came back to him, but he had been a callow greenhorn then; *now* he had become a soldier, an officer in Prince Edward's army, a trustworthy man on whom a helpless widow could rely. He glowed with satisfaction, and returned Dorine's happy smile.

Prince Edward's hasty retreat to Bordeaux after a less than glorious *chevauchée* had left his army disheartened and hardly in festive mood. They were therefore happily surprised and pleased at his convivial celebrations of the Feast which went on for ten days, into the new year of 1356. There were entertainments of different kinds, archery contests with prizes, hawking and hunting the boar on frosty mornings, and feasting at the banquets every night, where wine flowed freely. Some young men complained among themselves that the lack of a *Princess* of Wales meant that there was a dearth of ladies-in-waiting and their maidservants, but they found that their Prince had made provision for this lack. For officers of his inner circle there was a discreetly separate building where they could visit carefully chosen young women who had arrived apparently from nowhere with a black-clad Madame who watched over them with a maternal, all-seeing eye, allowing no debauchery or excesses.

'Have you been over to the *house of beauty* yet, Sir Galahad?' joked Jean-Pierre, but Wulfstan had no desire for a stranger's bought kisses; he preferred to visit his billet at the house of Madame Merlette, taking sweetmeats and such dainties as he could stealthily remove from the laden table at the palace, to present to Madame and her daughter. In return a blushing Dorine had let him kiss her in the wintry herb-garden at the back of the house, and he needed no sweeter reward. It had happened quite suddenly at twilight, without any contrivance on his part, though he later wondered if she had been lingering at the back door, hoping for him to encounter her there. When he saw her, he had impulsively taken hold of her hand.

'I have been very happy here in your mother's house,' he told her, wondering if he dare raise her little hand to his lips.

'And you have been so kind to us, Monsieur,' she answered with a shy smile that he found encouraging.

'I shall be very sorry when I have to leave Bordeaux, Dorine.'

'I shall be sorry too, Monsieur,' she whispered, lowering her eyes. He cautiously drew her towards him, and she hid her face against the woven woollen tunic he wore. He at once pulled his fur-lined cloak around them both, encircling her in its generous folds. She nestled against him, and he felt her slender body trembling within his gentle embrace, half fearful but willing. This was a moment that might never come again.

'Dorine . . .' He bent over her, willing her to raise her head. 'Look at me, Dorine.' As she lifted her face to meet his, his lips brushed the tip of her nose, then found her rosy mouth. Their kiss was the sweetest sensation imaginable, and sent a tremor through his own body like a flash of lightning. He saw himself as an experienced man after la Gouvernante's lesson in love, but by all the rules of chivalry he was bound to protect this innocent girl from harm. He was about to whisper her name again, when they were suddenly interrupted.

'Dorine! Dorine, where are you?' her mother called from

the kitchen, and she hastily pushed him away from her with a muttered, 'O, mon Dieu!' Aloud, she called out, 'I'm coming, Mother!' And she was gone, leaving Wulfstan standing uncertainly in the flowerless garden, like a guilty schoolboy caught playing dice in the classroom. Dorine never breathed a word to her mother, but her blushing glances showed him that she too would welcome an opportunity to exchange such another kiss.

The days of feasting came to an end, and the Prince prepared for another *chevauchée*, this time calling upon all waverers to declare or renew their allegiance to his father King Edward III, ruler of extensive territories in France. He began by splitting his army into three units, fanning them out over a large radius, to the limit of Gascon jurisdiction to the north, and eastward along the river Garonne.

'We're to be in the middle section, Wulfstan, under the Prince's own command,' said Eric. 'And if he has to leave us to take charge of the others, we'll be under Sir John Chandos, a great soldier with years of service to the King. I can't wait to be up and into the saddle!'

Suddenly the time had come for Wulfstan to take his leave of Madame Merlette, and he found himself strangely tongue-tied as she thanked him for his consideration and kindness to them, by which she meant his respectful attitude towards a widow and her daughter.

'Will you be coming back to Bordeaux at some future time, Monsieur Wulfstan?'

'I . . . I really don't know what Prince Edward intends to do next, Madame – but if I do return, I will certainly call upon you – and Mademoiselle,' he assured her, not allowing himself even to look at Dorine, though he felt her eyes upon him. 'We are to set out tomorrow on the *chevauchée*, and I . . . I'm sorry that I must bid you farewell.'

And so the Prince's detachment took to the road, and the young soldiers laid wagers about the conduct of this wide-ranging raid, anticipating what the Prince was planning to do. The first town of any size they reached was Périgueux, and when they marched into it, the leaders of the townspeople begged the Prince to spare them, but received a stern answer, 'that the Prince desired to do only that which he had set out to do, which was to discipline and punish all inhabitants of the duchy of Aquitaine who had rebelled against his father.'

Eric Berowne nodded with grim satisfaction to Wulfstan. 'You can see that our Prince intends to repeat his exploits of last year, with a great marauding raid into all those territories under English rule, to ensure their loyalty – only this time with better success.'

The town was not therefore sacked, but the men of the Prince's army were given permission to help themselves to food and any valuables that took their fancy. Some of the soldiers took this to mean that they could also help themselves to pretty girls and violate their maidenhead, to Wulfstan's horror. He pictured his pretty Dorine Merlette trying to fight off such an attack, and for her sake he swore that he would never take a woman by force, no matter whether she was a friend or an enemy of England.

The progress of the advance into France on three fronts proved to be much slower than at first expected, and men began to sicken through cold, and to grumble at the lack of information. After a freezing winter of inaction, the army's supplies had run low, and the Prince had to wait some time for supplies and reinforcements to be sent out from England before he could continue to move forward. With the welcome advent of spring, the relief forces at last arrived: several hundred archers and horses to carry them, longbows, bowstrings and arrows. Among the new faces were a father and son very familiar to Wulfstan, and he rushed to welcome them with unconcealed joy.

'Count de Lusignan, how glad the Prince will be! And my brother-in-law, we shall be soldiers together!'

The Count and his son Charles were equally delighted, though Wulfstan learned that they had at first decided not to join the Prince's army, Charles having lost his elder brother at Crécy and not wanting to be involved with more warfare and killing, especially now that he was married to Wulfstan's sister Ethelreda, and father of a growing family. The Count had also listened to his wife's pleas and decided against more military service; but the urgent message from the Prince for more men had overcome their reluctance, and so here they were. They had been personally welcomed and thanked by the Prince himself, for they brought the news that the Prince's cousin Henry, Duke of Lancaster, had landed in Normandy with an army to carry out a similar disciplinary raid there, and which, it was hoped, would link up with the Prince's in due course. It became known that the Prince had sent a message to the Bishop of Hereford to hold daily Masses for the soldiers under his command, and to ask both clergy and laity to go twice a week in procession through Hereford town, praying for divine aid.

With renewed heart the Prince drew his forces together, to head for the heart of France. This brought Jean-Pierre Fourrier and Robert Poulter to reunite with Wulfstan, Eric, and newcomer Charles, following the Prince and Sir John Chandos at the head of some six or seven thousand men, foot soldiers, bowmen and mounted men-at-arms, advancing at about ten miles per day. They passed through a series of towns – Brantome, Rochechourat and Châteauroux – and it was the Prince's policy to halt at any well-provisioned town and rest there for a few days to refresh themselves, then to proceed, taking their plunder with them, piled high in their carts and horse-drawn wagons full of booty, taking the same course of action at the next town. Wulfstan could hardly question the rightness of his Prince's policy, but his conscience troubled him more with each township they entered.

'God's bones, I hope there'll be some willing women at the next town,' said Robert, grinning. 'Otherwise I'll have to make do with a couple of unwilling ones.'

'You don't mean you'd take a Frenchwoman against her will, surely?' Wulfstan asked, his tone both disbelieving and disapproving.

'Why not? They're our enemies, aren't they? Oh, come off your high horse, Sir Galahad, just because your blood runs thin! There are red-blooded men who need to satisfy their appetites before going into battle, the better to conquer!'

Wulfstan had no answer to this, having heard from others around him that a man was allowed, and indeed encouraged to ease his natural lusts when away from home in all-male company. For his part, he took refuge in remembering the sweet sensation of Dorine's shy response to his kiss, and to know that she thought of him in her prayers. To force a stranger to supply his carnal needs was utterly alien to him, but he did not care to argue with Robert, or to mention Dorine's name; after all, it was Robert who had first appraised her and been ousted by himself in her affections. Dear, sweet little Dorine! It was the thought of her, the memory of that moment of closeness that gave him strength to follow his Prince to a glorious victory – though it might cost him his life. Such thoughts he was unable to share with Robert or Jean-Pierre, or indeed with any of the other young officers serving under their Prince.

Except perhaps for Charles de Lusignan, whose thoughts were with his wife Ethelreda and young Piers, Norval and little Sofia, soon to be joined by another.

Five

The weeks dragged by, turning into months, and Wulfstan was not the only officer of the Prince's men to grow impatient with the conduct of the war, which seemed only concerned with safeguarding the English king's territories in France. Contradictory rumours abounded, one being that the French king, John II, was marching south with a large army to join up with his troops stationed at Chartres. There seemed to be some confusion as to how Prince Edward intended to proceed.

'You surely don't expect the Prince to publish his plans to all and sundry,' said Fourrier, who had heard from Sir John Chandos, the Prince's second-in-command, that King John's so-called army was mostly made up of mercenaries who would fight on the side of whoever paid them the most, and would desert in their droves if faced with the prospect of defeat.

'Besides, we know the Prince is waiting for news of his cousin, Duke Henry of Lancaster, to swell the numbers,' said Poulter, though his friends had learned not to give too much credence to his boastful assertions. He had appropriated several casks of wine from the towns through which they passed, and like the rank and file in times of inaction, was often drunk, giving his friends cause for amusement or irritation.

'He's bored,' said Eric with a shrug. 'He'll mend his ways when we go into battle.'

Yes, but *what* battle, and *when*? The mutterings got louder as time went on.

Then came some unexpected action. On an afternoon in early summer Sir John led an exploration to the fair-sized town of Vierzon to assess the situation there and the mood of the people. He chose Robert Poulter and Wulfstan to take charge of a dozen men each, carrying their swords but without armour except for helmets to protect their heads. Nobody knew how the French got wind of this venture, but Chandos's men suddenly found themselves ambushed by a detachment of French militia, and Wulfstan was faced with a soldier's choice: to kill or be killed. A sharp skirmish took place, and Wulfstan felt his sword sink into human flesh; he heard his victim's cry of pain, and at the same time Troilus reared up in terror, nearly unseating his rider. The French took flight, but Chandos ordered his men to pursue them into the citadel of the town and fight to the last man. Wulfstan was feeling sickened and reluctant to give chase, but at that moment, as if by some supernatural intervention, the Prince himself appeared among them, and the very sight of their royal leader in his black armour spurred them on. Under his command they set about capturing the citadel and taking two prisoners of rank. The Prince's presence alongside his men gave them enormous encouragement, and when he singled out Wulfstan to compliment him on his swordsmanship, the young officer had to bow and looked suitably honoured. This incident, however, brought him to a decision: to exchange the faithful Troilus for a destrier, one of the great warhorses that had carried men into battle for centuries past. What to do with Troilus? There was no way of shipping him back to England, and on the advice of Poulter Wulfstan decided to offer the horse as a gift at the next monastery they drew near; the brothers would put him to farming duties and treat him well, but Wulfstan was troubled, feeling that he'd behaved treacherously to a faithful friend of seven years' service.

'Better that than be shot with a French arrow and lie for hours dying in his own blood,' said Robert briskly, while most of Wulfstan's companions thought him too much affected by the loss of a horse unsuitable for warfare.

Still the Prince waited for news of Lancaster, hoping that he would cross the lower Loire in time for them to form a united front against the French king's greater numerical advantage.

'Why in God's name this damnable delay?' asked Eric impatiently. 'Our Prince is a match for any French king, no matter what the numbers under his command.'

Wulfstan nodded, having no answer. He was increasingly

disturbed by what seemed to be a confusing cat-and-mouse game, and more weeks passed, until one day a shout went up at the approach of a scout, riding into the camp as fast as his steed could gallop.

'Thank God, an answer from the Duke of Lancaster at last!' shouted Charles de Lusignan, and the officers crowded round the Prince as he studied the message. He drew in a sharp breath of dismay, for it was not Lancaster, but King John who had crossed the Loire with his army. Wherever there was a bridge they streamed over it to the south bank, 'like a great hunting pack', reported the scout. Closer at hand, the French were entering Tours.

'There's only one way for us to go, my liege,' Wulfstan heard Count de Lusignan say, 'and that's south, and quickly.' In two days the Prince's army had covered thirty miles, but by then King John's men were a bare twenty miles away. The Prince was confronted with a hitherto unconsidered threat, that King John might march his army of thousands into the English-held territory of Aquitaine in a *chevauchée* that would repay the English and Gascons in their own coin, turning their tactics upon themselves, including the plundering. After a brief consultation with Sir John Chandos, the Prince turned his army round, abandoning their cartloads of booty, to lead his men-at-arms across the Poitiers road, stringing them along the fringe of Saint-Pierre wood; but at that very hour the King was entering the town of Poitiers, and there was a scuffle when the Prince's vanguard came upon straggling groups of the King's rearguard. The English killed a few and took prisoners, while the remainder of the French escaped down the road towards Poitiers. The Prince's men were jubilant.

'At least each commander now knows where the other one is,' Poulter remarked drily.

'Aye, but the Prince's first concern must be to prevent the French from cutting him off from Bordeaux,' answered Eric Berowne, while Wulfstan and Charles caught each other's eye and shrugged, thoroughly confused.

Action came at last. Late on a summer evening and very early the following morning the Prince led his troops up to a commanding position north of a Benedictine abbey, looking down to the Poitiers road, with their backs to the wood and divided into three columns: the right side was commanded by the Earl of Warwick, the left by Suffolk, while he himself with Sir John Chandos and the Count de Lusignan took command of the central column. Ten years before, King Edward III accompanied by his son, this same Prince aged sixteen, had used this tactic to conquer the French at Crécy, but this time the enemy was in full array before him, ready to attack. Wulfstan, Robert Poulter and Charles de Lusignan were among the men-at-arms in the central column, supporting the archers, and as dawn broke on that Sunday morning, a Dominican friar led them in a prayer for victory. Wulfstan bowed his head and prayed silently under his breath, begging that his courage might not fail him, and to die honourably if this should be his fate. Secretly, shamefully he felt afraid. What was happening in King John's tent? Were they also praying that God would be on their side?

The sun rose upon the two opposing forces standing ready for the order to attack and be attacked, but then, incredibly as it seemed, there came yet another delay. A group of clerics on horseback came galloping into the space between the Prince's and the King's men, led by Cardinal de Perigord with a message from the Pope, ordering that the battle be delayed until sunrise on the following day, to avoid bloodshed on the sabbath. King John, in spite of protests from some of his leaders, agreed to the request, and his men were ordered to rest and spend the day in prayer. The Prince also agreed, for to him this was a valuable breathing space for his troops to dig ditches and strengthen barricades. That evening his Dominican friar led them in prayer again, and he addressed the men in a stirring speech of encouragement. Wulfstan was on foot, having tied Troilus to a tree, with the intention of offering him to the Benedictine Abbey after the battle. He wore a helmet and a hauberk, a tunic of chain mail that came halfway down his thighs, and carried a six-foot lance held horizontally as in the jousting tournaments, but instead of being blunted, it ended in a lethal two-edged blade.

On the Monday at sun-up the opposing forces faced one

another, waiting for the signal to attack. Wulfstan stood with bated breath, and heard the shouted order from the French side, swelling to a roar of 'For France and St Denys!' as the heavy cavalry of the French thundered forward, led by the Constable of France and two Marshals, swords flashing and pennants flying. On the English side the Prince called, '*Now!*' – and the archers drew back the strings of their longbows, took aim, and filled the air with arrows flying over and down upon the French cavalry, finding a target in men and horses. The latter reared up in terror, and refused to go forward; they turned back and stumbled, some falling upon their riders in huge confusion.

'*Now!*' called the Prince again, and a second wave of arrows whistled through the air. One of the Marshals was killed, likewise the Constable of France. Wulfstan watched one man fall after another, and then the Prince gave the order to advance. The middle column moved forward, yelling at the tops of their voices, 'For England and St George!' Wulfstan was carried forward and lost sight of Robert and Charles, though he thought he could see the Prince in his gleaming black armour riding ahead amidst the noise: the blaring horns and clarions, the thunder of hooves, the screams of wounded men and horses added up to a deafening din that robbed Wulfstan of any sense of direction on the field of battle. He clutched his lance and moved blindly forward, hardly knowing friend from foe.

A sudden blow on his helmet and a furious kick in the groin below his hauberk sent him staggering, bent double and clutching at his vital parts.

'Damned English cur!' was hissed in his ear. 'By God, we'll fill our ditches with your blood, damned sons of English whores!' The hatred expressed in the words was almost as frightening as the physical assault. Wulfstan's head whirled and the man's curses sounded strangely in his ears, for he recognized the voice. He straightened himself up and held his lance upright, signifying that he had no wish to use it.

'Léon!' he gasped, 'Léon Merand, my friend, don't kill me. You saved my life at Sailly, remember? We are comrades from the Maison Duclair!'

'So I thought then!' came the contemptuous reply. 'I was a

fool among other fools, and forgot my true allegiance, to my shame. But now I'm vowed to defend the sacred soil of France to my last breath. Prepare to die, English worm!'

He lunged at Wulfstan with his sword, and instinctively Wulfstan deflected it with his lance, unable to believe this was really happening, for surely he was in the grip of a nightmare. Another swish of his lance knocked the sword from Merand's hand, and with a skill learned at the Maison Duclair he thrust the point of the lance beneath Merand's hauberk just beneath his right arm; he felt it meet flesh, and crying out aloud for God's pardon, he pushed it with all his strength, sinking it into the chest to cut asunder heart and lungs.

Merand gave a sigh and sank to his knees, staring sightlessly at his erstwhile friend. Wulfstan groaned as if he were the victim, and would have knelt beside the body, had not another Frenchman attacked him with a battleaxe.

From then on it was hand-to-hand fighting. Wulfstan used his lance to knock the axe out of the man's hand, and picked it up to use it against its owner, but the man disappeared into the crowd. All around Wulfstan there was bloodshed and death. Then he heard a voice above the chaos and confusion.

'Wulfstan! Where have you been? We've got the French army on the run!'

It was Robert Poulter, blood-smeared but triumphant. 'King John has retreated, and the Prince has won the day!'

Unable to take in this news, Wulfstan stumbled after him, back to the line of Saint-Pierre wood, where he found that on the Prince's orders, the surviving men were carrying their dead and badly wounded to the camp at the edge of the wood, laying them under bushes and hedges, in the shade. From the dead they took their spears and swords to use again, and arrows were drawn from men's bodies and their stricken horses. Somebody held a water-bottle to Wulfstan's lips and told him that the Prince was high in his praises, but he hardly heard, so incredible, so horrible was the knowledge that he had killed a former friend. A great weariness came over his spirit, and he felt drained of all emotion as he stood among the dead and the injured in their death throes, and heard their pitiful groans all around him.

'Mother – mother, are you there? Help me, dear mother.'

'Damn them all to hell, French fiends – they've done for me. May Christ have mercy on my soul.'

'Water! For the love of God, give me water!'

And then another voice he recognized, calling out, 'My son, where are you? Have pity on your grieving father, show me where you're lying. Oh, my son, my son, forgive me!'

This agonized plea was from the Count de Lusignan, seeking Charles who had never wanted to go to war again. It was one more tragedy among so many, and all Wulfstan could think of was his sister Ethelreda; how could he comfort her when there was no comfort to be found? It was a scene from hell. And the Battle of Poitiers was far from over yet.

A lull in the fighting had been mistaken for victory by the English. King John of France had indeed retreated, but was re-forming his army, calling upon reserve troops at Tours to join him at Poitiers. The English were unprepared for the sight of the French king advancing again, leading an augmented army of fresh men, pennants flying and bright armour shining. Helmets were donned again, and hauberks hastily pulled over tunics. Wulfstan saw the Prince in his black armour, sitting astride his horse, defying their approach, and at this moment a man blurted out, 'Alas, we are overcome!' The Prince rounded upon him in fury.

'Liar! Coward! Never say we can be overcome as long as I live!'

So Wulfstan was again thrust into battle under the Prince's command. No sooner had his column fallen into line than a volley of arrows from French crossbowmen darkened the sky. The English, short of arrows and desperately tired, seemed scarcely a match for the advancing horde, and Wulfstan saw the Prince exchanging words with the Earl of Warwick, who then led his column of archers and men-at-arms away from the field, to disappear down a gully and into the trees. Could they possibly be fleeing the field after such a declaration from the Prince? It must look like it to the French, thought Wulfstan, who again prepared himself for death, uttering a silent prayer for courage in defeat, and committing his soul and all of his friends to God's judgement.

He heard the Prince give a tremendous shout: 'Let us go forth – you shall never see me turn back! Advance in the name of God and St George!'

Wulfstan, a foot soldier, was swept forward on the tide of battle, as likely to be killed by his own comrades as by the enemy in the chaos of this black Monday. He fought with sword and lance, spurred on by the thought of Charles de Lusignan, his friend and brother-in-law, lying dead somewhere on this bloody field. Separated from his friends, breathless and ready to drop in sheer exhaustion, he suddenly looked up to see his Prince, who from this day would be known as the Black Prince by friend and foe, sitting up astride his black steed, and looking ahead with an expression of undisguised relief. Wulfstan followed his gaze, and saw what the Prince had been waiting for: a glint of steel emerging from the west side of the wood. It was the Earl of Warwick with his longbow archers, who had turned a half-circle and now came up behind the French. He gave his men the signal to fire their murderous arrows, and Wulfstan stared up at them, weapons of fearful destruction, recalling what Monseigneur Duclair had said: that the Englishmen's use of the huge, clumsy-looking longbows which stood on the ground, double the span of the crossbow, had won for them the Battle of Crécy ten years before. The crossbow might be light, easily carried and easily fired, but the longbow, its bowstring drawn back by a well-practised hand, shot heavier, deadlier arrows with an impact to knock a man off his horse and fell him to the ground. Wulfstan grabbed his lance to continue to attack the French, but the field was thinning. The King's army was now being attacked from the front and the rear, and his men, demoralized by the two-pronged assault, were beginning to quit the field in increasing numbers. The end of the battle was in sight, and Wulfstan stood on bloodstained heathland, his heart pounding, his breath coming in rapid gasps, his mouth dry; there were no more Frenchmen left to attack.

It was evening. The Prince removed his helmet, and wiped his face; his standard-bearer helped him to take off his black armour, and from now on he would be known as Edward, the Black Prince. He set his banner in the top of a tree, and gathered his knights and commanding officers around him as they returned from the battlefield. Wine was brought forth on a tray.

The field was strewn with bodies of men and horses, and a roll call showed that though the French had come to the battle with much higher numbers, they had lost many more than the English and Gascons. Twenty dukes and counts lay dead, and hundreds more men-at-arms. But there was one important name absent from the list of dead and captured: the vanquished King John II of France. The Prince ordered the Earl of Warwick to take two officers with him to go out and seek for news of the king, who was said to have his fourteen-year-old son with him. If they found him alive, they were told to escort him back to the Prince's tent, and to show him every courtesy befitting an anointed king.

Red-eyed with exhaustion, Wulfstan stood on the field of death, thankful at least that he had not brought Troilus into such mayhem. When he became aware of raucous voices some hundred yards away, he turned to see a ring of English soldiers of the lower sort, yelling at a man who was valiantly defending himself with a battleaxe while a young boy cowered beside his horse. Wearied and bloodied as he was, Wulfstan saw that this was no ordinary French soldier, but a strong, fine-featured man, intent on fighting to his last breath rather than give himself up to these rowdy assailants, though he and the boy would inevitably be killed.

'Grab his axe, and club the old ruffian over the skull with it!' shouted one of them.

'*No*, lads, don't kill 'im!' yelled another. 'He's more use to us alive! He's worth a king's ransom, ain't he? Come on, grab hold of 'im an' tie 'im up with the boy!'

A king's ransom? In a flash Wulfstan realized that this was the beleaguered King John II of France, the enemy of England and the Black Prince, but worthy of a more dignified end than to be clubbed to death by this rabble, or tied up like a felon. And the boy must be fourteen-year-old Prince Philippe. Something must be done, and there was only Wulfstan to do it. He stepped forward, pointing his blooded lance at the mob.

'Get off him, you knaves, leave him to be judged by the Prince! Leave him alone, I say, or feel this metal in your guts!'

They turned to look at him, recognizing an officer but not inclined to obey.

'Who d'ye think *you* are, a bloody Frenchman? You ain't 'avin' 'im, he's ours!'

There was no time to bandy words. Wulfstan charged straight at the defiant men, who got out of the way of his lance, but were not in a mood to obey him. Turning quickly, Wulfstan aimed his lance horizontally at a big fellow who seemed to be a ringleader of sorts. The man jumped aside with an oath, and roared at one of the others, who stealthily came up behind Wulfstan with a battleaxe, bringing it down on his left shoulder in a tremendous blow, accompanied by a sickening crack of bone which caused Wulfstan to cry out and reel backwards, unable to get his breath. The men jeered as he staggered and clutched at his left shoulder, groaning like an animal in pain.

'Told yer to stay out of it, serves yer right!' the big fellow shouted, but some of them looked alarmed. This was an officer, and there might be trouble when his injury was known.

'Come on, lads, run for it! *He* won't know who we are!' A few of them made off with speed, but three or four stayed to take grim vengeance on the interfering fool who had spoiled their sport.

'Let's shut 'im up once and for all!' he heard through a flaming red cloud of pain. 'Don't leave 'im alive to tell what he's seen – finish 'im off, and then tie up the ol' king and his boy, and take 'em to the Prince an' claim our share o' the ransom money!'

They advanced towards him, brandishing knives and axes; he was helpless to save himself, and for the third time that day Wulfstan prepared for death.

That was the moment when the Earl of Warwick rode up with two men-at-arms, sent by the Black Prince to seek out the French king if he was still on the field of battle. As soon as they saw the earl and heard his shout, Wulfstan's tormentors fled, leaving him half-fainting. One of the officers came to assist him, while Warwick approached the king.

'I come from Prince Edward of England, Your Grace,' he said.

'Be assured that he wishes you no ill.' He then invited the king to remount his horse, calling on Wulfstan to follow them, his right arm over the shoulders of the man assisting him, his left hanging down uselessly at his side. Adjusting his pace to Wulfstan's, Warwick led the defeated French king with his son to the Prince's tent, where he was received with the respect due to a fallen foe who had fought valiantly. The Prince bowed before an anointed king, and called for wine to offer him and his son, and also to Wulfstan who sipped it in spite of the searing pain. He was never more impressed by the Prince's chivalry than now, for showing courage in battle and magnanimity in victory.

After exchanging words with the Earl of Warwick, the Prince came over to speak to Wulfstan, commending his actions and ordering a surgeon to examine the broken shoulder. When the left arm was straightened out, Wulfstan screamed in agony, but after it had been firmly bandaged to his body, the pain was slightly more bearable. This having been done, the Prince rose, took his sword from its sheath and ordered Wulfstan, assisted by the surgeon, to go down on his knees. What was this? Was he about to be executed? He bowed his head, and felt the sword lightly touch his right shoulder, broadside on.

The Prince spoke. 'Arise, Sir Wulfstan Wynstede, noble knight of Poitiers field!'

Even the excruciating pain could not detract from such an honour from the Black Prince, and having been helped to his feet, Wulfstan bowed deeply. He then asked for permission to return to his camp where the dead and wounded English had been left before the second phase of the battle had begun. The Prince at once ordered an escort for him, as walking wounded, and on his arrival he was jubilantly greeted by Sir John Chandos and Robert Poulter with the news that Charles de Lusignan had been found alive on the battlefield, though badly wounded and likely to lose his right leg. The Count would have embraced Wulfstan in his joy at his son's survival, but checked himself on seeing the bandage and the young man's deathly pallor. Charles, though weak from blood loss was still able to whisper his sympathy, and the news of the knighthood, told by Wulfstan's escort, was greeted by a cheer from Robert Poulter.

'Is there anything I can do for you, Sir Wulfstan?' he asked with a smile, and when his friend, feeling a little steadier after the wine, asked to be taken to see and untie Troilus, Robert gladly agreed, adding that he would then take the horse to the Benedictine monastery east of the field of battle, to offer him as a gift to the brothers; but when they reached the tree where the horse had been tethered, he was not there, and Wulfstan could not hide his distress. Robert sympathized, but said it was not surprising.

'Stands to reason, a man who's lost his own horse will be only too pleased to find another tied up and waiting for him,' he gently pointed out, for he knew of Wulfstan's deep attachment to his steed, a gift from his brother Oswald some seven years previously, before he had come to France and the Maison Duclair.

'I can go and look for him among the fallen,' he went on, 'but first I'll take you back to the camp.'

But Wulfstan absolutely refused to return to the camp, and insisted on going to look for Troilus on the field of battle. Hanging on to Robert with his right arm, and gasping with pain at every step, he managed to walk for several hundred yards, down to a shallow depression in the ground where dead and wounded horses lay in their own blood, flies buzzing over them, some twitching in death throes, some still crying out weakly, a sound more like a man in pain than an animal.

'Oh, my Troilus, what suffering I've caused you,' groaned Wulfstan, fearful of what he might find, and fervently hoping that the horse had escaped into the countryside around Poitiers.

They found Troilus, an arrow through his head and a deep wound in his belly from which his guts protruded. And Sir Wulfstan Wynstede, newly appointed a knight of the realm in his nineteenth year, eased himself down beside his faithful friend and wept aloud at such an end to a noble horse, and for all the innocent beasts around them who suffered because of man's thoughtless cruelty.

Six

After such a resounding victory, there were many among the Black Prince's army who wished he had progressed to the gates of Paris and entered the city in triumph, a conquering hero. He decided against such a gesture, for his men had gained so much booty, piled into their carts, that there was no room for more; and there was one trophy he dared not risk losing, and that was the King of France, who with the young Prince Philippe rode immediately behind him, treated with courtesy but not allowed to forget his captive state.

And besides, the Black Prince was tired after such a long campaign, and so were his men. There were some severely wounded who had to be carried on litters: men like Charles de Lusignan and Sir Wulfstan Wynstede, for whose sake the retreat to Bordeaux was slow, with frequent stops for overnight lodgings. The people had no choice but to supply them with bed and board, though they shrank back from them, fearful of being robbed or worse by their unwelcome guests.

Wulfstan was made as comfortable as possible, and shared the attentions of the Prince's own surgeon; a sweltering fever set in after two days, and he muttered incoherently about Troilus, pleading for his horse to be brought to him so that he could serve the Black Prince. He was given infusions and herbal elixirs to ease his pain, and these clouded his wits further but gave him the respite of fitful sleep for short periods until pain stabbed him back to wakeful delirium.

They reached Bordeaux in early October. The French king and his son shared the Black Prince's lodgings in the archbishop's palace, as did Sir Wulfstan; Charles de Lusignan was also kept under observation there, and his friends shook their heads at the gravity of his condition. There was some disagreement between his attendants as to whether his injured leg should be

sawn off above the knee, and there were those who advised
the Prince that young Sir Wulfstan would recover more quickly
without his lifeless, useless left arm. The Prince was reluctant
to agree to either of these drastic measures, and the consensus
of opinion for the time being was to wait and see how both of
them progressed or failed to do so.

By mid-November Wulfstan began to improve; he became
aware of his surroundings and marvelled at the comfort provided
for him by the Black Prince, who visited him from time to
time, bringing a gift of wine and words of encouragement.
Some of the officers with families in occupied France began
to leave Bordeaux, among them Jean-Pierre Fourrier; Eric and
Robert wanted to return to England, but the sea voyage was
difficult and dangerous in winter.

'We're thinking of crossing the country to Normandy and
sailing from Calais,' Robert told Wulfstan. 'It's the shortest
route across the Narrow Sea, and we'd avoid the storms of
Biscay. There isn't much we can usefully do here.'

'And the antics of the common soldiers, like the ones who
nearly murdered the French king, are giving us all a bad name,'
added Eric. 'They've emptied the fat purses they came back
with, and they're roving around in lawless bands, terrorizing
the local people, helping themselves to farm produce and wine
– and not only that. Respectable families are having to lock
up their daughters when these conquering heroes appear over
the horizon.'

Hearing this immediately alerted Wulfstan to the danger that
Madame Merlette and Dorine might be in, and he longed to
get up from his bed and visit them. Robert was again staying
in lodgings with their former landlady, and told his friend that
the mother and daughter were safe with him to protect them.
Wulfstan was partly reassured, but remembered that Robert
had been the first to notice Dorine in a lustful way, and being
a drinker might lose his inhibitions one night and try to take
advantage of her.

There came a dark day in early December when Charles de
Lusignan's condition began to deteriorate, and black areas on
his injured right leg showed that the flesh was dying. The Prince's
surgeon at once prepared to saw off the leg above the knee, and

the Count and the Dominican friar were present when the desperate remedy took place. Charles was given wine and sedative infusions of valerian roots, but he was barely conscious anyway. The huge unsuppressed groan that was heard by Wulfstan in his room and others in the vicinity was not from Charles but from his father as the bone-saw did its work, and an assistant stood by to cauterize the stump with a red-hot iron; the friar held up a wooden Cross and said prayers for Charles and his father. The next few days would decide Charles's fate, whether he died or lived to recover, and Wulfstan's thoughts were deep. Even if Charles survived he would be a cripple with a wooden leg, unable to fight under the Black Prince's banner again; and similarly, Wulfstan's left arm, even if the shoulder joint healed, was not likely to regain its former strength in the service of Edward the Black Prince who had so recently bestowed a knighthood upon him. What use as a knight would he be now? He was deeply disappointed with himself on this account, and confessed as much to the Prince when he came to speak with him after visiting Charles.

'There are other ways of serving your country, Wulfstan,' the Prince answered with a smile. 'I have heard from Monseigneur Duclair that you can both read and write in French, English and Latin, and that you have some dexterity with numbers. If this is the case, let me appoint you straightway to assist my scrivener, for he has broken his right wrist and can't use his hand.'

'I shall be more than happy to serve you in that way, my liege, though I pray that my left arm will soon be healed,' replied Wulfstan gratefully, but embarrassed and ashamed when his eyes filled with tears; this was no behaviour for a knight of the realm! But the Prince, knowing how close to death he had been, and the pain he had suffered, chose not to notice this weakness, and took his leave, appointing Wulfstan as assistant both to the scrivener and the Keeper of the Purse in the Prince's household as soon as he felt able.

Ten days before the Feast of the Nativity Wulfstan happily presented himself before his Prince in that capacity; and at the same time his friend Charles de Lusignan was pronounced to be out of danger. Eric Berowne and Robert Poulter decided to travel north-eastwards to Calais, to sail from there to England. Wulfstan became anxious about Madame Merlette and her daughter, left without protection from lawless soldiers bored with nothing to do but make trouble.

A week before the Eve of the Nativity, Wulfstan went to visit Charles in his room, and was shocked by the young man's appearance, so thin, and his face scarcely recognizable, chalk-white and drawn; he nevertheless greeted his friend with pleasure.

'Sir Wulfstan, old fellow! A pretty pair of soldiers we make now, me with one leg and you still hanging on to your arm! How are you? Have you been in much pain?'

Wulfstan glanced from Charles to the Count de Lusignan who spent practically all his waking hours at his son's bedside; he looked almost worse than Charles, having aged ten years, haggard with guilt and bitter regret.

Wulfstan winced at being called *Sir*. 'The pain is bearable,' he said lightly, 'though I wish the Prince had not been so ready to make me a knight, for I fear I may never serve him again as a soldier.'

'Neither will I, Wulfstan, but we must thank God for sparing our lives.'

At this point the Count rose and strode round the room in great agitation. 'I am blameworthy, Wulfstan! I talked Charles into going to war when he did not wish it or believe in it, having already lost my elder son Piers, his brother, at Crécy. Oh, may I be forgiven, though I'll *never* forgive myself – what shall I tell his wife? What can I say to his mother? *They* were opposed to this from the start!'

It felt strange to Wulfstan to be addressed as if on equal footing with the Count. As a boy, his family had looked up to the owners of Castle de Lusignan as greatly superior to the impoverished Wynstedes. The horrors of Crécy and the death of Piers had levelled the social barriers between the two families, and Charles had married Wulfstan's sister Ethelreda, to raise more de Lusignans. Under these changed circumstances, he attempted to offer some comfort to the Count.

'Charles has survived, sir, and will in time recover his strength to assist you at running the castle estate,' he said gently. 'His sons Piers and Norval will grow up to be his . . . your inheritors.'

'I hope you may be right, Wulfstan,' said the Count in a voice choked with regret. 'I'll do all I can for him when we get home. I'll send for that infirmarian at the Abbey, what's his name . . . Valerian – to see Charles and give advice. Everybody speaks of his skill.'

Wulfstan was conscious of an echo in his mind at hearing that name from his childhood. Friar Valerian had come to the aid of the Wynstedes in their times of trouble, but had always disappeared again into his life as a mendicant friar.

With a few more determinedly jocular exchanges with Charles and his father, Wulfstan left them and walked slowly down the spiral stairs of the palace; he went out into the inner courtyard, breathing in the air of a cold but clear December day and thinking of another visit he soon had to make, to Madame Merlette's modest boarding house. He had mixed emotions, longing to see Dorine again, yet fearing the meeting with her and her mother. It had been a whole year since that stolen kiss in the wintry garden when he had cut a fine figure in his military tunic and mantle. Now with his left arm bandaged to his side, and a constant pain in his left shoulder that sent sharp shocks down his arm, reflected in the frown lines on his forehead, he was much less impressive, and half afraid to appear before her. What would she think of him? What would she say? Would she be disappointed? There was only one way of finding out, and he walked resolutely down into the town.

His mouth was set in a straight line as he knocked at the door. A maidservant opened to him, she of the snub nose and button eyes. She gave him a suspicious look when he asked to see Madame Merlette, left him standing on the doorstep while she went to call her mistress, and returned to ask him to step into the kitchen as being the warmest room in the house. He followed her in, and stood by a window looking out on to the back yard, uncertain whether to sit down or remain standing. When Madame Merlette entered the room, he bowed to her. She did not offer him her hand to shake, much less to kiss.

'Good day, sir,' she said without smiling. 'I've heard that you have a wound, a broken arm that it was feared might be lost.'

'It is my shoulder that is broken, Madame, and my arm is affected by it. But how are you, Madame? And Dor-Mademoiselle – are you both well?'

'We are well enough,' she said. 'Thanks be to God, we have no English soldiers taking up room in our home at present.' Her voice was cold.

'Oh.' He paused, hardly knowing how to reply. 'Master Robert Poulter has left you.' It sounded unclear as to whether this was a question or statement of fact. 'I have thought often of you and . . . you and your daughter.' He winced as a stab of pain shot through his shoulder and down his arm to the useless hand. 'I would have come earlier, had it not been for this injury. Is it possible that I may speak to Mademoiselle Merlette? I have a small gift for her, and also for you, Madame.'

'Master Poulter tried several times to offer us gifts,' she said stonily. 'We did not accept them. We have no wish to receive plunder stolen from our own countrymen.'

'Oh, this is not plunder, Madame, but honestly bought and paid for, I assure you.' He had two rings of solid silver, one with a single opal set at its centre, intended for Dorine, the other with a garnet, for her mother. He now took them from his pocket, each wrapped in a little black velvet pouch, which he opened to show to her. She glanced at them briefly, but said nothing. He spoke again, hesitantly.

'If I may speak with your daughter, Madame—'

'I'll fetch her, but she's working and can't stay here talking.' She left the room, leaving him standing awkwardly. What could have happened since they last met, to turn her friendship and generosity to such cold disapproval? Several minutes passed before she returned, followed by Dorine. He caught his breath at the sight of the girl, now sixteen, and even prettier than he remembered. Her figure was maturing into womanly curves, but there was no smile for him, only a rather scared look. After a quick glance at Madame, he bowed to her daughter and held out his hand which Dorine warily took, also glancing at her mother as if for permission. He did not dare raise her fingers to his lips.

'Mademoiselle Merlette,' he said, releasing her hand. 'I have thought of you often over the past year, and prayed for your health and . . . er . . . well-being. Madame tells me that you are well.'

'No thanks to Poulter,' broke in Madame. 'And no thanks to the common soldiers who have been in here, drinking and behaving indecently. I have had to lock Dorine in her room on occasion, for her protection, for fear of her being ill-used by such rabble.'

'Oh, I am so sorry to hear that, Madame!' cried Wulfstan, at once outraged. 'I thought that Robert . . . that Master Poulter would protect you both, as he told me he would. Did he not intervene?'

'Poulter was all right when sober, but he was drunk nearly every night,' retorted Madame. 'And when he'd filled his belly with wine, he was as bad as any of them.'

Wulfstan was appalled. 'I did not know of this, and he has left for England now, or I would thrash him for a liar and a lecher!'

'And may all English riff-raff follow him there, the sooner the better! He tried to enter Dorine's room on the night before he left, and I had to heave the drunken brute away from her door. Would that he had fallen downstairs and broken his neck!'

This was worse than anything Wulfstan had feared. He straightened himself up, causing a sharp pain to stab his shoulder. 'I am deeply grieved to hear this – I apologize on behalf of my countrymen – and a man I looked on as my friend.' His face was pale as he faced the two women. 'If I can make amends in any way . . .'

'Only to go away and leave us alone,' replied Madame. He looked at Dorine who lowered her eyes. At sixteen she must be already disillusioned with the world of men, he thought. Her mother had spoken for them both.

'I am sorry from my heart, Dorine,' he said. 'And I beg you not to associate me with any of these men – or with Poulter.' He turned to Madame, pleading with her. 'Will you allow me to visit again – and escort you to the Mass on the Eve of the Nativity, as last year?'

'We shall not be going this year,' replied Madame. 'We shall say our prayers at home, and ask the Lord to drive out all English and Gascon scum from our city of Bordeaux. Good day to you, Master Wynstede,' she added, knowing nothing about his new status as a knight.

'But Madame, dear Madame Merlette, I would protect you both from such scum!'

Her eyes were hard as she looked at him. 'With only one arm? You'd hardly be able to defend a dog. Good day, Wynstede.'

His pale face flushed at the sneer, none the less painful because it was true, and had come from Dorine's mother. Dorine herself had not uttered a single word.

The Feast of the Nativity was lavishly celebrated in the archbishop's palace, and the Black Prince's famed generosity was shown by the gifts he showered on those commanders who had fought at the Battle of Poitiers and the long campaign which had preceded it. The Duke of Lancaster sent a message of deep regret that he had met with unexpected military defiance among the men of Normandy and Brittany, and had been forced to remain there instead of marching southwards to meet his cousin; he received immediate pardon. The Prince's newly appointed scribe and treasurer was privy to these messages, and knew that the administrative work still to be done would prevent his master from returning to England until the spring; and whereas this was a disappointment to many officers who wanted only to go home, Sir Wulfstan was delighted to work so closely with the Prince, greatly preferring this to life at Ebbasterne Hall. Discussions were going ahead for a truce with France, and negotiations regarding the amount of ransom to be demanded for the most important prisoners taken, the greatest prize of course being the French King John II and young Prince Philippe, currently staying in the archbishop's palace and treated more like honoured guests than captives.

Wulfstan began to feel his natural strength and energy returning, although the pain in his shoulder gave him little respite; the surgeon advised him to exercise his left arm gently, but it had neither power nor feeling, and now seemed to be shorter than his right arm, which was constantly employed in his lord's service, and his reward was the praise the Prince bestowed upon him.

Charles de Lusignan was recovering more slowly, not yet fit to make the sea voyage home, and when the Count offered Wulfstan a permanent position at the castle, to assist Charles on an equal footing as a brother, he eagerly accepted the offer, for it solved the problem of where he would live and what he would do when back in England. Once the stump of Charles's leg had healed, Wulfstan was determined to get his brother-in-law back on to a horse, a gentle mare such as he would choose for himself in their circumstances. By then he hoped that the Prince's official scribe, a Master Hugh Baldoc, resentful at being ousted from his position, would be ready and able to resume his duties.

'My son and I will be forever in your debt, Sir Wulfstan,' said the Count, scarcely able to control his emotion. 'When your good sister Cecily brought you up to the castle as a boy to be trained as a squire, we little thought that you would be made a knight at nineteen! God grant that the broken shoulder will heal, and restore you to full health and strength.' His voice shook.

Wulfstan smiled and gave a little bow – then gasped at the pain caused by this slight movement. It showed no sign of abating, and caused him much secret agony.

The situation regarding Dorine Merlette still troubled Wulfstan, and if Robert Poulter had not left Bordeaux, Wulfstan would have challenged him and demanded a full apology from him to the Merlette ladies; yet he would have been humiliated by his inability to engage in combat with his one-time comrade-in-arms. He tried to banish the matter from his mind, but continued to smart under the unfairness of it; he had for so long anticipated a renewal of friendship, and perhaps more, with Dorine.

One afternoon when he was at work in the room set aside for official business, the Prince entered in a jocular mood.

'What's on your mind today, Sir Wulfstan?' he asked, seating himself on the table, covering the parchments. His face was flushed, and his breath smelled of wine. 'Why all this frowning and turning down your mouth? Is it a disappointment in love?

Has some shallow-hearted miss turned you down because of your arm? If so, she's not worth fretting over!'

'It's nothing, my liege, nothing to speak of,' Wulfstan replied hastily, not wanting to make any confessions that the Prince might repeat in his cups.

'Nothing? So it *is* an affair of the heart!' said the Prince, laughing at Wulfstan's reticence. 'Is she English or French?'

'Really, sire, it's of no importance,' said Wulfstan, unable to stop himself from flushing deeply. The Prince regarded him for a minute or two, then heaved a heavy sigh.

'Ah, my boy,' he said with the air of a father towards a son, though they were but eight years apart. 'It may interest you to know that I too love a woman who can't be mine, so I can share your chagrin – and it is a bitter draught indeed.'

Wulfstan was surprised at hearing such an admission from Edward, the Black Prince, that universally popular figure, for surely no lady could resist him. He would need to be careful in answering, however, for the Prince might later regret making such a confession when not completely sober.

'Indeed, my liege,' he replied, hoping that he was not going to hear more details.

'How long have you known *your* fair lady?' asked the Prince. 'Is she a Frenchwoman?'

'Yes, sire, and I met her when I arrived in Bordeaux, just over a year ago.'

'Ah, that's not long. *I* have yearned for my beloved Jeanette ever since we were children playing together,' confided the Prince, and pulled from an inner pocket a short length of pale-blue silk. 'She wore a gown made from this, look – the sweetest lady I've ever known, and yet I have to foreswear her.'

Wulfstan's expression was blank as the Prince continued, a little wryly.

'My parents have done their best to find me a suitable bride, for they say it's important that I marry and raise up heirs to claim the crown when I depart this life. They've offered me a princess of Portugal, and the daughter of the Duke of Brabant, any number of young virgins with half a spoonful of royal blood – but I'll have none of them.' He stuck out his lower lip in defiance. 'If I can't have my beautiful Lady Jeanette, I'll have no other queen.'

For a minute or two he stared moodily into space, then gave himself a little shake. 'But come, Sir Wulfstan, 'tis your turn to name your ladylove. You say she lives here in Bordeaux?'

'Yes, sire, she is the daughter of the widow Merlette who keeps an inn. She is but sixteen, and—'

'God in heaven, boy, have you been paying court to a wench of sixteen, a mere innkeeper's daughter? Would you really tie yourself down to such a one? If she were older, I'd suggest you take your pleasure of her, then leave her for some neighbouring French butcher or baker to claim.' He looked hard at his scribe. 'But you wouldn't do that, would you, Wulfstan?'

'Indeed I would not, sire. And she wouldn't have me.'

'There you are, then – forget her and look for an English rose when you're home again. I must stay here until March, till England and France sign this peace treaty for two years – but we'll be setting sail in April, and you'll be a conquering hero – your wound will be your badge of honour. All the comely girls will be throwing themselves at your feet!' He laughed and clapped his hand on Wulfstan's left shoulder, causing him to clench his teeth in pain, though he managed to conceal it, at the same time resolving to follow his royal master's advice not to look back on his lost opportunity with Dorine. He straightened his shoulders to show his confidence in himself – and immediately had to stifle another gasp.

'It's nothing, sire, only a passing twinge,' he muttered as the Prince stared at him, for he could not hide his grimace. Poor boy, thought the Prince, he's in no fit state as yet to go seeking for a wife, but I'll keep him at my side until he regains the use of that arm and shoulder – or until he has to lose it.

Seven

1357

Land! A cheer went up from the crowded and slow-sailing vessel on which the Black Prince was returning to a grateful nation. It had been a tedious voyage from Bordeaux, sailing against the wind. Wulfstan narrowed his eyes at the distant outline, turning from misty grey to green as it came closer.

'There she is, Sir Wulfstan,' said the Prince, 'our homeland. Does the sight of it touch you in the same way?'

'I shall be glad to set foot on dry land, my liege,' answered his newly appointed knight and scrivener, weary of the rolling deck, crammed together with other military officers of the Prince's inner circle, not including the Count de Lusignan and his son who had sailed on an earlier, smaller vessel. To feel the earth firm beneath his feet was what Wulfstan most yearned for, and to continue his career as official scrivener and Keeper of the Purse to the Prince, much to the chagrin of Master Hugh Baldoc, now demoted to assistant scrivener. Wulfstan was sorry when he thought of the de Lusignans, for his new position in the Prince's household meant that he could not accept the Count's invitation to assist Charles's recovery at the castle, and to get him on to a horse again.

When the Prince had heard of this invitation, he flatly refused to allow it.

'What? Waste a valuable young fighter as nursemaid to an invalid?' he had said to the Count. 'Certainly not! I have plans for Sir Wulfstan's future at my court. There are plenty of able men looking for just such an opportunity to be squire to your son.'

Wulfstan's conscience smote him, pleased though he was at being a member of the Prince's household; he knew that he was said to be a 'favourite', and Hugh Baldoc made no secret of his resentment towards one he considered a young upstart.

'I'll visit Castle de Lusignan at the earliest opportunity to see you, Charles,' he promised, but even as he spoke, he felt disloyal to his brother-in-law, who through their shared experiences in France had become a close friend.

The landing at Plymouth was a ceremonial occasion, for the Mayor and chief burghers were waiting to welcome them, and a cheering crowd of townspeople jostled to get a glimpse of the Black Prince who stood up on a platform by the jetty to address the company. He named and presented to them the men who had been closest to him in the Poitiers campaign; the first was Sir John Chandos, and the last Sir Wulfstan Wynstede, honourably wounded in battle.

It was a strange experience for Wulfstan, hearing the cheers and shouts of his name: here he was, a newly appointed knight of the realm, sworn to serve his country, his King and his Prince, surely the luckiest youth in England and France! Dismounting from his horse gave him a jolt which sent a sword-thrust through his shoulder; his arm, now supported in a sling around his neck, was as lifeless as the arm of a corpse. Yet as the Prince had foretold, his wound was a badge of honour, and he saw some admiring looks from women and girls in the crowd.

On the following day a procession was formed with the Prince at its head. Taking a southerly direction, they skirted the great forest of Dartmoor and reached Totnes before evening, where they were offered good board and lodging. The next lap of their journey took them to Exeter, where the Prince commanded every man to enter the massive cathedral to give thanks for their deliverance and commend the souls of the fallen. Wulfstan duly knelt to give thanks for the Prince's victory, and begged for a return of strength to his left arm, and relief from the pain in his shoulder, now eight months after the blow that had broken it. The cathedral choristers sang *Non nobis Domine, sed tuo da gloriam,* and a great wave of patriotic fervour filled Wulfstan's heart; this was surely where his future lay, here in his native land. He had been away too long.

A long journey followed, mostly through untamed heath and forest, often through steep and difficult ways. The earth was awakening after its winter sleep, and fresh green foliage decked the trees; the distant grey, blue and green horizons of England seemed to beckon them on. Sometimes they came upon great open fields divided into narrow strips farmed by the tenants of gracious manor houses; sturdy yeomen's cottages of wood and stone contrasted with the single-roomed hovels made of wattle branches daubed with clay and cow dung, which housed the families of the labourers who toiled in the fields. As they approached a dark, dense forest, the Prince came to ride at his side.

'Well, Sir Wulfstan, are you glad to be back on English soil? Are you content to serve the house of Plantagenet in an English court as well as in a French one?'

'I would serve the King and his heir wherever they were lodged, my liege, but I'd prefer to serve in England.'

'Well said, Wulfstan! Your wish will be granted for at least the two years of the truce!'

Their progress along the edge of this wilderness eventually ended in a steep north-easterly climb which brought them out on to a wide open plain, where stood a circle of upended standing stones, some supporting other stones placed horizontally across them.

'There are many ideas about how these stones came to be here,' said the Prince, seeing Wulfstan's amazed stare. 'Some believe that they date back to a time when giants ruled the land, and others say they were here at the Creation of the world, but got swallowed up in the waters of the Flood, and strewn around as we see them now.'

They came to Salisbury, its newly completed cathedral spire pointing heavenwards. Once again Wulfstan followed the example of his Prince, and knelt to pray. The Dominican friar came over and touched his right shoulder.

'See over there, Wynstede, the tomb of St Osmund where men with broken bones come to be healed by putting their arm or leg through one of those three openings in the stone, do you see? Being close to St Osmund's bones may bring you healing from him.'

Wulfstan sprang to his feet, causing another stab of pain to shoot through his shoulder. Lying on the marble floor, he removed the sling, and using his right hand, pushed his limp left arm into one of the three holes, pressing his shoulder against it, while the friar said a prayer to St Osmund. The pain was so intense that Wulfstan had to withdraw his arm and confess that the saintly bones had not had the power to heal him. He began to despair of a cure, and prayed that he might continue to walk, write, ride a horse and put a brave face on his affliction; he had no wish to become known as a cripple.

From Salisbury they traversed miles of heathland, and by now were saddle-sore; Wulfstan's right arm ached from having to hold the reins for hours at a time, doing the work of two. They reached Winchester and another vociferous welcome; the Prince did not tarry there, but continued to lead them eastward, through sandy soil and tall pine trees, to Kingston where they crossed the river Thames. And then, on the twenty-fourth of May they were met by the Mayor and aldermen of the capital, who led them through decorated streets and cheering crowds to Westminster where King Edward and Queen Philippa awaited their triumphant return. The King embraced first his son and then King John of France and his son. For Wulfstan it was the culmination of a year and a half of high adventure, of serving the Black Prince and fighting under his flag. It was also time for rewards, and the Prince celebrated his successes with his customary lavishness, handing out gifts of land, horses and armour, gold and silver for the religious institutions, rare silks and brocades for the ladies. He paid public tribute to them all.

'You have excelled yourselves in battle, my friends, and now you may enjoy the rewards of peace,' he told them, and they needed no second bidding. Their days were spent hunting and jousting, and at night there were games of chess, draughts and backgammon; many bags of gold sovereigns changed hands at dice, especially after heavy drinking. Though unable to joust or shoot an arrow, Wulfstan became a skilful chess player; he had little patience with the men who were drunk every night, and his own one experience of over-indulging in wine had been a salutary lesson. Reeling back to the room he shared with three others in a similar state, he collided with something, a door or a wall or even another man silly with drink, which caused such agony in his shoulder that he howled out loud, and his friends feared the devil was after them. Never again! Besides, a drunken man was not attractive to the ladies of Queen Philippa's court who were more inclined to look with favour on such as himself, a courtly young knight with the advantage of natural good looks.

In the evenings when the musicians played for those who wished to dance, Wulfstan was soon persuaded to join in the slower, more formal dances currently in fashion, treading a measure to the low-pitched, melancholy sackbut and rhythmic beat of the tabor, holding a lady's hand with his right, while she placed her other hand on his shoulder for lack of a hand to hold; it caused him many a stab of pain, but he was learning to conceal it, compensated by the smiles of the ladies who were happy to dance with a handsome young knight, honourably wounded in battle. He had noticed one in particular, with laughing eyes as blue as cornflowers, and golden hair she sometimes wore loose, rippling over her shoulders, signifying her virgin state. He tried to find a reason for speaking to her, but she always seemed to be deep in conversation with others, and he would hear her peals of laughter from across the hall or the courtyard, wishing in vain for an opportunity to share the joke.

During the day he rode, sometimes alone, sometimes with others, mounting without help the docile mare he had chosen from the Prince's stables. A frequent companion was Sir Ranulf Ormiston, a cheerful, well-turned-out man in his twenties, shorter than Wulfstan, and with a squarish, blunt-featured face and floppy brown hair. He always made allowances for Wulfstan's lack of a left arm, and took particular care when crossing streams, avoiding steep and stony paths, which he knew jogged Wulfstan's shoulder.

Returning from one such ride, they went into the courtyard beside the great hall where the tables were laid for a banquet. Groups of people were standing around talking and laughing – and Wulfstan saw the lady he had admired from afar. She was wearing a high-waisted, low-necked gown in blue brocade, caught in folds beneath her breasts, and fashionably close-fitting sleeves.

'Tell me, Ranulf, that lady in blue, talking to Earl Holland? Who is she — his wife?'

'Oh, no, *he's* married to the "fair maid of Kent", lucky man; they say she's as kind as she is lovely to look at,' Ranulf replied with a grin. 'No, *this* beauty in blue is Lady Mildred Points, daughter of old Sir Humphrey Points, a Crusader in his time, and very jealous for his daughter. Some armful, eh? Imagine coming up behind her and putting your arms round under those two — ah! There'll be plenty of competition for her favours, so you'd better stake your claim early. Go on, offer to escort her in to supper!'

Wulfstan frowned at his friend's mockery. The young woman was indeed a beauty, slender and graceful; her fair hair was plaited this evening, and wound around her head, kept in place with a jewelled circlet. And she was looking straight at him. He felt a curiosity, a sudden strong attraction to her, an arousal of his manhood that took him completely by surprise: he stared as she smiled and took her leave of Earl Holland who bowed to her in return. And then — and *then,* incredibly, she began to walk towards Wulfstan and Ranulf, smiling and holding out her hand! Ranulf bowed to her, but she addressed Wulfstan, who hastily bowed, wondering what on earth she would say, and how he would answer.

'I have heard that you won your honourable wound by the part you played in the capture of the French king, Sir Wulfstan,' she said, taking his right hand and looking up at him with interest in her large blue eyes.

'My lady,' he said, taking her hand and blushing, much to his annoyance, aware of his body's swift response.

'Sir Wulfstan, I am happy to meet you — such youth and such courage! Will you be dining at the Prince's table, sire?'

'Yes . . . yes, of course, my lady,' he stammered, bewildered by her condescension. Was this some kind of invitation? With Ranulf's teasing in mind, he drew a breath and asked her outright, 'Will my lady permit me to escort her — to escort you to dine with the Prince?'

She smiled, her blue eyes dancing, and keeping hold of his hand, she replied, 'She will be more than happy to permit you to escort her, Sir Wulfstan.'

And so he took her little hand in his, and led her into the great hall, leaving Ranulf to gape open-mouthed at their retreating backs. Dinner was not yet served, and he led her – or did she lead him? – to a seat against the wall; she sat down, and he sat on her left, aware of the warmth of her, the fragrance of her body that made him think of ripe, sun-warmed fruit. In response to her questions about the Battle of Poitiers and capture of the French king, he said he had only been at the scene by chance. King John and his son were now living at the magnificent Savoy Palace in the Strand, under house arrest.

'Though they'll probably be sent to some great manor house when the Savoy's needed again,' she said. 'There's an enormous ransom on their heads – a king's ransom indeed!'

Wulfstan had hitherto privately thought it hardly fair to demand such a huge amount from a country which had already been so pitilessly plundered, but he simply nodded, entranced by her smiles, her voice, her obvious interest in him. Surely he must be dreaming! But no, she was speaking to him, asking him questions.

'Does your wounded arm hurt very much?' she asked him. 'I pray that it may soon be healed.'

Wulfstan had faced the fact that he might never regain the use of his arm which was shrinking and becoming discoloured, though he still hoped for the shoulder to heal and stop giving him pain; but he thanked her for her kindness, and said he hoped that it might be so.

'Such bravery deserves reward,' she said, smiling up at him, and he could think of no reply, merely inclined his head.

Dinner was being served on the long tables, and at her prompting he led her to the smaller round table where the Prince sat with members of his inner circle. The lady immediately gained the Prince's attention.

'Ah, Lady Mildred, I see that you have captured the bravest of my knights, and the comeliest! I trust that you will grant him the favours he has earned!'

Wulfstan coloured, and lowered his eyes, unable to meet hers; but she gave a little silvery laugh and told the Prince that she had several favours to ask of Sir Wulfstan, at which the company laughed. If he was being teased, Wulfstan did not mind, for to be seated beside this exquisite creature who so openly displayed the warmth of her feelings for him was a new and heady experience; and knowing that the wound he had gained in battle was the reason for her attention, he felt some compensation for the pain. He would find it easier to bear, a burden turned into a blessing, a badge of honour nobly won and to be nobly borne, for her sake. She was enchanting!

Looking at the faces around the table, he saw some of them whispering to each other; were they speculating on the favours the lady was to bestow on him? His head whirled.

'I beg your pardon, Sir Wulfstan,' said a young gallant seated near to him, 'but would you care to look some time at a specially fine broadcloth made from the wool of English sheep and woven here in London? There is no finer cloth in Europe, and a whole bevy of sempstresses make it up into tunics and cote-hardies for the court.'

Lady Mildred nodded towards the speaker and added her approval.

'Yes, Sir Guy Hamald is quite right, Wulfstan, and I insist that you take up his offer! You're no longer just a soldier returned from the war, wearing a worn black cloak with the seams unravelling, and though it has done you good service, it is time that such chivalry be rewarded by a new wardrobe. Show him the material, Guy, and I will match it with silk and velvet – and call upon my embroidresses!'

Wulfstan murmured his thanks, bewildered though he was by such generosity. He felt her blue gaze upon him, and returned her smile, suddenly conscious of his dull colours, his undoubted shabbiness in comparison with the rich fabrics of the others at the Prince's table; why had he not noticed before? The Wynstedes had never been ostentatious in their dress, being solid country gentry who managed their estates, working with their bailiffs, the women sharing the upbringing of their children with their nursemaids. But now he was a knight of the realm, seated at table with the heir to the throne, and it was time to look worthy of his status. He thanked Sir Guy Hamald for his recommendation of the broadcloth, and Lady Mildred for her offer of help with the stitching and embroidering. He did not notice the smiles that passed between the diners. Lady Mildred's smile was the only one he saw, and he basked in its glow.

A new wardrobe was duly designed for him: with the help of the Lady Mildred and the young knight known as Guy Hamald, he became the possessor of three colourful tunics, three soft linen shirts and a fur-edged russet cote-hardie that hung from his shoulders to the floor, its sleeves wide and flowing, with the fashionable dagged edging, cut into points.

Ranulf Ormiston was both amused and impressed. 'You'll be leading the fair Mildred in the dances,' he remarked, and immediately checked himself, remembering his friend's injury, his lack of an arm. Wulfstan had already thought of this, and told Ranulf not to worry on his account, because he could dance well enough, and hold his lady's hand as they trod the measures to the music of sackbut and cymbals. 'The difficulty is knowing what to do with my left arm,' he confessed. 'Shall I keep it under my clothes, and tuck the sleeves inwards, so that my lack of an arm can be seen by all? Or should I push it into the sleeve, and let it hang loose, for it has no movement? I could wear a glove on the hand – or cover it with extra lace on the cuff. What do you think?'

In envious admiration of his friend for gaining the Lady Mildred's favour, Ranulf tried first one way, and then the other, but drew in a breath of shock and dismay when he saw the left arm uncovered. It was shorter than the right, and shrunken; the flesh was discoloured, mottled white and brown, and the fingers curled inwards – like a claw, thought Ranulf, and hurriedly hid the thought under a grin, suggesting it might be better to put the arm into a sleeve, and then support it with a sling; that way there could be no misunderstanding.

'The lady can put her left hand into your right, and off you'll go, prancing side by side down the line of dance,' he said. 'Yes, with such fine apparel, she won't be able to resist you, Sir Wulfstan!'

'At least the damned arm doesn't hurt any more,' said Wulfstan wryly, 'but I fear it may never heal to do its work like the other.'

Ranulf did not reply. He saw and knew beyond any doubt

that the withered arm would never be of use, but thought his friend should be left to face this fact for himself.

As the spring advanced, Wulfstan lived in a world of incredulous joy. Surely it could not be true that Lady Mildred loved him as he knew he loved her – and yet it *must* be true. He saw it in her eyes, her responses to his shy advances; when he put his arm around her slender waist, she drew close against him; when he daringly covered one of her soft, ample breasts with his hand, she sighed and whispered his name. It was the first time he had experienced the heady sensation of being in love, and to be loved in return. His seduction by Madame la Gouvernante had been coldly and deliberately planned by Monseigneur and Madame Duclair, and pretty little Dorine had been too young and innocent – and too much under her mother's rule – to return his advances. But Mildred, beautiful, ravishing Mildred, made no secret of her feelings, and when they kissed in a corner of the corridor near the door of her room, he felt that life could hold no greater bliss: but he wanted more, much more . . .

And so did she, unashamedly, not pretending to any false modesty. She clung to him, leaning her head upon his left shoulder, and he gave no sign of the pain it caused; he would have endured torture rather than rebuff her in the slightest degree. They stood there, listening to each other's heartbeat, and then she whispered, 'Come to my room tonight, dearest Wulfstan, after dark when they're all either in bed or drinking and gaming downstairs. I shall send my maid away, and be there, waiting for you.'

'I'll be there for you, sweetest Mildred. Kiss me again.' They exchanged one last, lingering kiss before parting, and he was transported into a different world: surely heaven's high bliss held no greater happiness than this? He wanted no supper that evening, nor could he settle to any kind of activity with his companions; he wanted only to be alone until he could be with her. He went outside and gazed at the sunset, herald of a fine day tomorrow. Oh, Mildred, Mildred – how suddenly you have come into my life, and taken it over! Let me be worthy of you . . .

★   ★   ★

The hour came at last. The palace was quiet except for the distant sound of voices down in the hall. He climbed the stone stairs leading to the corridor at the end of which her bedchamber lay in darkness. He took off his shoes, and stood before the door, bracing himself to knock softly: she immediately murmured on the other side, 'Come, Wulfstan.' The door was unlocked and he entered, closing it behind him – and then stood transfixed at what he saw. She was waiting for him, her eyes dark in the light of a single candle by the bedside. And she was completely naked; her golden hair cascaded on to her shoulders, her beautiful breasts were waiting for his touch, her lips were parted ready for his kiss. His knees went weak in the presence of the enchantress. She drew him towards the bed, gently lifted his tunic off over his head, and began to unlace his shirt. His left arm was covered by a sling that hung from his neck. He hesitated a moment, then carefully took off his shirt, removed his braies and hose, and got on to the bed beside her. They were panting with anticipation, breathless with their mutual desire. Her hand was on his belly, then lightly slithered down to touch his member, erect and rigid, for he was ready to enter her and know the supreme pleasure of sharing his body with a beloved woman. Soon, soon, he would be *there*!

'Wait, Wulfstan,' she whispered, pulling herself up against a feather pillow. 'Let me love *all* of you – your poor arm, wounded in the service of the Black Prince. Let me take off the sling and kiss it – oh, let me kiss it, Wulfstan.'

'No – no, Mildred,' he almost groaned, not wanting any further delay; but she pulled the sling from around his neck, and his arm flopped on to the sheet, mottled and leathery as the arm of a corpse and as lifeless, the fingers stiffened into a claw. As soon as she saw it she recoiled with a suppressed shriek.

'Oh, my God, what is it?' she cried. 'Is it a snake? Oh, don't bring it near me!'

This was an unforeseen interruption to Wulfstan's all-consuming lust. Her desire which had matched his own had given place to something very different, and he put out his right arm to soothe her, to take her hand and reassure her. His Mildred.

'Don't touch me with that thing! Get off my bed, go away!' she shouted in panic.

Her voice rose hysterically, and he withdrew his hand, moving further down the bed, away from her; but his privy member, heavily erect, could not contain itself, and he groaned involuntarily as it emptied warm, sticky fluid on to the sheet and over her feet. She screamed again, covering her face with her hands.

'Go away! Leave me alone! For God's sake, go, go, go!'

Shaking with the aftermath of losing his seed and seeing the look of revulsion on her face, he got off the bed and found his braies on the floor. Blindly trying to reorientate his thoughts, he pulled them on and picked up the rest of his clothes.

'Go away!' she shouted again, and he had no choice but to leave the room, dressed only in his braies and carrying his new and costly garments over his much put-upon right arm. He prayed that he would not meet anybody on the corridor as he made his way back to the room he shared with Ormiston, carousing with companions in the hall below. He sat down on his wooden-framed bed, his senses still reeling, his heart still pounding in his chest. His head began to clear, and he realized that the beautiful Lady Mildred Points was no longer his. She would never be his, not now; he could not be her gallant knight and defend her. The cruel words of Madame Merlette came back to him: *Defend us? You couldn't defend a dog!* He was a cripple, a one-armed man, no use as a soldier, no use as a lover. He would have to leave the palace and the Prince's service, for his war wound counted for nothing now, less than nothing; it had become a hideous curse. He sat on the low bed and stared into space, rejected and abashed.

Queen Philippa was shocked and disbelieving.

'But it's so out of character, Mildred. My son has always praised Sir Wulfstan for his chivalry, his courtesy to ladies of high and low degree.'

'I thought so too, Your Grace – I was pleased to be noticed by such a noble knight,' sobbed her lady-in-waiting. 'But last night was so shocking, so shaming – I cannot bear to recall it!'

'Calm yourself, Mildred, and answer me. What time was this? Was it after the household had gone to bed, apart from those foolish young men who spend half the night carousing in the hall?'

'Yes, Your Grace, I was retiring to my bedchamber, and he followed me there.'

'Followed you? Into your bedchamber? Where was your maid?'

'I told her she could go to her sister's room and minister to her. She has a fever and a cough, Your Grace.'

'Really? Didn't you think that the maid might bring back infection with her?'

'Yes, that's why I told her she could stay overnight in her sister's room, Your Grace.'

'So you sent your maid away, and Sir Wulfstan followed you to your bedchamber. Did he attempt to enter it with you?'

'Yes, Your Grace, he overcame my resistance and said he . . . said he wanted to make love to me,' replied Mildred with a fresh outburst of crying. 'I thought he would show more restraint, but he picked me up and threw me on the bed, and . . . oh, Your Grace, it was so awful, so shameful, I was frightened out of my wits!'

The Queen looked upon the distraught young woman, and foresaw the enormity of the scandal that would ensue if her words were proved to be true. Sir Wulfstan might be disgraced and stripped of his knighthood, banished from the Prince's circle for ever.

'Were there any witnesses?' she asked.

'No, Your Grace, not at that time of night, or I would have cried out for assistance.'

The Queen nodded, pursing up her lips as she considered the situation. 'I must ask you, Lady Mildred, if you encouraged him in any way?'

'No, *no*, Your Grace, I—'

The Queen held up her hand. 'Listen to me, Mildred. We all know that you and Sir Wulfstan have been much in each other's company, and have thought you to be in love. In fact, many men have envied Sir Wulfstan for his conquest. It would not be so remarkable if you had decided to make love, though it would need to be confessed to a priest. I shall ask you again

– was it your intention to couple with him?'

Lady Mildred hesitated, then answered tearfully, 'It was *his* intention, Your Grace, but not mine – oh, the sight of that horrible fleshy thing, all wrinkled and discoloured and dangling over the bed – it was . . . oh, Your Grace, it was such a hideous sight!'

'Good God, Mildred, do you mean that he was undone and showing his privy member?' Queen Philippa remembered court gossip about Lady Mildred Points on past occasions, and doubted this was the first time the lady had looked upon a man's nakedness.

'Er, no, Your Grace, it was his arm, a hideous thing like a poisonous snake—'

'His *arm*, Mildred? You mean his left arm, injured by the wound he received at Poitiers? Did he take it out of the sling? Speak up, young woman, for it sounds as if there was horseplay on both sides.'

'Forgive me, Your Grace, I never expected to see such a fearsome thing!' Mildred started sobbing again, but Queen Philippa's face was stern.

'I'll ask you again, Mildred, and I want the truth. Did Sir Wulfstan remove his arm from the sling, or did you?'

'I'm sorry, Your Grace, please forgive me, he let me untie it, and I . . . oh, the sight of—'

'Enough. I shall have to tell my son the Prince what you say happened, and he will deal with Sir Wulfstan. He was at fault in entering your bedchamber, but I suspect you must take your share of the blame, and I shall have you sent back to Sir Humphrey Points.'

'*No*, Your Grace, *no*!' pleaded Mildred. 'I trusted him, I never thought he would attempt to ravish me! Please, oh *please* let me stay at court—'

'You may leave me, Mildred,' the Queen replied coldly. 'My son will question Sir Wulfstan, and take what steps he sees fit. You are dismissed.'

'Oh, *please*, Your Grace, I'll take back all I said, if only—'

'Be quiet. You may leave me – *at once*.'

'So, Sir Wulfstan Wynstede, I have heard shocking news of you from my mother the Queen. Yes, I see you're ashamed, and so you should be. Have you anything to say in your defence? Come on, boy, speak up!'

'My liege lord, I am ashamed indeed,' mumbled Wulfstan with bowed head, so not seeing the Prince's teasing eyes. 'I ask permission to leave the court as soon as I may.'

'What? Take away my scrivener and treasurer? Poor Baldoc is hardly a substitute, and I shall soon be moving my whole household to my castle at Berkhamsted. *Must* you desert me at such a time?'

'I cannot stay to be the butt of the court, my liege.'

'Ah, so you admit to being a very poor lover, then, failing to please a lady.'

On hearing this, Wulfstan's humiliation was complete. 'It was not my intention to uncover the accursed thing, my liege.'

'What? Are you saying that the lady uncovered it? And that it was as wrinkled as leather and shrunk to half its size? God's bones, I don't wonder that it frightened the poor woman!' The Prince could no longer suppress his laughter, and Wulfstan raised his head to see the merriment on his master's face. A remnant of dignity stirred his response.

'You may find my withered arm amusing, my liege, but I have no wish to provide the court with entertainment, nor do I want to see the Lady Mildred again. Dismiss me now, or I shall have to quit the court without permission.'

'Sit down, sit down, Wulfstan, and let us be finished with misunderstandings. I beg your pardon for my misplaced mirth, but won't dismiss you. You're far too useful to me.'

Wulfstan stared back at him, at first completely mystified, but then the realization dawned upon him that the Prince had been jesting with him from the beginning of their interview, and now laid a hand on Wulfstan's sound right shoulder.

'My mother is well acquainted with the lady in question, and has sent her home to her old father to try out her story on *him*, the lying little hussy. Meanwhile, Sir Wulfstan, there is much work to be done, and I shall need your services more than ever, starting now. Are your quills ready sharpened?'

Eight

'The holy monks must have been praying for fine weather!' exclaimed Sir Ranulf Ormiston, and indeed it was a perfect May morning for a royal wedding. A huge crowd was assembling before the king's palace at Reading, where the banner of St George fluttered from a flagpole on the roof.

'The sun itself will be outdazzled by so many princes and dukes,' he grinned as he and Sir Wulfstan Wynstede rode up the avenue. 'What with the king and queen in their royal robes and crowns, and his grace Prince John bedecking himself as bridegroom on his wedding morning – peacocks on parade!'

Sir Wulfstan nodded. 'Yes, it's a good time to bring all the family together. There's our Prince Edward of Wales over there with his brother John, and Prince Lionel. And look at their little brothers! The youngest can be scarcely four years old – but there he is, gambolling with his little sisters, all dressed up for the great day!'

'The bridegroom looks happy with his parents' choice for him, as well he might! The Lady Blanche has a good pedigree, co-heiress to the Duchy of Lancaster, and only her father and elder sister stand between her and her inheritance – and our excellent Prince will be looking to claim the lot in due course!'

Sir Wulfstan frowned. He disliked Ranulf's over-familiar tone when speaking of the royal family, but what he said was probably true. The nineteen-year-old Prince John of Gaunt, fourth surviving son of King Edward III, was known to be as ambitious as he was handsome, and now here he was dressed in a gold gipon open to the waist to show a gold-embroidered shirt and white silken braies, with a white fur cloak which swirled around as he moved. By contrast his elder brother Edward, the Prince of Wales, was dressed in his usual sombre black, relieved by silver trimmings and embroidery. He wore a coronet upon which three black ostrich feathers waved, reflected in the embroidery on his gipon, the fleur-de-lys which was his heraldic symbol. He waved to Wulfstan. 'Come and join the festivities, noble knight!'

They had reached the resplendent crowd of guests, and were hailed by acquaintances, among them Theobald Eldrige, now in the service of the king as a soldier. He was delighted to meet his one-time leader of a *chevauchée* from the Maison Duclair.

'I only went back there for a year, Sir Wulfstan,' he said, 'and then went home to help my father – but now with talk of war, I decided to improve my skill with the longbow. There's going to be some great jousting here after the wedding – no better way of keeping bored soldiers up to the mark, don't you . . . oh.' He gasped and cut himself short when he saw the tucked-in sleeve that replaced Wulfstan's left arm, strapped to the side of his otherwise strong and healthy body under his clothes. 'I'm . . . er . . . sorry.'

'Don't worry, Theobald, there's more than one way of giving service,' Wulfstan said with a half-smile. 'At Berkhamsted Castle I keep myself well occupied by serving the Black Prince as scrivener, treasurer and as his envoy, a sort of itinerant visitor to his estates.'

'And you ride a horse, I see,' said Theobald, anxious to make amends for his tactlessness.

'Yes, with the help of my two legs and a very strong right arm, I can mount her and dismount without assistance.' Wulfstan said nothing about the after-effects of his wound at Poitiers; the two vertical frown lines between his eyes gave him a stern appearance which added to his authority at the castle, whereas in fact they were due to the almost constant pain he endured in his left shoulder, but which he had become adept at concealing.

Ranulf broke in on their exchange with a knowing grin. 'Look over there, gentlemen, see, Earl Thomas of Kent, one of the king's finest soldiers, and his wife they call the fair maid of Kent – the most beautiful woman in England, with virtues to match, or so 'tis said. He's a much-envied man, is old Thomas Holland of Kent!'

Wulfstan glanced very briefly at the group, but did not want to stare; his eyes had fallen on another lady of the court, the Lady Mildred, now wearing the wimple and hair-concealing pointed headdress of a married woman. She was big with child, and her eyes were weary; across the crowd she caught sight of Wulfstan, and they both quickly looked away. How far away and long ago his days at the court now seemed, and how brief their romance! The fact that he had no feelings at all towards her now, except for a kind of pity, led him to conclude that he had never truly loved her at all. And now there was Beulah . . . the very thought of her brought a secret smile to his lips, which Ranulf noticed.

'Oho, Sir Wulfstan, I see that you still admire the Lady Mildred! Can it be that you have an interest in the burden she carries?'

Wulfstan glared. 'Such an ignorant, ill-mannered question does not even merit a reply,' he replied coldly, turning away to talk with Theobald and catch up on each other's experiences in the four years since the adventure of the *chevauchée*. Theobald had returned to his family home in south Hampshire to assist his father in running their estate, but he was eagerly looking forward to joining in the jousts which were to be part of the wedding celebrations for the next two days.

'We need to keep in training for the next invasion of France!' he said, then again remembered Wulfstan's lack of his left arm. His embarrassment was saved by the Prince himself, who strolled up at that point to speak to Wulfstan. He was flushed and seemed somewhat agitated; his breath betrayed his indulgence in wine.

'A word with you, Sir Wulfstan,' he said, making a beckoning movement with his head.

'My liege,' Wulfstan replied with a bow.

'D'you see that lady over there, the sweetest of all women, smiling at my brother John the bridegroom, but with never a smile for me?'

Wulfstan looked at the lady who had been pointed out by Ranulf, but hardly knew what to say.

'Don't you see her, the Countess of Kent over there talking to my sister? *Look* at her, Wulfstan, beside Thomas the Earl of Kent, and their children. An angel here on earth!'

Wulfstan now fixed his eyes on the Kents, and saw that the Countess was indeed beautiful, smiling and talking to the princess while her husband the earl regarded her with satisfaction, the mother of his five children.

'She is just as you say, sire.' Wulfstan could sympathize with the Prince for his lost love, married to one of his warrior noblemen, a virtuous wife who would never stray from her husband and the children she had borne him. The Prince continued speaking, as if in a rage.

'Today I am to watch my younger brother John marry the Lady Blanche of Lancaster, while I, a warrior prince of the blood, cannot claim my own true love, my own Jeanette,' he said, as if it were Wulfstan's fault. 'May you be spared the pangs of suppressed love!'

Then to Wulfstan's relief he turned away to talk with the bride and groom and help himself to another beaker of mead.

With the ceremony over, there was a feast at the palace, and the young men were impatient to begin the tournament, in which the king's grown sons and members of his standing army were inviting all comers to compete with blunted lances to unhorse their opponents.

'Make no mistake, the king's on the lookout for new military men, and before this year's over, there'll be a new invasion of France!' said Ranulf, and the young men's eyes brightened. Wulfstan knew this to be true; the two-year truce between England and France made in the March of 1357 had run out, and the king was known to be preparing to make a further claim on French territories held by the English crown. This royal wedding might well be the last celebration for some of the valiant men, royal, noble or commoner, who would win their spurs at the tournament, and Wulfstan knew himself to be an object of sympathy. Ranulf and Theobald certainly thought it a shame that such a proven knight and military hero should now be reduced to a pen-pushing scribe, adding up columns of figures, a task just as well performed by an older, retired soldier. And yet . . . was *he* sorry to be out of the combat when it took place? He sometimes worked by the light of a midnight candle, to complete documents for the Prince who had come to realize his worth – so much so, that he trusted Wulfstan with further duties, making him responsible for collecting dues from the many estates owned by the Prince: thus he became a tax collector, a character notoriously unpopular since biblical times. He visited landowners in their manor houses, merchants who rented town houses and practised trades in premises on land owned by the Prince; even a few monasteries held land that was his from birth.

Thus Sir Wulfstan had become a familiar figure in the shires, riding straight-backed, long-legged, controlling his mare with the reins held firmly in his right hand. When he arrived at great houses he was usually received as a guest by owners wanting to ingratiate themselves with the Prince, while others complained at what they considered unjust demands upon their incomes. Wulfstan treated them all the same, judging each case on its own merits and always aiming for fairness. He was never tempted to accept bribes, neither did he bargain; each householder got his rights, according to the size of the estate, and changes of family situation, births, bereavements and marriages. *Yes!* He *did* enjoy his life as the Prince's envoy, and had no desire to go to war again: his ever-painful shoulder and withered arm were constant reminders of the dangers as well as the glory, even in victory. So he threw himself into his triple duties, and his standing with the Prince rose steadily higher.

And there was Beulah. Sweet, gentle, pious Beulah, who at seventeen seemed quite unaware of her beauty, and the effect it might have on a man. She was a younger daughter of a landowner who maintained his income by judicious farming, and though Greneholt Manor in Hertfordshire was modest by the standards of the usual great houses of landed gentry, the estate was well managed, and Sir William Horst thought nothing of getting down to ploughing, hay-making and harvesting with his tenants who farmed their own strips in the great field set aside for that purpose. He allowed them to own, or share ownership of a pig, a goat and a few geese, as long as the livestock did not stray on to their neighbours' vegetable patches. Sir William and Lady Judith Horst reminded Wulfstan of his own parents at Ebbasterne Hall in his childhood, true country dwellers with no pretensions; like his father, Sir William shared the management of the estate with his bailiff, and Lady Judith had worked with the nursemaids in caring for the children, as his own mother had done. Consequently they were respected by their tenants, though on occasions they could also be feared, for their morality was stern, and being regular attendants at Mass in the parish church of St Mary Greneholt, they frowned upon ungodly sins of the flesh, especially fornication and drunkenness, and wrongdoers did not go unpunished.

Beulah had been brought up to share her parents' piety. Her clothes were neat, practical and modest, and her light-brown hair was tied up in a white twisted scarf around her head, out of sight. Yet notwithstanding these precautions against vanity, and protection against lechery, Wulfstan was drawn to her modest beauty at first sight when she shared the dining table with her parents and their important visitor from Berkhamsted Castle, and found himself suddenly thinking about her as he went about his duties, and as he settled down to sleep at night he would remember her soft brown eyes that had looked at him before she had modestly lowered her head. Two years had passed since the disastrous affair of Lady Mildred, during which time he had avoided any entanglement with womankind because of his accursed left arm, as hideous as it was useless. He could have no designs on shy, modest little Beulah, but just to think about her, and on occasion to look upon her, gave him a special delight, a lifting of the spirit he had not experienced before. He began to think of reasons why he should ride to places reasonably near to Greneholt, and while in the vicinity, to pay a call at the manor and tell its occupants of new trends in farming; for instance, while he talked with Sir William about matters concerning the estate, he would offer to obtain for him some seeds of a new, recommended crop of wheat or barley – or a new device for scaring birds away from the growing crop. Once, he brought Lady Judith a present of dried figs from abroad, and every time he came to the manor, Beulah would hear of his arrival and come to curtsey to him as Prince Edward's envoy. When he caught her eye she blushed and turned away, but as the days and weeks went by, she began to return his smile; and then one sunny day in June while riding through the Hertfordshire countryside, he admitted to himself that he loved her, though without expecting any return of love. Dear, sweet, virginal Beulah! She would never know his hateful secret, but he could at least allow himself to dream . . .

But he under-estimated the sharp eyes of her parents and their vigilance to guard their daughter from the lechery of men and those who would dishonour her.

After the excitement of the wedding and the tournaments that followed the feasting, the Black Prince returned to Berkhamsted with his knights, and found an occasion to speak privately with Wulfstan as they rode, dismissing Ranulf with a wave of his hand.

'You know already the rumours of renewed warfare with France,' he said, and Wulfstan nodded, for his friends had talked of little else. 'So let me tell you of what has been brewing on the other side of the Narrow Sea. That fellow the dauphin, an older son of King John of France, has set himself up as regent, to rule in his father's place – a sickly creature by all accounts.'

Wulfstan nodded. It was acknowledged that the king of France had left this son at home during the campaign that had culminated at Poitiers, because he was heir to the throne in the event of his father's death. Now with his father imprisoned in England, he had ruled over France for two years.

'There are reports that he is raising an army, a mixed bag by my spies' accounts, of men-at-arms, archers with their silly crossbows, no match for our longbows, and as many mercenaries as he can get to accept his money. He has not yet paid a quarter of his father's ransom, and *my* father questions his patriotism – does he wish to keep the king in captivity, so that he can continue to wield power as regent?'

Wulfstan nodded assent, as he was expected to do. He already knew much of what the Prince now confided in him, being scrivener at Berkhamsted, and thought he could guess what was coming next.

'My father the king is losing no time. His sheriffs are collecting stores of necessary victuals for an army, and the royal arsenal at the Tower of London is making and storing new weaponry. All our best men are to be mobilized, and the dauphin will get the shock of his life before this year is out!'

Wulfstan winced at the words 'our best men', for he could play no part in the coming invasion. As if reading his thoughts, the Prince went on, 'You will be left in my place at Berkhamsted while I'm away. There is a good household of servants and cooks, mainly women – and out of doors there is an excellent bailiff, under-bailiff and reliable grooms; but I'll leave you a handful of guards to call upon if there is any trouble, and your word will be law. Our friend Hugh Baldoc will assist you as scrivener, for he now has a tolerable right hand. My mother the Queen will be the official head of the household, but I hope you will not have to appeal to her. I know you, Wulfstan, and believe that I can trust you to look after my favourite royal residence. What have you to say?'

Wulfstan was trying to marshal his thoughts together, to give his Prince a proper answer. He knew about the proposed invasion of France, but his own promotion was an honour he had truly not expected.

'Well, Sir Wulfstan Wynstede, what have you to say?' repeated the Prince, smiling.

'I thank you, my liege, and will gladly serve you with all my heart,' he managed to affirm. 'Will I . . . Will you continue to use me as envoy to your estates?'

'Certainly. Who else could do it as well? There will be less time to spare, you will simply collect their dues without accepting hospitality – and you had better not be away from the castle for more than two nights at any one time.'

Then I shall still be able to see Beulah, thought Wulfstan.

'You do me high honour, my liege.'

'Well and good. Now, I intend to move down to Northbourne Manor with my senior commanders, to oversee the preparations for men and provisions. My father will remain at Westminster until we sail, probably a couple of months later.'

'Very good, my liege,' replied Wulfstan a little breathlessly, for his head was whirling as he tried to absorb all that the Prince was telling him.

'I'm asking a great deal of you, especially as you have not left my service for a single day since we returned from France.'

'Er . . . even so, my liege.'

'So I'm setting you free for a month before I move to Northbourne. Hugh Baldoc will have a chance to show his skill, and we shall all have to see how we fare without you. I've appointed an under-bailiff to do the rent collecting, while you visit your family at Hyam St Ebba, with one of my archers, Theobald Eldrige as your squire. It's about time.'

And more than time since I visited my brother-in-law Charles at the Castle de Lusignan, thought Wulfstan.

'How does that suit you, Sir Wulfstan Wynstede? Let's agree on the month of June for your escape from the grindstone, eh?'

The Prince was smiling, and Wulfstan could only smile back. 'I thank you, my liege.'

And had he not been sitting astride a horse, he would have bowed.

The interview with Sir William Horst, by contrast, took place in that gentleman's study.

'Pray be seated, Sir Wulfstan. As envoy of the Prince of Wales, and honoured by him for valour in the field of battle, I'm fully aware that you take precedence over me. Yet I dare address you as an equal in a personal situation such as we are in.'

Every muscle in Wulfstan's body tensed, for he saw where Sir William was leading. He assumed an expression of gravity to match the older man's seriousness.

'Have you any idea why I wish to speak to you, Sir Wulfstan?'

It was a direct approach, and demanded an honest answer.

'I dare to say that you are thinking of your daughter Beulah, sire.'

'Ah, I see that you do know, and I have to remind you that at seventeen years old she is far too young to consider marriage. She is totally ignorant of the ways of men, as innocent as a young child, and Lady Judith and I are much concerned over her.'

Wulfstan flushed darkly. 'Indeed, I know this well, sire, and I have nothing but the deepest respect for her maidenhood.'

'I am sure of it, and told my lady wife as much. I believe

you to be an honourable man, grievously wounded in battle, but still able to give valuable service to the Prince. We have the greatest trust in your integrity, but Beulah is our youngest daughter, and we think she should wait until she's twenty-one, and we look for a husband at least five years older than herself. May I ask your age, Sir Wulfstan?'

'My age? I am twenty-one, sire, exactly four years older than Beulah,' Wulfstan replied, utterly amazed at what he had just heard. He had been content just to look upon Beulah as a knight looks up to his lady – but here was her father talking of *marriage*! To be married to Beulah, with her innocent wifely virtues would be as happy a match and as prudent as could be imagined – in other circumstances, if the man were whole and sound in body, not carrying around an accursed arm, as hideous as it was useless.

'I am honoured beyond all telling, sire, and I understand your reluctance to—'

But Sir William interrupted him, his face beaming with joy.

'Good, Sir Wulfstan, my wife and I welcome you! Our beloved daughter could have no better husband, and so we ask that you will enter into a betrothal to Beulah, who I may tell you returns your feelings for her. Are you willing for a betrothal to be declared here at St Mary Greneholt church, and be further willing to wait four years? For I must tell you that if you are not thus willing, we could not allow you to see or speak to Beulah. Only as her future husband can we permit her to meet you, and we trust that you will protect and respect her virtue. Are you agreed to this?'

The prospect of meeting and talking with Beulah as a welcome guest of her parents was a pleasure that Wulfstan could not reject. Perhaps in the course of four years he might be able to tell her father the truth, and show him the hideous blemish on an otherwise fit and healthy body, that gruesome dead arm that hung from his ever-painful left shoulder – a sight that had terrified an older, experienced woman. And then perhaps her father would tell her mother, and her mother would tell Beulah, so that she might be prepared . . .

But Sir William was shaking his hand and calling for Lady Judith and Mistress Beulah to come to the study and hear the news; in another moment the sweet girl stood before him, her shining eyes leaving no doubt of her happiness. Prompted by her mother, she held out her hand and he pressed it to his lips. What should he say to her?

'Dearest Beulah . . .' was all he could manage.

'Dear Sir Wulfstan,' she whispered in return, and the promise was made and sealed. Later he might have doubts and question his fitness for her, but now, as she stood before him with her parents' glad approval, he resolved to banish such dark thoughts in the light of love.

Within three weeks the betrothal was formally declared and blessed in the church of St Mary Greneholt in the face of the congregation, and later that day, in the presence of her parents he was allowed to kiss her on the cheek. Her complexion was clear with a faint, rosy blush, and when he placed his hand on her shoulder, she gladly put her arms around his neck – at which Lady Judith hurriedly stepped forward and made her withdraw them. Beulah blushed and curtsied to the man whose wife she would eventually be, but her soft brown eyes sparkled. It was a moment to savour and remember for life, and he did not anticipate the emotional strain that lay ahead, the coming years of separation and frustration.

Nine

Heads turned to look at the two young men on horseback as they rode westwards out of London on a clear June morning; passing through Staines they reined in to stop at an inn for refreshment, and were very civilly received.

'D'ye reckon one of 'em be a prince?' the innkeeper's wife whispered. 'That handsome one in the russet tunic and leather belt with a sword at his side?'

'No, can't ye see, woman, he handles everything with his right hand, and that's 'cause he ain't got no left arm,' replied her husband. 'He must be some young nobleman who's lost it in the service o' the king, though he's scarcely twenty, neither be the other one. See to them horses, boy, and don't stand staring!' he added to a lad standing by.

The other young rider was similarly dressed in darker colours, and both wore elongated hoods; the swordsman had his twisted around his head in the style of a lord, while the other's hung down his back in a liripipe, denoting his servant status. Both men had short, clipped beards, and seemed on very friendly terms.

The swordsman thanked the innkeeper and paid him in good coin before they continued on their way; by mid-afternoon they crossed over the Bourne river into Hampshire, and proceeded along the valley until they rounded a bend and came in sight of Castle de Lusignan, perched up on a rocky outcrop above where the river Bourne meets the Dene.

'Well, there it is, Theo,' the young knight said to his squire as they crossed the bridge over the Bourne above the meeting of the rivers. 'The Castle de Lusignan. We'd better dismount and start climbing.'

The squire took the reins of both their horses as they toiled slowly up the steep-sided cliff to the forbidding castle.

'It's one of those built by William the Conqueror after his victory in 1066, more fortress than home,' he told his squire, for that was how young Sir Wulfstan remembered it from childhood days when the de Lusignans had considered themselves far superior to any of the families in the hundred of Hyam St Ebba.

'Times have changed a lot since this war with France,' Wulfstan continued as he made his way upward with the use of his one arm. 'Their sons fought side by side with us, and lost their first son Piers at Crécy, where my brother Oswald was also . . . er,' he hesitated and then went on, 'and their second son Charles was wounded at Poitiers three years ago and lost a leg. He's the man I'm going to see.'

Looking up at the castle, Sir Wulfstan's spirits rose, for here he was at last, given permission from Edward, known as the Black Prince, to visit his relations – and better still, his friends. He patted the neck of the docile grey mare which he had named Jewel, a gift from the Queen. She was sturdier than she at first appeared, and a bond of mutual trust had grown up between master and mount; she seemed to know that Wulfstan needed to avoid steep and difficult pathways, choosing to travel a longer way if it was easier. By his side was his squire, Theobald Eldrige, strong and reliable, happy to attend on Sir Wulfstan as his squire before joining the king's army later in the year.

Count Robert de Lusignan and Lady Hélène received their visitor civilly enough, though Wulfstan sensed a certain coolness in their greeting.

'We have long waited for a sight of you, seeing that you said you would visit Charles and help his recovery,' said the Count. 'Yet we have scarcely had news of you, other than your favour with the Black Prince. Our son has been much disappointed, and has not regained his strength as we were led to hope he would.'

'Even so, he will still be glad to see you, and Ethelreda will take you to his room,' said the Countess, and Wulfstan was taken aback by the sadness in her face; both of them had considerably aged during the intervening years since Poitiers,

and Wulfstan felt a sword thrust of conscience towards this
family who had treated him with much kindness in the past.
He bowed and murmured an apology, at which they nodded
briefly, and retired to their room, leaving it to his sister to do
duty as his hostess.

Ethelreda greeted him with kisses and tears, and the children
gathered around him, Piers, Norval and Sofia, and also a smiling
toddler that Wulfstan assumed had been inside his sister's belly
on his last visit.

'What happiness to see you again, Wulfstan! I thought you'd
forgotten all about us!' she cried. 'Charles has been wanting
to see you so often, but we thought you had grown too grand
for us, now that the Prince has made you his right-hand man
– so come and see him *now,* and tell him all about life at
Court!'

Wulfstan had expected Charles to come out to greet him,
on crutches or at least with a stick; but when he saw his friend
and fellow soldier lying on a couch in a room that was clearly
set apart as a sickroom, he understood only too well, and could
hardly conceal his shock at seeing Charles, once so vigorous,
now so pale and thin. He did not rise, but smiled a welcome,
holding out a hand whichWulfstan took, smiling back at this
shadow of the man he had known.

'So, what's the news from Berkhamsted?' asked Charles,
raising an eyebrow. 'Is it true that our gracious King Edward
and his warlike son Prince Edward are planning another
onslaught on France? Tell me it isn't so!'

Wulfstan told him regretfully that the rumours were indeed
true, but that he of course would not be going; instead he had
been given the privilege of overseeing the day-to-day running
of the castle at Berkhamsted with regard to expenses, and
answerable to the Queen.

'So you see, Charles, my wretched arm has spared me from
further slaughter of other men's sons,' he said, and Ethelreda
shot him a warning glance.

'Come, Charles old friend,' he continued with forced bright-
ness, 'we've still got three arms and three legs between us, and
I've been lucky in gaining a good position in the Prince's
household. I'll still be able to ride out to collect rents for him,

and I'll come over whenever I can.' He made a movement towards the couch, then gasped and winced. Ethelreda noticed.

'Are you in pain, Wulfstan? You have frown lines between your eyebrows. Is it since your arm was lost? Charles says he feels pain in his missing leg.'

Wulfstan did not want to go into any details about his own health while Charles lay languidly on a couch.

'I have not actually *lost* the arm, Ethelreda, it's still there, and 'tis a horrible sight, shrunken and discoloured.' He shuddered involuntarily. ''Twould frighten you if you saw it.'

'But that's not right, Brother! You must have it seen by a surgeon, and ask if anything can be done for it.'

'I have had the services of the prince's own surgeon, and I know that the pain will be there in my shoulder joint for the rest of my life.'

'Then you must go up to the Abbey St Ebba, and ask for Friar Valerian to see it,' she told him. 'He's the infirmarian there, and is known to have a healing touch. I always have him to see the children if they have a fever or rash, and so does our sister-in-law at Ebbasterne Hall – he comes at once.'

'But this is ten miles away – why should he come all that distance just to see your children, or Janet's? Shouldn't he stay within the Abbey?'

'He's not a monk, but a *Franciscan friar*,' she explained, 'used to travelling from one place to another, like St Francis himself, and he will come at any hour to see a Wynstede. He lives at the Abbey now, because his rigorous life has aged him, but he has a healing touch – though I've heard he's something of a law unto himself.'

'Is there any reason why our family should be so privileged?' he asked curiously.

For a moment she hesitated, then answered, 'He has always had a close bond with the Wynstedes since we were children. He can't give Charles his leg back, nor restore him to vitality of body – but he raises Charles's spirits by his wise sayings. I *insist* that you go and consult him!'

'Well, Sister, I shall do as you say, though I would hardly think my trouble to be compared with . . . with Charles's. And first I must visit our brother at Ebbasterne Hall, and his lady wife.' He grinned as he spoke of Janet, a Blagge who had acquired airs and graces since her marriage, and Ethelreda smiled and nodded.

'And you'll go to see Kitty and Aelfric at Blagge House, of course?'

'Of course, if that appalling old man will let me over the threshold – if not I shall arrange for Mistress Keepence to bring them to me at Ebbasterne Hall.'

'No, Wulfstan, command that they be brought *here*, to the Castle de Lusignan,' said his sister. 'Let them have a few days getting to know their Uncle Wulfstan and their cousins. They're fine young people; she's thirteen now, and already a beauty. Give them a holiday from their grandsire!'

'I'd better get my duty done first, and call at Ebbasterne Hall. You'll have to remind me of all the children's names, which I've completely forgotten.'

Ethelreda reminded him that the Wynstede twin girls were Lois and Joanna, and their three younger brothers Denys, Elmete and the latest to arrive, Cedric.

'I'll never remember, though I'm as much their uncle as I am to yours – and to Kitty and Aelfric,' he replied. 'And what's the name of your youngest, this little toddling fellow who keeps falling over?'

'Robert,' she said, her eyes softening with maternal pride. 'He's the joy of my life, Wulfstan – our youngest son, and the last – aren't you, my precious boy?'

She folded the smiling two-year-old in her arms, and Wulfstan looked at her keenly. She was no longer the roguish playmate he remembered from those far-off days of childhood. Though not yet five-and-twenty, she had lost the sparkle of her youth; and how did she know that Robert was their last baby? The answer was painfully obvious: Charles no longer took her as his lawful wife because of his weakness. Wulfstan sighed over the far-reaching ill consequences of war, and his thoughts turned to Beulah – dear little pious Beulah, willing to accept a long betrothal, all unaware of his misgivings about his secret disfigurement. He partly confided in Ethelreda, though he would not show her the arm, and she said that if Beulah loved him as she said she did, she would not be upset by the blemish of a withered arm, and wished him well. Yet it remained his deepest fear; for if the bold, experienced Lady Mildred had been terrified by it, how would it appear to Beulah – and her parents?

Abbot Damian received Wulfstan with the courtesy befitting a knight of the realm, and when Wulfstan asked if he might see Friar Valerian, a kind of recognition came to the Abbot's eyes, and he sent a lay brother to the infirmary; back came a message that the friar would see Sir Wulfstan straight away in the herb garden adjacent to the infirmary.

Friar Valerian had aged considerably since Wulfstan had last seen him as a child. Tall and rake-thin, with deep lines around his eyes and mouth, a livid ridged scar ran down the right side of his face, pulling down the skin around the eye; the once red-brown hair was grey, tonsured over the crown and hanging down to his shoulders. Nevertheless, Wulfstan knew him at once, even before the friar held out both arms to embrace him.

'Sir Wulfstan, little brother, I would have known you without being told. I thank God for letting me see you again as a man!'

Wulfstan returned the embrace, so close did he already feel to this man of God.

'I heard that you lost an arm at the Battle of Poitiers,' went on the friar. 'Tell me, how has it healed, my son?'

Wulfstan had grown accustomed to making light of his wound, and usually answered this question with stoic endurance; but now he spoke the plain truth.

'I still have the arm, good Friar, and suffer constant pain in the shoulder on that side.'

'Let me see it, Wulfstan. Come, take off your tunic and shirt – here, I'll help you.'

His touch was firm but gentle, avoiding direct contact with the left shoulder. Wulfstan obeyed his instructions, and felt a curious sense of relief when the withered arm was free of its bandage and hung down in all its ugliness.

'You poor boy,' muttered the friar, gently raising the arm and regarding the dark, claw-like hand and very lightly feeling the irregular shoulder bones, wrongly knitted together. He asked Wulfstan to stand up, sit down and then lie down upon a trestle table; a very light traction on the arm caused Wulfstan to moan involuntarily.

'My son, this will have to come off.'

Wulfstan nodded mutely. He had suspected this for some time, but only now did he admit it. The friar's eyes were filled with pity.

'You'll have seen arms and legs cut off after battles?'

'Yes, Friar. My brother-in-law Charles de Lusignan lost his right leg after Poitiers, and he has not recovered well after three years.'

'Ah, yes. Poor Mistress Ethelreda and their children.'

'I've heard that you visit my nieces and nephews when they're ill, Friar.'

'I do what I can for Cecily's children,' said the friar, crossing himself. 'And I'll do what I can for you, though it will not be without danger. You are otherwise young and strong, which is greatly in your favour.'

'I'll face danger, Friar Valerian – I'll risk death for a chance of losing this horrible thing.'

'Hm. You must speak to your brother Oswald, and obtain his permission.'

'I am my own man, Friar, of one-and-twenty years, and need no man's permission.'

'Even so, your brother and sister must know what you are prepared to undergo, and the risk of bleeding and of putrid suppuration after the limb is severed. They must be told of the danger, and I am reluctant to take this step without their knowledge.' The friar's voice was low. 'How long will you be staying at the castle?'

'For the whole month of June.'

'Have you a competent manservant?'

'Yes, my squire Theobald is strong and sensible.' There was only one question left. 'Suppose I do not submit to the knife and the saw, Friar, suppose I go on living with this withered arm, what would happen?'

'It will eventually blacken and may drop off, my son, but not before spreading its poison throughout your whole body. Already it begins to smell of dead flesh.'

'Thank you, good Friar. I believe that I was sent to you for this purpose. I shall tell my brother and sister of my decision, and absolve you from all blame if I should die.'

It was all settled. The Abbot, Sir Oswald and the Lady Ethelreda were told, and Wulfstan was lodged in the Abbey infirmary with Theobald Eldrige. An early date was fixed, and prayers were offered up at Masses held the day before and early in the morning of the day itself.

A scrubbed table was set up on trestles in the infirmary which had been cleared of all other patients, a clean sheet was spread over it, and on this Wulfstan lay down, wearing nothing above his waist. He was not given breakfast, for fear of him vomiting while the arm was being removed, and also to enhance the effect of the strong barley wine in a jug at his side, from which Theobald gave him frequent sips. On another table Friar Valerian placed clean towels, washed lambswool, two sword-sharp knives and a small saw. A fire was burning in the hearth, though it was a warm summer day. The friar stood at Wulfstan's left side, with Abbot Damian behind him with his Prayer Book, and Theobald sat at Wulfstan's right side. The friar handed him a wooden spoon with a white kerchief wrapped around it, to place between Wulfstan's teeth for him to bite on when the pain got very severe. He gave his master another sip of barley wine, and took firm hold of his hand.

Just before he began, Friar Valerian sent up a silent prayer. *Blessed Saint Cecilia, intercede for me.*

And then the Friar took up a knife and sliced it through the arm to the bone, about two inches above the demarcation line of withered flesh. As muscle was cut away from the bone, Wulfstan groaned through clenched teeth on the spoon, and Theobald murmured to him in a low tone.

'I'm here, Sir Wulfstan, your squire Theo. Hold my hand, and bite hard.'

Lord Jesus Christ, have mercy upon me, a sinner.

Side by side with Friar Valerian, the Abbot mopped up the brisk flow of blood with lambswool, and the friar reached for the saw.

'The bone will be severed further up, to give me enough

loose skin for a flap to fold over the stump,' he explained quietly, and then there was no sound but the scraping of the saw against bone, backwards and forwards as if sawing wood, until it was through, and the severed arm thrown into a bucket. Theobald whispered encouragement, but Wulfstan was deathly pale, his eyes were closed, his mouth half open.

'He's fainted from the pain, Friar!' his squire cried in alarm, but the friar was calm.

'That will give him a respite,' he answered, 'and 'twill lessen the bleeding.' He threaded a needle with the strong black linen yarn used for repairing monks' habits, and dabbing away blood between every stitch, the skin flaps were completely sewn together. A large lambswool dressing soaked in salt water was placed over the stump.

'That will have to be held in place and checked until the bleeding stops,' ordered Valerian, 'and then we can put on a tight bandage.'

Theobald Eldrige, flushed and perspiring, assured him that he would not leave Sir Wulfstan's side. The Abbot murmured his thanks to the friar, and together they took wine, offering a cup to the squire.

'We cannot rejoice too soon,' said the friar. 'We must wait to see if he runs a fever, or starts bleeding from the stump – or if pus forms in it, which God forbid.'

Abbot Damian nodded. 'Thanks be to God thus far.'

And thanks to blessed Saint Cecilia who watched over us and guided my hands, Friar Valerian prayed silently.

Surfacing up from a red-hot glare of pain, Wulfstan slowly began to regain his senses. A cup of cold water was being held to his lips, and the sips were balm to his parched tongue. He heard voices as if from a long way off. One he knew was the friar's.

'Your dead arm has been severed from your living flesh, my son.'

'May God be thanked that he has come through the ordeal.' It was the Abbot.

'I'm here at your side, sire, your squire Theo – take another sip of water.'

Wulfstan swallowed a gulp of water and coughed. 'Thanks

be to God,' he croaked, as the realization dawned upon him that it was *gone*, that hideous unclean flesh. He was free from its curse, and in spite of the pain he closed his eyes in relief and thankfulness.

The friar told Wulfstan he must stay at the Abbey for at least a week, in case of bleeding or festering. During that week, Sir Oswald and Lady Janet Wynstede rode up to visit him, and Mistress Keepence walked up from Blagge House with Kitty and Aelfric Blagge, Cecily's own children, born to her first husband, and now living with their Aunt Keepence and their embittered grandsire, who stayed away. Wulfstan became aware of an easy, friendly understanding between Maud Keepence and the friar, and assumed it was because she had willingly taken over Kitty and Aelfric and brought them up as her own after Cecily's death.

Mercifully there were no complications, and Wulfstan made a steady recovery, thanks to his youth and natural vigour, the friar said. Each day he felt a little stronger, a little more able to respond to visitors; the wound stopped oozing blood, and the friar applied a bandage that wound fairly tightly around the upper part of his arm, which caused Wulfstan some discomfort – but to his incredulous joy he found that the chronic pain in his left shoulder was lessening. Without the dragging weight of the useless arm, it began to improve, and the friar gently rubbed the skin over it with oil of comfrey, which he prepared himself in the little pantry attached to the infirmary. He smiled and shook his head when Wulfstan eagerly announced the merciful disappearance of the pain.

'Don't rejoice too soon, my son,' he warned. 'You will never be quite free from it, but it will become easier. I will pray to my blessed patron saint, Cecilia, for her intercession.'

Cecilia. Wulfstan had heard of her as a virgin and martyr who had lived in second century Rome, and he noticed a softening of the friar's stern features when he said her name. He mentioned this to Maud Keepence who nodded, like one familiar with a long history.

'It's true, she's his patron saint – and he looked upon your

sister Cecily as the embodiment of her on earth,' she said in
a low voice, her eyes smiling at a memory. 'They met again
on board that fated boat, only to be finally parted again.'

Wulfstan's heart gave a leap, like a seeker on the verge of a
discovery. He remembered Dan Widget's words about Cecily's
last night on earth, the shipwreck which dragged her down
into the deep. He gazed intently into Maud's eyes.

'When did Friar Valerian rejoin the brothers at the Abbey,
Maud?'

'When he returned from France, soon after we lost Cecily.'
She turned to him with sudden emotion. 'Oh, Wulfstan, your
sister was a good, virtuous woman, a faithful wife and mother
– and Valerian was always true to his vows, for theirs was a
chaste love, far above the earthly desires of men and women,
a lifelong devotion. Let her rest in peace!'

Her voice rose, and Wulfstan begged her to be calm. He
promised that he would never repeat what she had told him,
but for which he thanked her. He now saw why Dan Widget
had concealed the name of the other survivor of the shipwreck
that had taken Cecily's life; Friar Valerian had also been there,
and his life, like Dan's, had been preserved. Dan had wanted
to protect her good name and the friar's from the slightest
breath of rumour, and for this Wulfstan was grateful; it explained
the closeness he felt towards this man of God who had taken
away his curse.

For now he could return to Beulah, his betrothed, with no
need to be ashamed of the clean severance of an arm lost in
the Black Prince's service; it would be a badge of honour, a
sacrifice to be displayed with pride.

Ten

1360

It was the first day of the year. The Feast of the Nativity had been marked by daily Masses in the Castle chapel, and a haunch of roasted venison in the Great Hall, but there had been very little festivity at Berkhamsted without the Prince and his retinue of military men, and the weather had been freezing cold. Wulfstan stared moodily out at the rain now pouring down on the carpet of snow; the air was warmer at midday, but by the early dusk it would be freezing again, with the likelihood of more snow, creating treacherous ways for men and for horses. It would be foolish to walk or ride very far in these conditions, for fear of falling and risking injury to both man and animal.

From being a hive of activity, preparing for the new invasion of France, the castle now seemed silent and empty. Up until the end of October, victuals were being collected from the Prince's residences: oat flour, salt pork, cheese and beans. New arrows and bowstrings were being made to replenish the armoury at the Tower of London; ash and yew, horsehair and hemp were sent by river to the port of Sandwich, and wheelwrights worked round the clock to make more carts, all over the south of England. There was much sewing and stitching of garments for the men of war, not only by sempstresses but also by noble ladies, and much polishing of armour. Wulfstan personally paid for a steel hauberk for Eldrige, and a padded gipon to go underneath it; the lad had been sorry to leave his master, but could not hide his joy and excitement at the prospect of fighting under the Black Prince's banner, embroidered with his emblem of three ostrich feathers worked in silver thread against a sable background.

They sailed from Sandwich at October's end. By order of the king, the front line was led by himself and a trio of his

handsome, valiant sons: Prince Edward of Wales, the Black
Prince, ahead of his brothers, the newly wed Prince John of
Gaunt, named for the Belgian city of Ghent, where he had
been born, and Prince Lionel. Next came the Duke of
Lancaster, the king's cousin, followed by Sir John Chandos and
the Earl of Kent, still referred to as Sir Thomas Holland, a
seasoned veteran of Crécy and Poitiers; in one of these battles
he had lost an eye, and wore a white eye-patch. A genial man
in his fortieth year, he was an object of much envy, for his
beautiful Countess Joan was known as 'the Fair Maid of Kent',
and Wulfstan knew of the Prince's long years of hopeless love
for her. Thomas had been a founder member of the Order of
Knights of the Garter, for it was rumoured that at a ball given
by the king to celebrate the fall of Calais, Joan, then the young
Countess of Salisbury, had dropped her garter whilst dancing,
and the king (who, though married to the queen, was said to
be in love with Joan at the time) had picked it up and tied it
around his own leg with the words *Honi soit qui mal y pense*
(Shame on him who thinks ill of it!), which became the motto
of the Order. Wulfstan wondered what were the thoughts of
the Black Prince, watching Sir Thomas take leave of his lovely
wife and their children.

As well as Eldrige, Ranulf Ormiston was among the men-
at-arms, and without their high spirits and good-humoured
rowdiness, the castle seemed gloomy. Those left behind at
Berkhamsted were not such as Wulfstan would have chosen.
Apart from the bailiffs and servants, both men and maids, there
was Hugh Baldoc, painstakingly writing with his healed right
hand, and Sir Guy Hamald, in charge of the half-dozen guards
left to protect the castle and its occupants. Sir Wulfstan
Wynstede was generally liked for his fairness and feared for his
sternness towards any shirking of duty. He tried to be on civil
terms with Baldoc, but met with a surly response, and Guy
Hamald's over-familiarity amounted to insolence. Guy and his
guards would boast to each other of their conquests among
the maidservants, and lead the conversation round to Sir Hugh
Points, then with grins and nudges tell of his daughter's brief,
passionate alliance with Wulfstan, who restrained himself from
making any comment. He tried to ignore them, for he had

been vindicated by the queen herself from any misconduct with the lady, but they still made fun of him; he was either cast as a lecher by some who said he had led the Lady Mildred into temptation, or as a callow youth who had not known how to respond to the lady's bold advances. Either way he looked a fool, for by ignoring the insults he was condemned by his silence, and by denying them he gave Hamald and his friends more fuel for mockery, putting on solemn faces and saying that no insult had been intended, whilst laughing up their sleeves.

The news from over the Narrow Sea did nothing to raise his spirits. Having marched out of Calais in November, the king had arrived at Rheims shortly before the Feast of the Nativity, and laid siege to it. Reports were slow and sketchy, but it appeared that the citizens were determined to defend their city, and that the weather favoured them, being extremely wet and cold, matching the low morale of the king's men.

Wulfstan thought yearningly of his sweet, betrothed young bride, trusting that she remained as lovesick for him as he was for her. He despised himself for letting the rain keep him away from her, yet he could not subject his docile mare Jewel to such difficult, dangerous riding, beginning in the dark and ending in the dark of a dismal winter day, with a one-armed man astride her. There could be no hunting, jousting, falconry or any outdoor activities in such conditions – which left indoor games and pranks to pass the time. There was dancing, accompanied by musicians with flutes and percussion, and a shortage of ladies led to plundering the kitchen of its smiling maidservants, some of whom were more willing than others. Wulfstan's heart sank when he saw what would inevitably happen, and called upon the menservants to come up to the Great Hall and make sure that all the women were accounted for when the candles were extinguished and the revellers dismissed to their own beds and nobody else's. The rules were kept as far as Wulfstan could see, but he asked Hugh Baldoc to oversee the menservants and prevent any misconduct on their part. Gone was the light-hearted gaiety that had brightened the castle when the Black Prince had been at home, but Wulfstan was determined to keep order and maintain the Prince's household in his absence.

On a January day Queen Philippa arrived on a visit to the castle to enquire if all was well. She came in a carriage accompanied by a guard and a few of her ladies, and also a couple of empty farm carts. She took Wulfstan aside for a word about the food stores, confessing that she had heard from the king via special messenger that much of the army's food had been stolen or spoiled by the weather.

'I fear that if I cannot send out replenishments, they will steal from the peasantry and threaten to plunder houses and farms,' she confided anxiously. 'My son Prince Edward of Wales has given me permission to gather fresh supplies as you see fit.'

Easy words, but Wulfstan could not conjure up fresh supplies from muddy winter fields, and had no choice but to part with some of the castle's dry stores of salted meat, oats, cheese and beans, and to instruct the cooks to practise strict economy. He began to frequent the store rooms himself, to see how much could reasonably be spared. The maidservants were overawed by seeing their master among them, giving orders to take this or that sack for the men to load on to the carts; they were either shy and silent or saucy and giggling, and one shapely young girl answered everything he said with such ready wit that he laughed out loud, and found himself smiling into her bright, dark eyes. When he called on her to help him sort out the victuals and pack them into sacks and crates, she needed no second bidding, and when he felt her soft arm brush against his by accident – or had it been deliberate, and if so, had it been his will or hers? – he felt his treacherous, amoral manhood rising against his braies; his hands longed to touch her, to stroke her pretty face, to cover her little breasts. He drew a step away from her, but could not avoid her sidelong glances, the smiles that invited him to do as he – and she – wished.

He struggled with his baser self, trying to bring Beulah to his mind, but she now seemed far away, and he could not visualize her face. All he could remember were her mother and father hovering near, stopping him from touching her, making him wait for years – whereas this girl was here at his side, tempting him, teasing him . . .

'I don't even know your name, girl,' he muttered in a voice not his own.

'Miril be my name, sire, and it be a better name than *girl*,' she answered, looking up at him with such a saucy face that he had to laugh – he could not stop himself, and then he had to kiss her, and knew that it was only a matter of time and opportunity before he took her in his arms and kissed her lips, her breasts, her whole delicious body . . .

'Miril,' he said.

'Wulfstan,' she replied with all the familiarity of an equal, as at that moment she was.

He made a superhuman effort, releasing her and muttering, 'We must not be seen,' as he turned towards the stone passageway where guards and menservants were heaving sacks out to load the two carts. Guy Hamald and another guard were carrying a large crate, and he grinned at Wulfstan in a conspiratorial and infuriating way.

'Hurry up with your task, the Queen needs to be on her way before nightfall,' Wulfstan barked. Hamald stared after his retreating back, and spoke to the other man in a low tone.

'He'd better not try getting on his high horse with *me*, or he'll be sorry for it, the one-armed lapdog of the Prince.'

Before she left, Queen Philippa called Wulfstan to a private interview with her in the room he used for record keeping and the castle's accounts day by day.

'The news is not as good as could be wished, Sir Wulfstan,' she said, her kindly face tense with anxiety for her royal husband and sons. 'You know they laid siege to Rheims, and hoped to enter the city before the end of this month – my husband promised to spare all their lives if they would yield – but my special messenger now tells me that he has lifted the blockade and is retreating from Rheims, burning and pillaging the suburbs.'

'May God show mercy on them, Your Grace,' answered Wulfstan in dismay, able to imagine all too well the despoliation of the countryside, the terror of families made homeless, their plight made ten times worse by the merciless grip of winter.

'The King aims to reach Paris by a roundabout route,' she continued, 'and to lay siege to that city instead of Rheims within another month. The weather should be improved by then, and the days lengthening. With these extra supplies, the troops may not feel the need of such harshness.' Her eyes were full of pity, but she was unable to make the slightest criticism of her husband the king. Wulfstan knew her to be a good, tender-hearted woman, who had knelt to the king after the Battle of Crécy, imploring him to spare the lives of the six brave burghers who had come to offer their lives if he would spare the town of Calais.

Wulfstan bowed, and simply said, 'May it be so, Your Grace.'

'I am most grateful, Sir Wulfstan. I know that my son the Prince has every trust in you to govern the castle while he is away, even though –' she smiled – 'even though you are young. You won your knighthood by valour on the field of battle, losing your arm. I shall send my son a good report of Berkhamsted!'

Wulfstan bowed again and thanked her. He watched her departure and her retinue with a mixture of relief and regret that her news had not been better, and went to the empty chapel to pray for the king's army and such French citizens who were innocent, which he feared would be most of them. Kneeling on the cold stone and shivering, he resolved to visit Greneholt at the earliest sign of improvement in the miserable weather. The Queen's visit and her commendation of him had pulled together his wandering thoughts of Miril, and he accused himself of idle, lustful dreams, unworthy of a knight of the realm; he was determined to pursue the path of a celibate life until he could honourably take Beulah as his lawful wife.

That night he lay down on his feather-filled mattress, pulling the thick sheepskin over himself, waiting to drift into sleep. But he could not settle, and in spite of the heavy woollen wall-hangings there was a draught coming from somewhere, and the pain in his left shoulder returned if he lay on that side. His restless thoughts gave him no peace; when he tried to pray, all he could see was the tempting image of a woman's naked body. Cursing the ungodly desires of his treacherous flesh, he pulled the sheepskin up to his chin, and wished that he had Friar Valerian to counsel him.

Then there came a gentle tap on the door. At first he thought he had imagined it, and made no answer. Then it came again, tap, tap, tap . . .

'What?' he called out, sitting up and staring into the darkness. 'Who is this? Name yourself!'

'Here I am, Sir Wulfstan,' said a little voice as Miril entered, carrying a candle. She closed the door behind her. 'Here I am, Wulfstan.'

Snow and ice continued throughout February, and there were grim stories of travellers found frozen in the drifts; a horse trotted painfully up to a farmhouse with a dead rider on its back, stiff and staring. News from London was scarce, let alone news from across the Narrow Sea; even the Queen's special messenger was unable to set sail. Food supplies were low, and farm labourers and their families faced starvation. What life must be like in France for the army and the people, Wulfstan could only conjecture. He wondered how far the king had progressed to Paris, and whether he had yet come face-to-face with the dauphin who with his own troops remained within the city walls, and was said to be a weak, sickly young man.

March came in with lengthening days and a thaw set in; the skies cleared, the snow melted, and signs of new growth rejoiced the hearts of the people, their numbers diminished by the deaths of young children and old people during the bitter winter months, which had also killed many animals. Now the brooks and streams flowed freely, and the small animals, squirrels, hedgehogs and field mice began to wake from their winter hibernation. It was as if the earth had been released from icy chains, and the Queen ordered thanksgiving Masses to be said in all churches and the chapels of castles and great houses. Spring was on the way, and the birds were singing; surely there would soon be news from France!

Wulfstan was now faced with a dilemma. For two months he had shared his bed with Miril, and had been grateful for the comfort she gave to the uncontrollable needs of his body. In the winter darkness he had held her close, and knew the soft, moist cave between her thighs; her legs had embraced him as he thrust into her, gasping, crying out as each swelling wave of pleasure swept over him again and again.

'Oh, Miril.' It was almost a sob.

'Here I am, Wulfstan, all yours . . .'

He groaned and she laughed as the stream of life flowed. It was as if they were up above the world, whirling round and round in the night sky, all else forgotten, something beyond words, and Wulfstan did not want to come down to earth. He wanted to reward her, to show his gratitude, he wanted to tell her that he loved her—

This would have to stop.

'Wulfstan – do ye love me as much as any fine lady?'

He wanted to tell her that he did, but the words would not come.

It would have to stop.

And it did stop, but not through any virtue on his part. In the early dawn of the last day of March, as they lay sleeping in each other's arms, there came a loud knock at the door, and Baldoc strode in.

'Great news, Sir Wulfstan! The King has reached Paris and met the dauphin—'

He stopped speaking and stood stock-still, staring at the two heads on the bolster. Wulfstan stirred and passed his arm across his face; his eyes opened, and he returned Baldoc's stare. Miril slept on, or pretended to. Wulfstan sat up.

'Master Baldoc, I thank you for your news, and will hear the rest of it later. You may go.' Without another word, but with a certain gleam in his eye, Baldoc left the bedchamber.

Wulfstan got out of bed, and roused the girl. 'You must get dressed and go back to your kitchen, *ma petite*. I will see that you are not blamed, for the fault is all mine. Come, we must be as quick as we can.'

'Don't you want me to come to you again tonight, Sir Wulfstan?'

'Not tonight, Miril. Later, perhaps . . .'

He cursed himself for not being honest with her, for there would not be a *later*. He guessed that Guy Hamald had put Baldoc up to this, sending the unsuspecting scribe up to the bedchamber, to be surprised and shocked by what he saw – and to spread around the castle what he had witnessed with his own eyes. Now this liaison really had to stop, and he would have to tell Miril that she must never come to his bedchamber again. Not ever. His misdemeanour would be gleefully told to the Prince on his return, shaming him before the whole retinue; he could picture Guy Hamald smirking in the background, and the jokes that would be made and guffawed over, all the more humiliating for the strict attitude he had taken towards any misbehaviour on the part of those left in his charge: such hypocrisy!

There was also deep regret at using Miril to assuage the natural longings of his body, only to cast her aside – much as Eric Berowne had cast aside the maidservant Ange at the Maison Duclair. And as for Beulah, he dared not even think about how she and her parents would react if they knew. He was no longer worthy of her.

The news from France was indeed good. A peace treaty had been drawn up for King Edward and the dauphin, under which the King would gain complete sovereignty over Aquitaine, Gascony and Brittany. The ransom on King John of France, now a prisoner at Windsor Castle, was to be greatly reduced, and he would be allowed to return to France with young Prince Philippe. King Edward and his sons were expected to be home by April or May. There was great rejoicing all round, though Wulfstan's thanksgiving was marred by the entanglement with Miril. At his earliest opportunity he sent a message to her, asking her to attend him in the room where he kept his records and accounts, and as soon as she arrived he closed the door and asked her to be seated. Then he told her that though she would remain a maidservant at the castle, she must not come to his bedchamber ever again. The hurt and sadness he saw on her pretty face caused him yet more regret, but when she tried to protest he held up his hand.

'No, Miril, I admit that I was wrong, and you have no need to blame yourself at all,' he said. 'And I have here something to recompense you, I hope. Please take it.' And he held out to her a small leather bag containing five golden crowns, and as he tried to smile, he saw himself as no better than any lecher, paying off a whore. Would she see it in the same way? No, she carefully took the bag and looked inside it, then hid it in a fold of her gown.

'I thank ye kindly, Sir Wulfstan,' she said with a certain dignity.

'Good girl. And we'll keep it a secret between ourselves, Miril.'

'It be too late for that, Sir Wynstede; the kitchen maids talk o' little else, seein' they've missed me from my bed.'

Of course. He had been a fool to think otherwise. Another blow to his self-esteem. He rose and held out his hand.

'This has to be the last time, Miril. I thank you indeed for your . . . er . . . kindness.'

'That's good o' ye, sire,' she answered, also rising and taking his hand, hoping at least that he would raise it to his lips. He did not. She curtseyed and left the room.

There was another matter weighing heavily on his mind, one which would have to be settled now that there was no bar to his riding out to visit the manors from which the Prince received dues. The winter had left a backlog of money owing, and the King's treasurer faced the wrath of some of the heads of households when he demanded back payments. He tried to judge each creditor on his merits, and in some cases accepted only half the payment, allowing an extension of the time in which to pay the rest.

And he was due, overdue in fact to visit Greneholt Manor. After much thought he decided to ask Sir William to release him from the betrothal, on the grounds of his own unworthiness and uncertainty of his position when the Prince returned. He might be asked to accompany his royal master over to France on a peacetime mission, and so would be unable to offer Beulah a stable home like her father's. He could even admit that he had fallen into temptation with a maidservant, though he almost groaned aloud at the thought of what Sir William might say. Nevertheless, it had to be done, though Wulfstan put it off for week after week. Finally a letter arrived from Greneholt, and he opened it reluctantly.

Sir William Horst greeted his future son-in-law Sir Wulfstan in the Lord's name, and said that he feared that some mishap had befallen him, as they had received no word since the thaw had set in and the roads were passable. His quarterly monies to the Prince were ready for collection, and he and Lady Judith hoped for the happiness of seeing Wulfstan soon, or to receive a message explaining the delay. Meanwhile, he wished him good health and assured him of their daily prayers for him. There was no mention of Beulah at all, and between the lines was a reproach: on the following day he set out on Jewel towards Greneholt.

Sir William greeted him warmly, and asked him into a side room where visitors were received and offered refreshment.

'You are most welcome, Sir Wulfstan, and we thank the Lord for the sight of you. Lady Judith and Beulah will be joining us shortly, when we have finished our business.'

'Permit me to speak first, Sir William,' said Wulfstan hastily, feeling his face blazing red. 'I wish the lady Beulah nothing but happiness, but I have been shown, painfully, that I am unworthy of her, and don't deserve her . . . her love. I cannot marry her.'

Having spoken, he braced himself to hear words of dismay and disappointment, but they did not come. Sir William looked him straight in the eyes and nodded slightly.

'My dear Wulfstan, for I think of you as a son, your self-blame does you credit rather than otherwise. You are a young man of strength and courage, as proved by your loss of an arm in battle. I too was a young man once –' he smiled, and gave a little shrug – 'and I know of the temptations of the flesh, and the need to overcome them. I can guess at your difficulties, and can only advise you to pray daily for chastity of thought as well as in deed, and be assured of forgiveness from your Lord and Saviour who bore all our transgressions on his Cross.' He lowered his voice and spoke as one man to another. 'We shall say nothing of this to Beulah. Young women are not troubled in this way as men are. Their thoughts are engaged in anticipation of motherhood, for the bearing of children is their privilege and honour, such as we men cannot know. And now I will send for my daughter – no, do not say another word.'

Wulfstan was disconcerted that Sir William clearly thought his immoral behaviour was limited to impure thoughts, and before he could speak again, Lady Judith entered, holding out a hand for him to kiss, followed by Beulah, whose shining eyes revealed her feelings towards Wulfstan more than any words could express. He was overcome anew by her beauty and natural sweetness, and bowed to her, not presuming to take her hand. She curtseyed low before him, and to his utter amazement, reached out to take hold of his hand and press it to her own lips.

'Greetings, Sir Wulfstan, after such a long time,' she said softly. He took her hand and kissed it reverently, then held it in his own and looked into her eyes.

He could not utter a word of what he had planned to say to her and her parents, for he knew that he loved her as a man should love his wife, and their betrothal still stood, more firmly than ever. What he had to do now was to prove himself worthy of her, and never to give way again to his baser nature. And so the visit ended happily, with a promise of another within a month.

Throughout April the news from abroad continued to be good; the treaty was duly signed, and on the nineteenth of May the King and his three valiant sons rode into London amid cheering crowds. Several weeks of feasting ensued, but Prince Edward of Wales did not stay long, so eager was he to be back in his castle at Berkhamsted. A message was sent on ahead to expect him and a dozen knights of his retinue that had fought alongside him in the campaign, and the whole household was galvanized into activity. It was as if the Black Prince was already back in charge, as maidservants scurried to and fro, tables were scrubbed and pewter was polished; grooms prepared the stables to receive an influx of horses, and Wulfstan spent much of his time in the counting-house, bringing accounts up to date.

Came the day when the Prince rode into the courtyard, holding up his sword in a gesture of victory. Wulfstan saw familiar faces among his retinue, Ranulf Ormiston and Theobald Eldrige; two foot soldiers carried a litter on which a man lay.

'Good morrow, Sir Wulfstan!' shouted the Prince. 'We are right glad to set eyes on you, for we have sadly lacked your company and wise guidance!' Laughing, he leapt down from his horse and embraced Wulfstan, kissing him first on one cheek and then the other, in the French fashion.

'And has Master Baldoc done his duties, assisting you in the counting-house?'

'He has, sire.' Wulfstan reasoned that Baldoc would repeat his scandalous story to the Prince at his earliest opportunity, and then would come confession time. But not just now.

'Good! Well, you'll want to be reunited with your friends. Here's Ranulf and Theobald – and remember to call Theo *sire*, for he has been knighted on the field of battle, not that the fighting was half as fierce as at Poitiers. Oh, and we've brought a casualty home with us –' he nodded towards the litter – 'beyond our aid, I fear. He's Flemish, and I was for sending him home to die, but he'd never survive the journey. Then our brave new knight Sir Theobald said you knew him, and wanted to bring him home with us. I think he is not long for this world – and nor must he wish to live, poor devil.'

He turned away to join some of his close circle entering the castle, and Theobald pointed to the litter, beckoning Wulfstan to follow him.

At first Wulfstan did not recognize the deathly white bearded man who lay on a blanket slung between two poles; then he noticed the nose, now pale and pinched, but the bone structure was still large and prominent, such as Wulfstan remembered well.

'God's bones, Claus, is it *you*, my friend – Claus Van Brunt? Oh, welcome to Berkhamsted Castle, and I shall see that you are cared for.' One of the man's arms hung limply down, and Wulfstan lifted it and tucked it into the blanket covering the litter, but the man's eyes remained closed, as if in death. Wulfstan ordered the two foot soldiers to carry him into the castle, and called a manservant to show them the way to his own bedchamber. 'Be gentle with him,' he told them, 'and be very careful on the stairs.'

When the litter had been carried away, Wulfstan turned to Theobald. 'He looks more dead than alive. What happened to him?'

'It was a skirmish with brigands at Auxerre,' came the reply; 'not even the French military – those outlaws would have attacked either side for what they might gain.'

'He must have lost more than half of the blood in his body,' added Ormiston. 'His wound is stanched with clean sheep's wool. I think the bleeding's stopped now.'

'Where is he wounded, then?' asked Wulfstan. 'He has both his arms and legs, and I see no damage to his head.'

'He was wounded in the privities,' said Theobald, shaking his head in pity for their comrade's condition. 'His trinity was cut away completely with a sword thrust.'

'Oh, my God – oh, Mother of God, have mercy,' gasped Wulfstan in horror. His *trinity*, the male member and the two seed pods – all that makes for manhood, taken from this man, turning him into a eunuch. The Prince's gloomy verdict was explained, for what man would wish to live without his vital organs? Even so, Claus Van Brunt had a right to such care and comfort as was available with death approaching.

'Yes, he shall lie in my bedchamber,' murmured Wulfstan quietly. 'He must be given wine and water. He must not just be left to die.'

Raising his voice, he addressed his two friends. 'You go in and get refreshment after your journey, and we'll talk later.'

And turning on his heel, he made for his bedchamber and its latest occupant.

'Oho, Sir Wulfstan, what's this I hear? Such lewdness, such shameless goings-on in my absence – and with a poor little serving-wench, and you betrothed to the daughter of a knight – and a beautiful lady, so Dame Rumour has it!'

The words were stern, but the Prince's eyes were dancing with merriment. Wulfstan felt his face flush crimson, and he hung his head, unable to look his royal master in the eyes.

'I am—' he began, but the Prince cut him short.

'Don't try to excuse yourself, young lecher, don't tell me the old tale about how the girl tempted you, that she asked for it; I've heard that one too many times. Well? What have you got to say for yourself?'

With eyes still downcast, Wulfstan answered, 'The shame is entirely mine, my liege, and I was indeed tempted by my body's lustful cravings. The girl was not to blame, for I treated her like a whore, even to paying her off. I ask for the forgiveness of Almighty God, and for your pardon, my liege.'

He raised his eyes and saw a broad grin spread across the Prince's face.

'Say no more, Wulfstan, your guilt does you credit,' continued the Prince in a softer tone. 'Not many men would accuse themselves as you have done – but I wish I could have seen Master Baldoc's face when he came upon you taking your pleasure! Tell me, were you poised above her, holding your spear aloft, when he interrupted you?'

'No, sire, we were both sleeping.'

'How disappointing. Ah, well, Wulfstan my son,' he went on with all the seniority of eight years, 'I too have been tempted sometimes, when I've yearned for my heart's desire, the love of my life, married to another man, and a good man, too, Sir Thomas, Earl of Kent. My father has left him behind in France to oversee the English garrisons – and I am tempted, Wulfstan, I am sorely tempted! But she is as virtuous as she is beautiful, and so am I saved from the great sin of David.'

He sighed, and Wulfstan understood that he was referring to King David of Israel who had sent Bathsheba's husband Uriah into the thick of the battle to be slain, thereby removing the obstacle to David's lust. Wulfstan felt that he must answer.

'Even so, my liege, I thank you for your . . . er . . . kindness. 'We are . . . we are . . .' He hesitated, not presuming himself to be equal with the Prince.

'Brothers in adversity, yes, Wulfstan, we are.' He paused, and then added, seriously, 'But be warned – do not let temptation overcome you in that way again, or you could land yourself in real trouble and lose your lovely betrothed lady at Greneholt for ever.'

Wulfstan muttered, 'Even so, my liege. It will never happen again.'

To everyone's surprise the Flemish soldier slowly began to recover his strength. Wulfstan tended him daily, and ordered that he be given wine with water and simple gruel made from wheat and sweetened with honey until he could manage to eat bread and meat. The ghastly wound at the bottom of his belly appeared as a red, raw, bloody mess, but it began to heal, and new skin formed over it. Wulfstan took it upon himself to support Claus when he passed water painfully from what remained of the conduit from the bladder. This too began to heal, turning from raw flesh into scarred skin.

'I have to squat down to piss, like a woman,' said Claus weakly, overcome with thankfulness for Wulfstan's care, as firm as a man's and gentle as a woman's. Colour returned to his face, and strength to his limbs; his eyes brightened and he was able to share his thoughts with Wulfstan, to understand where he was, and the implications of his wound.

'Truly I thought God had deserted me, but now I see that he's led me to you, good friend,' he said. 'You have saved my life, and I'm learning to accept that my life will be limited as a eunuch. I cannot marry and sire children – but I'll still be able to work and be of use to England.' He sighed. 'I cannot return to Flanders as I am now.'

Wulfstan laid his arm on his friend's shoulder. As young men they didn't attempt to show their emotions, but both were aware of the strong mutual attachment that bound them together.

The summer months passed in peace and there were acts of goodwill towards the French, such as when the King and Prince Edward of Wales escorted King John II and Prince Philippe back to their native land after four years of exile, held under house arrest in various royal residences, the last being Windsor Castle. They all boarded a ship at Dover which carried them to Calais, and from there to Paris, with many assurances of peace between the two countries from now on.

Wulfstan enjoyed his journeyings on Jewel in the warm summer weather, and was able to visit Greneholt Manor and see the lovely Beulah; they were now allowed to walk together in the garden, bright with roses and honeysuckle, the fragrant rosemary and lavender that Lady Judith grew for use as nosegays and posies to sweeten the linen. Beulah would timidly put her hand in his as they strolled or sat on a wooden bench in the sun, and he felt that he had never known such a pure, unselfish love as this. Her beauty seemed to increase as the months went by, and he sometimes allowed himself to dream of the day when he would hold her in his arms as his wedded wife.

Until there came a blow that shattered all his wishful dreams . . .

He was in the counting-house when there came a knock on the door, and on being told to enter, one of the older menservants stepped in, closing the door behind him.

'Pardon me, sire, but may I speak with you on a private matter?'

Wulfstan was adding up the figures of the household incomings and outgoings, but nodded his assent.

'Begging your pardon, sire, but one of the maidservants needs help, and Mistress Dibbert says you ought to know.' Mistress Dibbert was a cook, in charge of the kitchen-maids. Wulfstan's heart sank. 'Go on,' he said.

''Tis the girl called Miril, sire, she's weeping all the time. Mrs Dibbert asks if you'll see her and . . . er . . . hear what she says, sire, or whether she should go to the Prince.'

The implication seemed to be that if Sir Wulfstan would not see the unhappy girl, her trouble would be made known to the Prince himself. With a sinking heart Wulfstan set aside his books.

'Very well, send her to me here.'

While he waited, he prayed that she was not bringing the news he dreaded to hear. He knew very little about the mysterious ways of female bodies, and he had not given much thought to the connection between the act of making love and the reproduction of children, but already he knew in his heart that the girl must be with child. He remembered from his days at the Maison Duclair that to dally with maidservants was to risk this consequence, and he had blamed Jean-Pierre Fourrier and Eric Berowne for what seemed to be their callous attitude towards the girls they had used and deserted. Dan Widget had bedded the maid Mab, but had wedded her and now had a happy little family. Wulfstan's own experiences had not run any such risk – Madame la Gouvernante had seduced him, and little Dorine's shyness and her mother's vigilance had prevented any closer intimacy, just as Lady Mildred's horror of his withered arm had cut short their eagerly anticipated pleasure. What must he do now to deal honourably with this kitchen maid?

Eleven

1360

When she entered the room, he was struck by her woebegone appearance, her usually bright eyes red and puffy with crying.

'Good day to you, Miril. Please sit down and tell me what ails you.'

More tears gathered in her eyes, and spilled down her cheeks.

'Oh, Wulfstan, don't be angry with me; we was so happy before that ol' scribe came in and caught us!'

'I won't be angry, Miril, just tell me what's the matter.'

'I . . . I'm with child, Wulfstan – Sir Wulfstan, and Mistress Dibbert said I was to come to you, seein' that . . .' She covered her face with her hands, and Wulfstan felt hopelessly caught in a trap. He cursed his own thoughtlessness.

'I don't know what to do, sire. Mistress Dibbert says it'll be born about November or December. Me mother won't have me home again; she says I got to marry as quick as I can.'

Marriage. It was unthinkable, this nightmare that had come about through his own selfish carelessness, but if it were the only solution, he must do his duty. But oh, Beulah, Beulah! It seemed he would never be worthy of her.

'Dry your tears, Miril. I'm not yet sure what had better be done, but I won't desert you, or try to deny that I'm the . . . er . . .' He could not bring himself to say the word *father.*

'Look, go back to your Mistress Dibbert, and tell her that I've promised to look after you.'

'Thank you, sire. I told her you was a good man.'

'All right, then, Miril. I shall have to think about this, and then I'll send for you again.'

He stood up, and so did she, her eyes pleading. 'Won't you kiss me, sire?'

It had to be done, and he did it, then she went back to the kitchen while he sat at his desk with his head in his hands.

The Prince was away with his father the King, consolidating the peace treaty with France. This latest turn of events would have to be confessed on his return, and Wulfstan suspected that the Prince would be much more severe in his attitude to Wulfstan's careless lovemaking: he would be more likely to judge than to tease. Marriage would surely be the only solution to this otherwise insoluble dilemma, a last resort to spare the girl shame and possible poverty and homelessness.

And there was Beulah, once more lost to him, for Sir William and Lady Horst would not show leniency if they knew about the poor kitchenmaid's plight; they would say that his duty was to marry the girl and never see Beulah again.

What else could he do? Pay Miril off with gold? No, for there could be no monetary compensation for bearing and rearing his child, losing her good name and having nowhere to live if her mother refused to shelter her, and she could not stay at Berkhamsted Castle with a child in tow. Memories of his mother, Lady Wynstede who had helped girls in trouble now came back to his mind. She would send for the man, usually a groom or manservant, and order him to marry the girl, offering some monetary assistance. There was no such lady at Berkhamsted, no kind mistress to intervene, but what would his mother have said if told that the girl's disgrace was due to *him*, her own son? He must accept his responsibility and acknowledge the child growing in Miril's womb. Meanwhile, he sent for Mistress Dibbert, the motherly cook who had charge of the maidservants; she appeared before him, red-cheeked and defiant, clearly prepared to argue. He asked her to be seated, but she remained standing. He took a breath and tried to speak quietly and reasonably.

'You did well to send Miril to me, Mistress Dibbert, and I intend to confess to the Prince about her when he returns,' he said, facing her accusing stare. 'I shall not blame her for what was my fault.'

She looked surprised at this unexpected admission, and had to revise her prepared speech. 'I thought she'd better tell you of her trouble, seein' as you was the one . . . er . . . sire,' she said. 'She's a silly little goose, but not a bad girl, and she was led astray. I'm willing to take care of her until she's brought to childbed, and then I'll try to make her mother forgive her – they usually do when they sees the helpless baby, and the Prince might sweeten her with money if you do as you say, and tell him you're the one.'

'Thank you, Mistress Dibbert, I am much obliged to you. I shall have to see what the Prince advises, and if he orders me to marry her, I . . . I shall obey.'

'Well, that's fair, and better than the usual fine gentlemen who deny they ever touched the girl,' she answered, clearly mollified. 'And there's no need to marry her before the babe's born, in case she miscarries or bears a dead child. Wait and see what comes out.' She took a deep breath, and looking straight into his eyes, said, 'She was right, you *are* a fair man, even though you're young to be made a knight. I didn't think you'd face up to your duty by her.'

She actually smiled and made a curtsey; he shook her hand and thanked her heartily, asking her to pass on his promise to Miril who would remain a kitchenmaid until she presented him with a son or daughter, 'before Christmas, I reckon', she told him, adding, 'Don't worry, sire, I'll take care of her, and won't have her made fun of.'

Good Mistress Dibbert, a true mother to the maids in her charge. Wulfstan was relieved at having made an ally of her, for he guessed she would be a formidable enemy.

But there was still Beulah. He would have to release her from their betrothal, and tell her father the reason why.

'There's something on your mind, friend,' Claus Van Brunt remarked as they walked out of doors, Wulfstan supporting Claus with his arm, and adjusting his steps to the other man's halting progress, for the extensive wound still gave him pain, though it had scarred over cleanly, with no dreaded infection pouring pus, as so often happened.

Getting no response, Van Brunt continued, 'Is there some trouble? Forgive me for asking, but we've become as close as brothers, and if you're carrying any sort of burden, I want to share it with you. Come, Wulfstan, I have a *right* to share it, as you've shared mine, and saved my life by your care.'

Wulfstan sighed and said it was a matter for him to deal with as his conscience dictated. 'I shall not speak of it to anybody, Claus, until the Prince returns. He must be the first to hear of what I fear will displease him. I have to face the consequences of . . . of my actions, so please, ask me no more. You will hear of it soon enough – all too soon.'

Claus nodded. 'As you wish, my friend.' After a short silence he asked, 'How is the lovely Beulah and her religious parents?' He smiled. 'When will you next ride over to Greneholt Manor and wander with her among the flowers?'

There was a long pause. 'Is it not well with her?' asked Claus, alerted by his friend's silence. 'Is she ill? Have her parents forbidden the marriage? Please, Wulfstan, don't suffer alone when you have a friend at hand – is your betrothal at an end?'

''Twill be ended soon,' Wulfstan replied heavily. 'And now, I beg you, leave me to bear it alone as I must – as I deserve,' he said, his voice breaking on the last words. 'Believe me, Claus, there is nothing you could do, nothing to help me bear it – so let us talk of other matters. You're walking better each day – is the pain also better?'

'Yes, thanks to you! I'm better in every way except one – and I can still live usefully here in England, for I have no wish to go to my homeland to meet my kin again, not as I am now. They'll assume that I'm dead.'

'My dear friend – brother – say not so. None of us know the future,' said Wulfstan quickly, putting his arm around his friend's shoulder. 'Let's enjoy the summer sun, and say no more of troubles past or present, just for this afternoon.'

Claus returned the gesture, putting his left arm around Wulfstan's shoulder and vowing not to plague his good friend with any more questions.

It was the day when Wulfstan called upon his reserves of courage to mount Jewel and set out for Greneholt to unburden himself of the latest turn of events, to confess the sin that must end his betrothal to Beulah. He dug his heels into Jewel's flanks – and then as she began to trot, sharply reined her in. He had heard the distant horn that heralded his master's arrival, and within minutes the Black Prince rode into the courtyard, followed by half a dozen of his knights.

'We should have warned you!' he called cheerfully, leaping down from his horse. 'I could wait no longer to see Berkhamsted!'

'My liege,' said Wulfstan, dismounting and bowing low. 'You are right welcome, sire.'

'Ha! Where were you off to? Have I interrupted a lover's tryst at Greneholt?' The Prince's eyes danced.

'No, sire, not at all. I will send word to the kitchens, and meat will be put on the spit.'

'Excellent, Sir Wulfstan. But first I need to wash and change my shirt, for I stink. How have you all been behaving yourselves while I was away? Better than last time, I hope!' He gave Wulfstan a broad wink, and Wulfstan quickly managed a smile, avoiding the Prince's eyes. The Castle would now be turned into a hive of activity on the return of its master, and inwardly he felt a guilty relief at the postponement of his ride to Greneholt; neither would there be an opportunity for an early confession to the Prince.

On the following day he thankfully turned to report on the castle's finances, and basked in the Prince's approval and admiration of the accuracy of his accounts and the general air of contentment among the hierarchy of the household, from guards and bailiffs to grooms, cooks, men and maidservants; the Prince greeted them all.

'Mistress Dibbert seems amiable,' he said, 'which is all to the good, for she can be a virago. I've known her ever since I was a boy, and am still fearful of her.' He grinned. 'You've made a good impression on her, Wulfstan. Well done!'

Wulfstan gave a nod and a half smile, thinking of the inevitable interview with his master; with every word of praise he dreaded it more than ever. Mistress Dibbert had been giving him some meaningful looks, reminding him of his promise to confess to the Prince.

Prince Edward of Wales looked older. Two vertical lines between his brows had deepened into furrows, and his handsome features had become hardened by warfare and rough living. When he had finished the work in the counting-house, he sent for wine and indicated that Wulfstan sit down with him by the table for private discussion.

'I shall be staying here for the rest of the year, I hope,' he said. 'Things are quiet in France for the time being. To tell the truth, I think King John was sorry to leave England – my father had made him very comfortable here, and I fear he's going to have trouble with that sickly, treacherous dauphin, a creature I wouldn't trust further than I can spit.' He shook his head, and added, 'My father has better hopes of *his* eldest son and heir to the throne.'

Wulfstan supposed that he should make strong patriotic agreement, but he remained silent, not wishing to be seen as an idle flatterer when his story was told. And now was the time to tell it, as May sunshine streamed through the window. There was no excuse for further delay. It had to be *now*.

'Forgive me, my liege, I have a certain matter to speak of,' he said, forcing himself to meet the Prince's eyes.

'What? Ah, your beautiful little maiden at Greneholt – what was her name? – you're about to tell me that the wedding date is to be brought forward, and you need to have leave of absence for the nuptials, am I right? Happy infant, to be born to such a couple! When is the little angel due? I shall expect to be godfather.'

Poor Wulfstan. This was worse than anything. 'Unfortunately, it's not like that at all, sire; the lady Beulah is entirely virtuous – but I must release her from the betrothal, for I cannot marry her.'

'*What?* Why not?'

'My wrongdoing has caught up with me, sire, and I have . . . my duty is towards another,' Wulfstan said miserably.

'*Another?* Don't tell me that you've gone back to the kitchen-maid! Surely, you could not be so foolish, Sir Wulfstan.' The Prince was genuinely puzzled.

'No, my liege, I didn't go back to her. I paid her five crowns and thought that was the end of it, but it seems I got her with child before dismissing her. Mistress Dibbert came to me and more or less demanded that I . . . that I admit my fault, and confess it to you. Mistress Dibbert says she will care for the girl until she is safely delivered, and then I intend to marry her.' He sat forward, his hands clasped between his knees as he waited for the Prince's roar of anger. Or contempt. Or both.

'*Marry* her? A knight of the realm, close to the King's son, to marry an unlettered kitchen wench? Don't be a fool, Sir Wulfstan! – though I wish I could have seen Mistress Dibbert making you shake in your shoes. Ha! When's the bastard due, do you know?'

'About the beginning of December, according to Mistress Dibbert,' muttered Wulfstan. 'And I have to do my duty by her, sire. I have to show that I'm not one of those men who take advantage of a girl and then forsake her. Mistress Dibbert said—'

'A plague upon Mistress Dibbert, she's too free with her opinions. Didn't your father teach you *anything,* Wulfstan? When a mistake like this is made, the usual course is to marry her off as soon as possible to a man of her own stock, be he servant or groom. For this a bribe must be offered him, and maybe haggled over, but be as generous as you can. I'll help you out; I always come back from France loaded with plunder. Now, let me see who we've got – there's Old Togs who waits upon the guards, somewhat of a drinker, he'd accept a bag of crowns to call the child his – and Willie One-eye who helps on the estate, harmless enough, but lacking more than an eye.'

Wulfstan was horrified. 'Do you mean, sire, that Miril could be married off to any ill-favoured hulk who'd be father to . . . to—'

'Your child, Wulfstan, yes. Married off and paid off is quite often the answer to a maid's dilemma, and 'tis a better fate than being left homeless and penniless. Leave it to me, I'll speak to Old Togs, and have a word in the ear of Willie One-eye's mother who's a laundress here. You just lay low and keep away from Miril and Mistress Dibbert.'

'*No!* I *won't* see the girl married to a drinker or an idiot! I'll marry her myself first!' Wulfstan almost shouted, flushed and trembling.

The Prince's features softened. 'Your anger does you credit, Wulfstan. It's infernally bad luck, just as you'd given her money and thought that was an end of it. I can't stop you marrying if you're set on ruining all your prospects – remember you're a knight of the realm and younger brother of another knight. If you were to inherit the Wynstede estate, think of the ridicule that'd be thrown at you and your kitchen-wench wife!'

'That wouldn't deter me, sire, I will not desert this girl.' Wulfstan's voice had quietened, but was firm and steady, his mouth a hard, straight line.

'Then for God's sake wait until the child's born and let Mistress Dibbert take a long, hard look at it. She's proved her worth as a wise-woman, usually able to name the father of a newborn when there's doubt. And Wulfstan – don't go galloping down to Greneholt with the bad news, not until the end of the month. I shall need all your help with the day-to-day running of the castle, and keeping the expenses within a reasonable limit.'

He stood up, and Wulfstan rose likewise. 'I can't afford to lose such a good brain and willing worker as yourself, young Wulfstan. And don't spread your bad luck around just to punish yourself – you'd be punishing the poor wench as well. Keep your mouth shut and leave the matter with me.'

And with that pronouncement Wulfstan had to be content, for the Black Prince's orders demanded obedience. He threw himself into his work, sometimes spending whole days in the counting-house, denying himself the outdoor pursuits of the Prince's men and the guards who practised jousting and hunting the boar. His only relaxation was to spend an hour or two with Claus Van Brunt, who understood that any further questioning about Wulfstan's secret burden would be unwelcome.

One afternoon he was surprised to find Mistress Dibbert in Claus's room, sitting beside him and apparently listening to his experiences as a soldier.

'Welcome, brother!' said Claus with a smile. 'Our master has sent this good dame to find out how I like my meat dressed, whether boiled, baked or fried, and we've been talking very happily. She says what this room needs is a woman's touch!'

Mistress Dibbert rose to her feet, and curtseyed to them both, smoothing down her apron and avoiding Wulfstan's eyes. 'I bid ye good day, masters.'

'Let's go for a walk in the sunshine, Wulfstan, and watch the Prince's soldiers learning how to deal with enemies of the realm,' said Claus Van Brunt, rising from his couch slowly but without grimacing. 'No, friend, I don't need your arm to pull me up, I can do it myself now.'

Watching Claus coping with his difficulties, Wulfstan experienced an odd, inexplicable sinking of his heart; when his friend no longer needed him, would he be limited to a life of scribing, adding and subtracting? He could no longer dream of a future with the lady Beulah, now that he was committed to marrying Miril after her baby was born, much to the amusement, no doubt, of Hamald and his kind. And then what would be his future? Would he still be able to visit Charles? How would Lady Hélène and Ethelreda receive his wife?

'*There* you are, Wulfstan, I've been looking for you! I need a trustworthy person to take an urgent message to my father the king, so prepare for a journey!' Wulfstan's thoughts were scattered as the Prince strode into the room. 'This is very important, the safety of the realm may depend upon it, and secrecy is essential. I know you to be trustworthy, and a one-armed man is less likely to be set upon by outlaws. Good day to you, Van Brunt, you are much improved. Come, Sir Wulfstan, there is no time to be lost.'

'But, my liege, my work here . . .'

'Baldoc can be scribe and treasurer; it's time he moved his backside and showed me what he can do – he's done enough grumbling, God knows.'

'But there are dues to be collected this month,' said Wulfstan, mystified by this sudden summons.

'I'll send a couple of guards out to do it, heaven knows it's not *that* difficult,' snapped the Prince. 'And some of my land-owners need shaking up, you are too easy on them. What I'm ordering you to do now is far more important. Go and get such clothes as you'll need to take, and saddle Jewel. I want you to leave for Westminster before the day is out!'

'But who's to care for Claus Van Brunt if I'm not here?' asked Wulfstan, at which the Prince completely lost his temper.

'How dare you argue with me! How dare you question a royal Prince! Any other man would be honoured to be entrusted with such an errand. As for Van Brunt, it's time he managed to shift for himself without your nursemaiding. Get yourself ready for the journey, and come to my room within the hour!'

He turned and left the room without a glance at Van Brunt who had listened in blank-faced silence, though a twitch at the corner of his lips betrayed his amusement at Wulfstan's stunned expression at this display of another side to the Prince.

'So much for those who say I'm a favourite of the Prince, a lapdog who can do no wrong,' Wulfstan said, shaking his head. 'I'll be more on my guard in future.'

'He's right, Wulfstan, you spend too much time with me, and it's time I started to walk without assistance,' said Claus, 'though you've saved my life, and given me back the will to live, and I'll always be grateful. But do as he says, my friend; it doesn't do to keep royalty waiting!' He smiled and then said more seriously, 'and it *is* a great honour to be entrusted with a secret message, it's a tribute to your trustworthiness.'

Wulfstan gave a grunt of acknowledgement, though his thoughts were in a whirl. Might the Prince regret confiding in him about his hopeless love for Joan of Kent? He shrugged, beginning to realize that the situation had certain advantages; he now had a good reason not to visit Greneholt and the lovely Beulah, she whom he could hardly face now, not before Miril had been found a suitable husband from her own serving class – or if none were forthcoming, he had promised to marry her himself. At the thought of such an outcome, he sighed deeply for the hundredth time, for with this urgent, secret business on his hands, the Prince would have neither time nor interest in seeking among the castle servants for a husband for poor, pregnant Miril.

As it was fairly late, Wulfstan's departure was fixed for dawn on the following day. He took leave of Claus Van Brunt and shook hands with an apprehensive Hugh Baldoc, suddenly thrust into Wulfstan's envied position in the Prince's household. He swung himself into the saddle on Jewel's back without help, and set off.

The solitary ride through peaceful Hampshire countryside was uneventful. It was at the end of May, evenings were long and morning larks ascended early. Wulfstan did not stop at any place in his journey, mindful always of the precious letter wrapped in a linen kerchief inside a leather purse tied to his body under his shirt. He carried a long-bladed knife in its scabbard on his leather belt, and would have used it without hesitation if waylaid, ready to kill rather than yield up the secret message he carried, the contents of which he had not been told, only that he must deliver it into the King's hands and no other.

'When you arrive at Westminster Hall, show the guard this ring which carries my seal, and demand to be taken to the King,' the Prince had ordered him. 'Do not wear the ring whilst travelling, but slide it on to your third finger when you arrive, and it will gain you admittance to the King's private chambers.' He had paused briefly, and added, 'Ride carefully, Wulfstan, and God go with you.'

When the tower of St Peter's Abbey came into view, Wulfstan saw two large birds, black against the bright sky, circling above Westminster with outspread wings. He thought of the ravens who were said to fly above the Tower of London at the time of an execution, and a shiver of apprehension ran down his spine: he hoped that these eagle-like creatures were not an augury of some nameless disaster. Holding his head high, he rode into the courtyard to face the guards, where sure enough, the sight of the ring with the Prince's seal of three ostrich feathers caused their suspicious looks to turn to deferential bows to the Prince's envoy, and to allow him passage to the King's quarters; a servant was then despatched to fetch the King who, when he saw the messenger, held out his hand for the letter which Wulfstan drew from under his shirt. He gestured towards a bench for Wulfstan to be seated while he opened the letter and read its contents. His face was grave, and he stroked his reddish-brown beard thoughtfully.

'These are grave tidings, Sir Wulfstan, and will have to be considered carefully. My son did well to choose you as messenger. I shall have to consult with my Privy Council as to what had best be done. Until then, you must stay here at Westminster as our guest.' He beckoned to a manservant to attend on Wulfstan and take him to a well-appointed bedchamber, where water was brought to him to wash, and a clean shirt and hose were supplied. When the manservant came to tell him he was to take supper with the King and Queen, he hurried to join them at the high table at one end of the great hall. Two huge dogs lay sleeping by the embers of a fire, for even in summer a fire was needed to cook meat and bake bread. By now he was intensely curious as to the message he had carried, but nothing was said, and he was left to speculate; was there to be more warfare with France so soon after signing a peace treaty? Surely not! Was it that France was planning to invade England? Never! The French were deeply thankful for the hard-won peace so recently secured.

Tired after his journey and rubbing his left shoulder which had begun to ache, Wulfstan was taken in hand by Queen Philippa, delighted to see him again, remembering their last meeting in January when she had come to collect army rations from Berkhamsted. She questioned him about his present duties in the Prince's household, and on hearing that he dealt with letters and accounts, her eyes brightened.

'I shall demand that my husband the King allows me to take advantage of your skills while you are with us!' she exclaimed. 'For my own court has need of a sensible secretary, and the King always says that he has no one to spare – but now he cannot refuse me!'

To his shame Wulfstan gave a great yawn which he could hardly conceal, and the Queen took pity on his weariness; she persuaded the King to let him go early to his room, accompanied by the manservant to wait upon him and see that he had clean clothing for the morrow. It was after Wulfstan had dismissed this attendant and blown out the candle beside his bed, that he heard men's voices drifting up beneath the open window on the warm air.

'He's lost an arm, so he's been in battle, though hardly more than a boy,' said one.

'He must be the one who brought a message from the Black Prince,' said another.

'Yes, he'll be the Prince's favourite, name of . . . er . . . Witstead or something. Watch out, lads, else he'll be carrying more tales to the King!' There was a general guffaw, and Wulfstan allowed himself a wry smile, but tired though he was, he could not settle to sleep. Images of Beulah floated before his mind's eye, pale and far away; Miril was closer, whispering in his ear and begging him to kiss her. It seemed that wherever he went, no matter how far he travelled, his misdeeds would always accompany him, accusing him, troubling his rest.

★　★　★

True to her word, Queen Philippa ordered the Prince's envoy to come to meet with her and her ladies in the solarium after breakfast. When she showed him the papers on which her private household accounts were written, he saw at once that they were badly organized and not in any order. No attempt had been made to gather them into some kind of sequence for easy reference, with dates for incoming monies and outgoings. She was granted an allowance by the King, but not on a regular basis, nor was it a constant amount, so would take him some time to untangle. He was not helped by her own charming presence and chattering ladies-in-waiting; she asked after Prince Edward, and deplored his choice of Berkhamsted as his home, rather than Westminster.

'He's either in France or buried in the depths of Hertfordshire,' she complained. 'It must be very dull at the castle, with no Princess of Wales to bring a little laughter and gaiety to that all-male establishment. Who can partner the gentlemen of his retinue when the musicians strike up after supper? With no ladies to dance with, they must be so *bored*!'

'It sometimes happens that the Prince sends for maidservants,' Wulfstan answered without thinking, 'but only if Mistress Dibbert gives them leave. She is the cook, and in charge of—'

'Good heavens above, Wulfstan, do you speak truth? Does my son allow his courtiers to dance with *kitchen maids*?' The Queen was clearly shocked. 'It's no wonder that there's trouble when one of them—' She broke off and shook her head, tut-tutting, and Wulfstan blushed painfully, unable to make a reply. Thankfully she did not pursue the matter, but leaned towards him, lowering her voice.

'The King and I are most anxious that Edward should find a suitable lady to wed and make Princess of Wales, to secure the royal line,' she confided. 'And he's more likely to find her here at Court than at Berkhamsted.'

He now became aware that a bevy of ladies had gradually drawn closer, smiling and eyeing him with some curiosity. One in particular, with milky-white skin and flame-red hair, was appraising him, a question in her large greenish eyes which sparkled with gold flecks. Wulfstan turned away from her glance, not wanting to show the slightest interest in her; he was in more than enough trouble already, thinking of his sweet, innocent Beulah, lost to him because of the hapless Miril who was carrying his child; the two were constantly on his mind, leaving no room for any other woman, however beautiful or willing.

The Queen noticed their brief contact, and lowered her voice almost to a whisper.

'Mademoiselle de l'Isle is indeed a beauty, and has Anjou blood in her veins. Would that my son the Prince would choose such a one as his bride! She would join our two countries together in the best possible way – it would be a matrimonial alliance!'

The lady in question moved away from her companions, giving Wulfstan a look of disdain. He ignored her, and got down to his secretarial and monetary duties for the Queen, thankful to have a demanding task to engage his thoughts.

It took Wulfstan three days to make some sense of the Queen's personal accounts, and she openly marvelled at his mathematical skill.

'The King has never allowed me a scrivener or treasurer of my own,' she told him. 'Dear old Dame Marilla, who was my nurse, does her best for me, but she's nearly blind, and I have to read out the numbers to her, loudly because of her deafness, and it takes hours. But *you* are better than the King's secretaries, so serve him right!'

Wulfstan bowed politely, though waiting hourly for a message from the King to send him back to Berkhamsted with an answer to the Prince's message, whatever it was; but two days passed, and then a third; the King's haughty scrivener told him that the King was much taken up with affairs of state, and when a message finally came from the King, it was to congratulate Wulfstan on his services to the Queen and invite him to take part in a hawking display the following morning, on common ground to the north of Westminster, unofficially named the King's Fields. At first Wulfstan was minded not to attend, having no interest in hawking, and a little irritated by the secrecy surrounding the important matter the Prince had sent to his royal father, but of which he, the messenger, had been told nothing.

Queen Philippa advised him to obey and attend upon the King, as a refusal would be discourteous.

'And you should learn falconry, Wulfstan. 'Tis a fine sport, without danger to life and limb, as is jousting. You could learn to be just as skilful as an archer!'

And reminding himself of the saying that when in Rome it was wisest to do as the Romans did, Wulfstan set out early the next morning to the King's Fields, and found that an enthusiastic crowd had already gathered. A number of men, some on horseback, and a few ladies, carried huge, fierce-looking birds of prey perched on their wrists, falcons and kestrels, and smaller sparrowhawks and goshawks. The birds had leather hoods over their heads, and most of them were lightly strapped to their owners' wrists, but some perched voluntarily, waiting for the signal to fly over their prey and seize it, kill it and bring it back to score points for their owners. The lady Mademoiselle de l'Isle was proudly showing off her pet goshawk, but Wulfstan did not look at her. He was more interested in identifying a tall, broad-shouldered man of about his own age, sporting a neatly clipped beard and moustache, though his face seemed familiar. An angry-looking bird perched on his wrist, which made Wulfstan unwilling to approach too closely, but the man suddenly smiled in recognition of him.

'Sir Wulfstan Wynstede, I declare! Don't you know me?' – and Wulfstan remembered the face of André Demoins, a member of his *chevauchée* from the Maison Duclair in Normandy which now seemed so long ago. He cordially returned the greeting.

'Well met, André! That's a formidable bird you have there!' he said, keeping clear of the cruel beak, the sharp claws. Demoins put a finger to his lips.

'Sssh, not so loud, you'll frighten her,' he warned. 'She's as fine a falcon as any here today. But is it really *you*, Wulfstan? What brings you here to the King's court? I heard that you covered your name with glory at Poitiers – but it cost you an arm, I see.'

Wulfstan gave a modest shrug. 'I happened to be in the right place at the right time to assist in the capture of the French king,' he said.

'God's holy truth, Wulfstan, that was lucky! But losing your arm – no more soldiering for you, then. What do you do with your time?'

'Scrivening and counting the Prince's money at Berkhamsted Castle, and running the occasional errand for him, as now.'

'Old men's work. What a waste of a soldier,' said Demoins, shaking his head, and Wulfstan was silent, feeling somehow diminished.

'Have you news of any others from that time?' asked Demoins. 'Did you hear about Léon Merand? After saving our lives at Sailly, he changed sides when the war began, and was killed by one of the Prince's own men on the battlefield, so it's said. Do you know anything more about that?'

'No,' replied Wulfstan, unwilling to confess to the killing of a one-time comrade in arms, though he wondered how Demoins would react if he knew just how Merand's life had ended. 'War's a bloody business, and I'm not sorry that I'm finished with soldiering.'

'Charles Lemaitre must have felt the same, for he left the King's service to enter a Benedictine monastery where no doubt he prays for us all,' said Demoins, and Wulfstan stared back in astonishment.

'Good heavens, *Lemaitre*? Whoever would have thought it? I suppose *you* would say that he too has become a waste of a soldier.'

'His choice,' said Demoins with a shrug. 'And did you ever hear what happened to that Flemish clown, what was his name, Van Bronk or something? God's teeth, what an oaf! I suppose he attacked one of our own men instead of the other side!'

Wulfstan found himself disliking Demoins more and more. 'I believe that Claus Van Brunt showed great courage, and suffered severe wounds,' he said coldly. 'Theobald Eldrige has been knighted for *his* courage on the battlefield, even though he is not yet twenty. Anyway, what brings *you* to King Edward's court, André?'

'Ah, that would be telling. Shall we say that I'm a courier between England and cities all over Europe. I work for several masters, and not without danger. And . . . er . . . well, there is another reason why I'm here today,' he added with a self-consciously knowing look. 'Queen Philippa is very kind, and allows me to speak to one of her ladies-in-waiting.'

'Indeed? And does the lady answer?'

'She pretends to be evasive, and I have competitors, but Lisette shares with me a love of sport, and she's here this morning with her little goshawk – over there!'

Wulfstan turned to see the lady de l'Isle in her clinging green gown with a gold-studded belt around her waist, expertly holding her hooded bird and talking with the Queen. So her name was Lisette.

'I wish you good luck, André. She's certainly a beauty,' he said, aware of her raised eyebrows as she gazed in their direction, and not sure which one of them was the object of those green-gold eyes.

'Come, Wulfstan, the King is about to give the signal for the first birds to be unhooded and set free. Do you see those baskets being taken up? One's full of live mice, and the other of rabbits. Let's see what my pretty bird will catch for me – get ready, my girl! Off you go!'

The sound of a horn was heard, two quick blasts followed by a great flapping of wings as the birds were released up into the clear air, and then began to swoop down. The crowd did not cheer, but waited in silence for the predators to return with their kill.

Wulfstan saw the lady Lisette de l'Isle welcome her goshawk back, its talons embedded in the body of a helpless rabbit as big as itself.

Twelve

The dusty track stretched ahead as far as the eye could see, shimmering in summer heat. Where the way ran close to woodland, Wulfstan chose to ride in the shade, but not too far in, for the woods were known to harbour outlaws, disaffected villeins who lay in wait for solitary, unprotected travellers, if only to steal their horses. Wulfstan carried a note for the Prince, and a jewelled necklet and bracelet, 'for a lady', the King had told him, 'a gift from the Queen'.

'Guard the written message with your life, Sir Wulfstan,' the King had ordered, 'and hand it only to Prince Edward.' Wulfstan had bowed deeply, and mounted Jewel with inward dissatisfaction. He had been at Westminster for nearly three weeks, spending most of his time as secretary to the Queen. The music, dancing and flirting at court had not appealed to him, though more than one of the Queen's ladies had tried to persuade him to dance, notwithstanding the lack of an arm. The lady Lisette had not approached him, though neither had she responded to Demoins' advances, and the latter's over-confident smiles had faded as she turned away, apparently preferring to converse with other ladies of the Queen's bedchamber. Wulfstan had learned a little about falconry from the grey-haired man who trained the King's birds, but he had avoided the company of André Demoins. As the days had gone by, his thoughts of Beulah gave him constant regret, for surely after all this time away from Greneholt, she and her parents must presume that he had broken his betrothal promises. To his further chagrin the King had given him no explanation of the nature of the message he had carried from the Prince, and there had been no signs of a political crisis.

As Jewel carried him across open common land where pigs rooted and farm carts lumbered along the winding tracks where the occasional beggar asked him for alms, his spirits sank lower and lower. What was he to do with his life, an ex-soldier with but one arm? There was no longer a place for him at Hyam St Ebba, nor did he relish the prospect of scribing and adding up numbers for the rest of his life, with Miril as his wife. The only truly close friend he had was Claus Van Brunt, tragically made a eunuch by the war; had he really done the man a favour by saving his life? His thoughts turned to Friar Valerian who had loved his sister Cecily: would the good friar be able to advise him? Was he, like Charles Lemaitre, called to enter a monastic life of prayer and discipline? The idea did not attract him, but he resolved to ponder and pray to be shown the direction his life should take.

The sight of the battlements of Berkhamsted Castle gave him no pleasure at returning to the place where he was a knight in the service of the Black Prince, with duties to perform. He turned Jewel's head towards the castle, and sat up straight on her back.

There was nobody to greet him in the courtyard apart from a groom who came forward to take Jewel's bridle as he dismounted without the man's assistance. Carrying his precious leather bag, he walked stiffly towards the archway leading to the passage and stairway to the Prince's private apartment and counting-house. The Prince was not there, only a harassed Hugh Baldoc sorting out various documents spread out on the table. He looked up in some relief.

'Thanks be to God, I thought you were never coming back, Wynstede. I've scarcely left this room since you set out for London. The Prince is relentless in his wants—'

'And you are infernally slow, Baldoc,' said the Prince, striding in at that moment. 'You may leave us, and wait outside. Well, Wulfstan, you're back, thank heaven. That man's got no sense, and is so slow, I might as well engage a snail. Now, I believe you have something for me, a message from the King.'

Wulfstan drew forth the note from its bag, and the jewellery. At the sight of the latter, the Prince's eyes lit up, and he held the necklet up to the sunlight which rippled like water through the polished stones – agates, topaz and onyx.

'Splendid! A perfect gift for a bride!'

Wulfstan did not dare to ask the identity of the bride, but

assumed that his master had given up yearning for the 'Fair Maid of Kent', and had decided on a second choice, a suitable woman to be Princess of Wales.

'I am happy to have fulfilled my duties to you and to the King, my liege,' he said coolly. 'I trust that the matter on which I was sent away has been resolved?'

'It appears to have been settled, and thank you for your part in it. Oh, and by the way, the man I sent to collect the dues from Greneholt came back with a complaint from Sir William Horst, asking why you have stayed away for so long. I sent word that you were away on important business for the King.'

Wulfstan sighed at hearing this, for it meant that he would still have to go to Greneholt and confess his shame. He bowed. 'Even so, my liege.'

'You had better go now to find refreshment. It must have been a hot, dusty ride.'

'Very good, my liege.' Wulfstan bowed again, and left the room feeling strangely empty. He was clearly not going to be told the nature of the secret messages he had carried. So, he would go to seek the one man who was his true friend, one who would welcome him back with real warmth.

Claus Van Brunt was not in his room, nor in the inner courtyard where there were seats in the shade. Wulfstan was puzzled; surely Claus must be much improved to be able to walk this far, he thought as he descended the stone steps to the carved wooden door that gave on to the sweep of level greensward used for jousting. A couple of the Prince's guards were practising with horses and blunt-tipped lances, and Wulfstan walked across to the groom attending them.

'Have you any idea where I may find Master Van Brunt?' he asked, at which the man smiled and said, 'Welcome back, Sir Wulfstan! Go down that slope and you'll find Master and Mistress Van Brunt sitting in the circular garden.'

Mistress? Wulfstan was puzzled for a moment, but thought the man must mean Mistress Dibbert who had become nurse as well as cook to the invalid.

'She's brought him a very long way,' he remarked, at which the man tapped the side of his nose. 'Aye, sire, but he's a different man since the wedding.'

Wedding? What was the man talking about? He stared in bewilderment, and the groom grinned. 'Haven't ye heard, sir? The Prince himself witnessed it for 'em. Look, they're coming back – see how well he walks with her holding his arm, he hardly needs that stick!'

Wulfstan stared open-mouthed as the couple drew near. Claus hailed him with a wave of the walking-stick, holding his wife's arm with his other hand. Beside him, blushing and looking extremely pretty, was Miril; a gentle curving beneath her gown showed that she carried a child. *His* child. What in God's name had the Prince been doing while he was away?

'Wulfstan! Thank heaven you're back, safe and sound! You will see that I have acquired the blessing of a wife since you left for Westminster. Miril, my love, make your curtsey to Sir Wulfstan Wynstede.'

Blushing and with a flutter of undoubted happiness, Mistress Van Brunt curtseyed low to her former lover. 'My liege,' she whispered, mistakenly giving him a prince's title, though Wulfstan did not notice, confronted as he was by this totally unexpected situation. In his head his whirling emotions were beginning to settle, and he slowly began to see and understand why he had been so summarily despatched to the court at Westminster. The Prince had told him that he would find a suitable husband for Miril, a man who would take her and accept the child she carried as his own; but *Van Brunt*? A man tragically made a eunuch by the sword of war? When Wulfstan remembered how Claus had begged to be allowed to share the burden that was so troubling him, and how for shame Wulfstan had refused to tell him, he now marvelled that the burden was not only shared, but taken from his shoulders and placed on Van Brunt's, he who for his friend's sake had married an unlettered maidservant. This being so, he owed Claus an over-whelming debt of gratitude, but how could he express it in front of the smiling bride?

Bride. At once he thought of the jewelled necklet and bracelet sent by the Queen to the Black Prince – 'a perfect gift for a bride'. So was the gift for Miril?

He must have been staring at the newly weds, because Claus Van Brunt now addressed him honestly and firmly.

'You need have no doubts or misgivings, my good friend. This sweet girl has consented to be my wife, and she will present me with a child in due course, and make me the happiest of men.' He lowered his voice and added, close to Wulfstan's ear, 'I shall be forever in your debt, my friend.' He smiled and Wulfstan smiled back, rather uncertainly. It now appeared that Mistress Dibbert had been sent to Van Brunt's room to assess his suitability as a husband for Miril and father for her child, and then to act as go-between – and that he, Wulfstan, had been hastily removed from the scene while the negotiations took place.

Another thought occurred to him: if the Prince had told Sir William Horst that Beulah's betrothed had been sent on urgent business with the King, he need make no shameful confession, but hurry to see his sweet love as soon as possible, and apologize to her parents for his sudden and prolonged absence 'on business with the King'. So Van Brunt was happy with his bride, Miril was happy with a kind husband, and Wulfstan was rescued from disgrace and free to renew his promise to marry his beloved in three years' time.

When he next met the Prince in the counting-house, he thanked him fervently for his intervention which had brought about such a happy state of affairs. The Prince gave him a curious look and took a document from a drawer beneath the table.

'You have complained at not being told of the important business for which you were sent to Westminster,' he said. 'This is the message my father the King sent back to me, the message you carried.'

Wulfstan stared at the brief note, hardly able to make sense of it at first, but then the letters settled into place, and he was able to read what they said.

Your young fool herewith returned. The Queen and I kept him as long as we could. Thank God for the Fleming, and may the girl bear him a son. The enclosed trinkets are for her from the Queen.

Wulfstan's face flamed. 'B-but Claus cannot take her—'

'God's blood, did your father teach you nothing at all? There are other ways of pleasuring a woman – he's got hands, hasn't he? And fingers?'

'I . . . if I could only thank you, my liege—'

'Oh, don't stand there stammering, get on your horse and gallop to Greneholt, where your ladylove awaits you, you lucky devil. And keep out of temptation's way in future!'

The grey stone walls of Greneholt Manor were bathed in warm midsummer sunshine, as was the nearby church of St Mary Greneholt; both had been built at the turn of the 13th century by the Horst family, now well established as landowners of the hundred of Greneholt.

Wulfstan dismounted, and looked upon the pleasing scene before him. In front of the entrance of the manor was a grassy area, edged with lavender bushes; a trellised archway to the right, covered with climbing pink roses, led to the right side of the house where a kitchen garden was planted with vegetables. To the left was a hedge formed of gooseberry and currant bushes, beyond which lay a small orchard of apple and pear trees, continuing round to the back of the house.

Wulfstan's heart gave a sudden jolt: there in the archway stood a young woman in a blue gown, picking roses, and surely she was Beulah! Yes, she had caught sight of him, and for a moment they stared across the intervening space, before she quickly disappeared round the side of the house, to tell her parents of the long-awaited visitor. He walked towards the front entrance with a thudding heart: how would he greet her when they were face to face? Would he be allowed to speak to her alone?

He soon found out that no such permission was given. He was shown into a cool room with tapestries hung from two walls opposite a window, its only furnishings a carved oak chest. Sir William Horst entered with a brief, unsmiling bow which Wulfstan returned, and came straight to the point.

'My daughter has been deeply distressed and my wife and I quite bewildered by your absence, Sir Wulfstan. We knew you were unable to ride over in the cold and darkness of winter, with your disability, but with midsummer now upon us, we thought to see you long before now. When one of Prince Edward's men came to collect our dues, I sent him back with a message for the Prince, asking about you, and he replied that you were away on urgent business with the King.

If the Prince could courteously send us this message, why could you not do so, Sir Wulfstan? If you could have seen the disappointment on the face of the lady Beulah, you would surely have been moved!'

Wulfstan hung his head like a condemned prisoner. Guilty as he was for neglecting his betrothed wife by his long absence, he felt ten times more guilty of his deception, about which Sir William knew nothing. What on earth would be his reaction if he ever found out, Wulfstan could not bear to contemplate. He had enemies in the Prince's household, Baldoc and Sir Guy Hamald – men who would seize on an opportunity to discredit him, show up his hypocrisy and make him a figure of ridicule.

Sir William had stopped speaking. Making an effort to raise his head and look the old knight in his eyes, he attempted to give an answer.

'I am sorry beyond all words, Sir William, that I have caused sorrow to your daughter the lady Beulah.' He paused, and when Sir William gave no reply, he drew in a long breath and continued. 'As Prince Edward explained, I was sent away suddenly to the King's court at Westminster on an errand concerning the . . . the safety of the realm, a . . . a very delicate matter. I hope that you and the Lady Judith can find it in your hearts to forgive me, and be assured that this will never happen again.'

The two men regarded each other for a long moment, and then Sir William Horst put his hands together and nodded.

'Because of the strong attachment my daughter has towards you, and the respect owed to your position at court, a soldier who has fought bravely in battle and lost a limb, I accept your apology and will instruct my wife to do likewise.' He held out his hand, and Wulfstan took it, sighing gratefully with relief, bowing and thanking Sir William. When Lady Judith entered the room with a shyly smiling Beulah, she followed her husband in shaking Wulfstan's hand, nodding to her daughter to step forward and do the same; but Beulah burst into tears and went down on her knees before Wulfstan.

'I never doubted you, dear Wulfstan; I knew there would be some good reason for you staying away. I've prayed for you morning and night—'

'Get up, Beulah, you forget yourself!' said her father sharply, and Lady Judith put out a hand to help her arise. The sobbing girl then ran from the room, and when her parents looked at Wulfstan they saw tears in his eyes, which had more effect on them in his favour than any words of regret.

'It appears that you have retained her love, Wulfstan, and so we will say no more. When she has composed herself, you may walk with her in the garden, accompanied by a trusted lady companion of my wife's.'

Wulfstan bowed, unable to speak, and half an hour later he took Beulah's hand, and they walked out into the orchard, with Mistress Craik the chaperone following at a discreet distance, and they kept their voices down, out of earshot.

'Thank you for your trust in me, dearest Beulah,' he said in a low tone. 'I will never again cause you grief, if you can find it in your heart to forgive me.'

'Don't . . . Please don't say any more, Wulfstan, there is nothing to forgive,' she whispered, hanging on to his hand, and he was overwhelmed by a sense of his own unworthiness. How happy he would be, he thought, how proud to be the object of her devotion, if he had only been as innocent as she believed him to be. But her adoration was another sword thrust of conscience, of self-accusation. Part of him would have welcomed a chance to confess, to unburden himself of the shameful truth, that he had got a maidservant with child, and consented to her being married to another man – his best friend. But this he could never do. He pictured the incredulous shock in those soft brown eyes, and the very thought of Sir William's anger and contempt made his heart shrivel as if burned by fire. All connection with the Horst family would be over.

No – he would have to keep such knowledge from them, and pray that it would never be revealed by ill-wishers. He stopped walking, and looked down into those shining eyes. She held up her face to him.

'Kiss me, dearest Wulfstan, let's kiss to seal our betrothal as a man and his wife!'

How could he refuse? She put her arms around his neck, and his arm encircled her waist. His lips brushed her cheek, but she turned her face so that his lips met hers in a kiss of sudden fervour.

Until Mistress Craik gave a cry of alarm, and forcibly thrust herself between them.

'In God's name, what are you thinking of? Beulah, let go of him at once! Shame on you, sire, for laying hands upon her – for . . . for . . .' Words failed the good lady as they drew apart – but they had sealed their love with a kiss that said more than a hundred words.

Mistress Craik took Beulah's arm and nothing more was said as she accompanied them back to the house, but Wulfstan saw from the corner of his eye that his betrothed was smiling to herself.

As the summer days shortened into an autumn of mists and early frosts, life at Berkhamsted went on much as usual. Wulfstan's secretarial duties kept him well occupied, and Baldoc assisted him with a much better grace than formerly. The Prince no longer sent Wulfstan on errands to collect dues, but ordered two of his guards to take on this duty, except for Greneholt Manor which Wulfstan was able to visit every three or four weeks. There was no repetition of the emotional scene in the garden, and any kissing between the betrothed pair was confined to hands; Beulah's eyes were kept modestly lowered, and Wulfstan had to tell himself to be content to wait for another three years, and count himself extremely fortunate to have escaped further censure. He could never forget his wrong-doing, being reminded of it daily by the sight of Master and Mistress Van Brunt who occupied a room in the castle to await the birth of their child. Claus's happiness was reflected in his good health and spirits, his constant care for his pretty little wife, now growing big with the baby; they were truly in love, though Wulfstan knew that he would not be sorry to see them go to Flanders after the birth, for Van Brunt now wanted to settle among his relatives as a married man and father.

Having now no especial friend at Berkhamsted, Wulfstan was delighted by the return of Sir Ranulf Ormiston, a sensible ally to counteract the insolence of Hamald. It was a relief to have him as companion and confidante in place of Claus Van Brunt who had no further need of his friendship.

The new peace with France appeared to be unruffled, and halfway through October the Prince joined his father on an expedition to their territories in France and the English occupying forces there, now inevitably fraternizing with the population and taking French wives.

'We shall be back before the year's end,' Prince Edward told Wulfstan. 'I can leave you here under the jurisdiction of the Queen – and you'd better get down to Greneholt to see your lady-love before the winter sets in. The country people say there will be storms. I'll leave Ormiston here to back you up.'

Wulfstan duly set out on Jewel for the place where he was now welcomed without reservation. He arrived as dusk was falling, and even Mistress Craik smiled upon the handsome knight betrothed to her lady's beautiful daughter. A strong wind had arisen, scattering the last of the summer leaves and whipping through the homes of the peasant labourers on the estate, blowing on their smoky fires, sending sparks flying up to threaten wooden beams and dry straw, which then had to be doused with water. Sir William set out with two manservants to bring distressed families into the shelter of the manor for the night, and Lady Judith ordered extra victuals to be set out on trestle tables for them.

Wulfstan was invited to sit at table between Lady Judith and Mistress Craik, though he would far rather have sat next to Beulah on her mother's other side. Outside the wind grew stronger, and soon there were flashes of lightning followed by deafening crashes of thunder, always a portent of trouble to come, and the sheltering villagers clung to each other in terror. Sir William stood up to ask for the Lord's protection and beg for forgiveness if any had offended him.

'Restrain thy wrath, O Lord, and have mercy on us thy penitent sinners!' he prayed aloud, but the tempest continued to rage, and the howling of the wind was joined by more sinister noises, crashes that caused the house to shake on its foundations, and moans that sent shivers of fear down their spines. Children sobbed and their mothers wept.

''Tis the wailing of the damned souls in hell!' somebody yelled, and Beulah cried out in fear. Wulfstan could not keep his seat, but got up to sit beside her and encircle her in his arm, holding her head upon his shoulder and whispering comfort, saying that God would take care of them; even so, he sent up his own silent prayer for safety. The storm thundered on, the shouting rose, and oaths filled the air; one woman cried out that she saw a dark figure holding a flaming sword.

''Tis the Devil himself come among us, seeking his own! Help us, save our souls! Lord, have mercy upon us miserable sinners!' she screamed as a lightning flash illumined the high windows.

'Be calm, beloved Beulah,' whispered Wulfstan. 'I'm here beside you. No evil can come near you.' Nevertheless he crossed himself and muttered a prayer of contrition for his own secret sins, holding her all the while, and though unable to stroke her hair, he kissed the top of her head. Her father and mother sat close together, and did not miss this intimacy, in spite of the darkness. Mistress Craik enfolded a frightened housemaid.

At last, after what seemed hours but in fact was less than an hour, the storm began to abate and die away. Prayers of thanksgiving were led by Sir William, kneeling on the stone floor, and gradually the company regained composure, and even to fall asleep, children in their mothers' arms.

When Sir William announced that he was going outside to assess the storm damage, he told Wulfstan to accompany him, with two menservants. A scene of devastation met their eyes, trees uprooted and lying on the ground, broken branches and peasants' homes collapsed in heaps of wet timber and clay. A couple of horses without a stable neighed their distress, and the lowing of cows accounted for the sounds heard during the storm.

'But it's over, Wulfstan,' said Sir William, 'and God has spared our lives.'

'So he has, sire, and for that we must rejoice,' answered Wulfstan. 'But it was a terrifying experience, and I had to comfort Beulah and bid her take courage. It made me realize how much I long to take her as wife and be near her.'

'Beulah is safest with us, Wulfstan, and here she will stay for the next three years,' Sir William replied sharply. 'Her mother and I would never allow you to break the terms of your betrothal.'

Wulfstan made no reply. The storm had awakened his discontent at this long separation from Beulah, and he might have disputed with her father and put the case for marrying her earlier if only he had been able to offer her a home at Berkhamsted, for the Prince would have no objection; but this was out of the question with Van Brunt and Miril there – and too many tongues to make mischief. And even if he had been able to offer her a palace, it was abundantly clear that her parents would never consent.

'We have a formidable task before us, to repair the storm damage and our tenants' dwellings without delay, with winter so nearly upon us,' remarked Sir William gravely. 'Until they have roofs again, the children and their mothers must remain in the manor. How long will you be able to stay with us, Wulfstan?'

Wulfstan was apologetic. 'With the Prince away I need to be at Berkhamsted, sire. I can only stay until tomorrow, but today you may command me to give what help I can. I regret that I can stay no longer.'

He then threw himself into working from dawn to dusk, side by side with the tenants and menservants in clearing away fallen trees and the collapsed roofs and walls of peasants' homes, scarcely stopping to eat. It left no time to exchange a word with Beulah until after supper, by which time he ached in every muscle, and she was concerned for him. After a night's exhausted sleep, he bid his hosts farewell and set off on a nervous Jewel to cover the distance to Berkhamsted by afternoon, wondering how the storm had affected the household there: would there be reports of the Devil appearing and gathering souls to hell? How would he be greeted?

As soon as he rode into the courtyard, he was aware that something momentous had happened. He dismounted and strode into the great hall. There were voices exclaiming and even laughing – and from a chamber above came the sound of the cry of a newborn baby. Wulfstan's heart lurched: his child was born.

Mistress Dibbert came down the stairs with a satisfied expression on her rosy face.

'The storm so affrighted Mistress Van Brunt that her travail came upon her and I've delivered her of a fine boy!' she cried in triumph. 'He's small, of course, he wasn't due to be born for another month or so, but he's strong and healthy, and has a great voice on him! Master Van Brunt is the happiest man in England!'

Wulfstan hardly knew what to say. So this was the end of his passionate embraces with Miril – a son. He thanked Mistress Dibbert for her good services, and sent his congratulations to the happy parents. She told him that the storm had caused little damage in Berkhamsted, but the noise had kept them all awake and brought on the birth of Mistress Van Brunt's child.

'I'll have refreshment sent to you, sire,' she said with a smile, and left the hall.

Wulfstan sat down wearily on a bench against the wall. His back ached and his legs were stiff; the old pain in his left shoulder had returned. A maidservant entered with a bowl of soup and a crust of yesterday's bread which she set before him, and he had just begun to start dipping the bread in the soup when he heard footsteps on the stairs; looking up he saw Van Brunt. Again, words deserted him, but his friend smiled broadly and thanked him for his good wishes. 'Mother and child are very well, thanks be to God,' he said.

'Ah, yes, I heard the child crying as I came in, Claus,' said Wulfstan awkwardly, disorientated by fatigue and not knowing how to react to this sudden news. Which was why he next said what he did.

'I shall look forward to seeing my son.'

There was a moment of silence, and it was as if the very air in the room had chilled to ice. Then Van Brunt spoke.

'Pieter is my son, not yours, Wynstede. His mother is my wife, and he is my son. I intend to take them home to Flanders as soon as they are well enough to travel. I thank you for your hospitality and the good care you gave me which saved my life. I am indebted to you, but I must ask you *not* to see Pieter. He is *my* son, and I don't want anything said otherwise.'

He turned on his heel and left the hall.

Wulfstan set aside the food. This must be the very worst day of his life, worse than the loss of his arm which had made a hero of him – or the shame of his encounter with Lady Mildred Points and its aftermath which had made a fool of him in front of his peers; *nothing* had been as painful as this cold rejection from the man he had looked upon as his closest friend. And he could make no claim at all on the son he had fathered, not even to set eyes on the babe who had been named without his knowledge.

After a while he accepted that what had happened was fair enough; he had handed Miril over to his friend without realizing what a strong attachment would grow between them. He had no cause for complaint, and was affianced to the lovely lady Beulah, of whom he was unworthy.

Only – he knew that he could not endure to share the castle with the new parents and their son, and the next day he rose early and rode to Westminster for an audience with the Queen, under whose jurisdiction he now held office in her son's absence.

Queen Philippa agreed at once to see him, turning away other suppliants and bidding him follow her into an inner chamber.

'What brings you back to court, Sir Wulfstan, so soon after my son's departure? Is there trouble at the castle?'

'No, no, Your Grace, I beg your forbearance in what must seem a trifling matter,' he said with a low bow. 'I have come to appeal to your kindness for a tender babe who was born untimely early because of the storm. It needs warmth and the care of wise women. If you can find room for it and the parents in a kinder lodging than Berkhamsted Castle, it would be a great blessing.'

'What? You have ridden all this way just to ask me to take a newly born babe off your hands?' asked the Queen with a curious look. 'Of whom do you speak?'

'A Flemish family named Van Brunt, Your Grace, who will be returning to their home after Christmas,' answered Wulfstan, fearing that this would be no easy interview.

'Who is this child's mother?'

'The wife of a Flemish soldier who served under the Prince at Poitiers, and was badly wounded, Madam.'

The Queen looked straight into his eyes. 'And the child's father?'

Wulfstan opened his mouth, but could not speak; he was unable to meet her eyes.

'Is this the lady who received a jewelled necklet from me? Ah, Wulfstan, you need say no more. So you cannot face your son?' Her tone was stern but not unkindly, and Wulfstan's face flamed. He abandoned all pretence.

'I may not see him, Madam. I cannot endure it, not under the same roof.' To his further shame, he blinked back tears. The Queen regarded him for a long minute before replying, and Wulfstan prepared himself for a rebuke. Her face remained grave.

'Very well, your request is granted. The three will be carried to Kennington Palace forthwith, where there is more comfort for a child born early, and women to attend on it and the mother. Take some refreshment now, and then return to Berkhamsted at once.' She held out her hand for him to kiss.

'I thank you from my heart, Your Grace. I shall pray for—'

'You may leave us, Sir Wulfstan.'

King Edward and the Prince of Wales sailed back to Dover on October 31st, and proceeded to the King's domain at Westminster. The Prince returned to Berkhamsted two days later, declaring the short expedition a success.

'I think we may hang up our swords or beat them into ploughshares,' he said with satisfaction. 'As soon as the French saw we were there to renew the peace, and not to stir up old enmities, they were happy to exchange civilities. The King has ordered Sir Thomas Holland, Earl of Kent, to start withdrawing the English garrisons.'

Wulfstan nodded discreetly, knowing that the name of Sir Thomas Holland, one of the founder members of the Order of the Garter, a respected leader of men and friend of the King, was fraught with emotion for the Prince.

'And is this your mind also, my liege?'

The Prince nodded. 'The men will welcome it. Winter lies ahead, and they'd rather be at home beside their own hearths

– and to bed with their wives, eh, Wulfstan? Have you been over to Greneholt while I've been away?'

'Once only, sire, for the weather continues foul. While I was there a great storm blew up and caused much damage. I have never known such a tempest – it raged as if the devil himself were riding on the wind.'

'I heard from my mother that it struck terror into people, and had some other results, like frightening women with child to bring forth babes before their time.' There was a meaningful look in his eyes, and Wulfstan endeavoured to give a reasonable reply.

'Indeed, sire, Mistress Van Brunt was delivered of a small but healthy son at the height of the storm. I asked the Queen if he and his parents could be taken to the royal palace at Kennington where he would have better care from women and more comfortable lodging than here. And now, sire, do you wish to inspect the castle income and expenses?'

'So you never saw your son, Wulfstan? You took no pride in fatherhood?'

'He was Van Brunt's child, sire, and I . . . I could not live under the same roof and not see him.' Wulfstan turned away to hide his agitation.

'Ah, my young friend, you have many years before you,' said the Prince with a sigh. 'The lady Beulah will give you more sons in the course of time, whereas I, Prince of the realm and heir to my father's throne, may not see or speak to the woman I have loved all my life, since we played together as children at court.' He smiled grimly. 'The good Sir Thomas, Earl of Kent, no doubt hopes to be home with his wife for the Feast of the Nativity.'

Wulfstan heard the unspoken words, and was silent. There seemed nothing more to be said.

Wulfstan could not remember a more miserable Christmas than that of 1360 at Berkhamsted. Bitter winds with flurries of snowflakes whirled around the castle, making outdoor activities impossible, and a great deal of drinking went on. Masses were held in the castle chapel on Christmas Eve and the morning of Christmas Day, the latter sparsely attended because of the after-effects of drinking into the early hours of the morning. The likes of Guy Hamald and his handful of cronies among the guards were not satisfied with dicing and indoor games, and the maidservants were summoned. Mistress Dibbert could protect the shy and innocent girls, but could not stop the bolder ones from escaping up into the great hall where music and dancing went on into the small hours. The Prince himself was seldom completely sober during the festive season, and Wulfstan found himself dreaming of Beulah in a lascivious way, for which he was ashamed.

The worst incident was in midweek between Christmas and the New Year celebration, when Guy Hamald and a few others, bored by the weather which prevented them from hunting, turned the lower greensward used for jousting into a pit for dog-fighting. They used the Prince's valuable pack of hounds, kicking the creatures and tormenting them with sharp pointed sticks, urging them on to tear at each other's eyes, throats and bellies. Wulfstan was alerted to the hideous spectacle by the agonized howls and snarls of usually well-tempered dogs. The Prince was drunk, but Sir Ranulf quickly came to his aid, and together they mounted their steeds and galloped into the pit with swords unsheathed, ordering the men to stop the fighting forthwith. Hamald and the ringleaders were seized and led down into the windowless cells beneath the castle. Others slunk away, denying all involvement in the mêlée.

'Let it be that in 1361 God sends us better times,' the Prince was heard to say at Mass on the eve of that New Year.

But the only news that arrived on January 1st was that Sir Thomas Holland, Earl of Kent and the King's lieutenant-general in France, had died of a fever at Christmas, aged forty. He left a widow, three sons and two daughters, and the King had ordered a month's court mourning.

Thirteen

Wulfstan felt almost personally affected by the news. He knew the Prince's heart, having heard the name of the Countess of Kent on his lips on many occasions, and of his hopeless love for 'my lady Jeanette', 'the Fair Maid of Kent', on whose account the Prince had rejected a series of brides chosen for him by his parents to be a Princess of Wales and future Queen of England. How would the Prince react to the news that the woman he loved was now a widow? And how should Wulfstan approach him now? He would have to maintain a blank expression and make no comment, to behave as if the death of the Earl had never happened.

His questions were soon answered. On the day the news was brought the Prince shut himself in his bedchamber and spoke to no one. On the following day he rose early and dressed himself for a journey. His face was unsmiling, his manner brisk in front of his household.

'I shall ride to Canterbury, and pray before the shrine of St Thomas à Becket,' he announced, adding in a lower tone, 'I need the prayers of such a saint to give me guidance.'

'Very good, my liege,' replied Wulfstan as the Prince strode forth to where a groom stood waiting with his stallion, saddled and bridled, and a mounted guard stood ready to accompany the Prince on his long winter ride. At the arched stone doorway, he stopped and turned back to embrace Wulfstan briefly.

'Pray for me,' he muttered.

'I will, my liege,' Wulfstan replied, and then his royal master was gone; but in that momentary grip, there had been tension, indecision – and joy, amazing joy!

'Our Prince has got something on his mind, for sure,' said Ranulf Ormiston. 'There are sparks coming out of his spurs. Was he deeply attached to the good Earl of Kent?'

'Sir Thomas was a man admired and respected by all.'

'So he was, but that doesn't answer the question. It seems that the man's death is going to have consequences that could affect us all.'

Left alone, Wulfstan was in no mood to celebrate the New Year, and took himself up to the counting-house where he checked over the well-kept records. At midday, when he usually expected a maidservant to bring him refreshment, it was Mistress Dibbert who climbed the stairs with the jug and trencher.

'Sit down, Mistress, and tell me what they're saying in the kitchen,' he said with a casualness which belied his true curiosity. This woman had known the Prince from childhood.

She obediently sat. 'You mean about the Prince riding off to Canterbury, sire?'

'You knew him as a child, I believe, and ruled him with a rod of iron, he told me!'

'He was a self-willed boy, to be sure,' she said smiling, 'and needed a firm hand!'

'Mistress Dibbert, let me ask you – the lady who is Countess of Kent was a playmate of his. Were they close to each other as children?'

'Ah – he told you this, sire?' She nodded slowly. 'Yes, they were devoted.'

'What was she like?'

'She was a dear, sweet little girl, and everybody loved her. She was his father's cousin, you see, daughter of the Earl of Kent. He died in mysterious circumstances, and our good Queen Philippa adopted her. She used to play happily with Edward and his two sisters, being a little older than he, and he would do anything to please his Jeanette, as he called her, but before he left the women's hall, she was married to William Montague, the Earl of Salisbury, so they were parted. She was a famous beauty, even then, and it was said –' Mistress Dibbert lowered her voice, though there was nobody in the room to overhear – 'it was said that the King himself was in love with her.'

'Was that true?' asked Wulfstan in surprise.

'I don't know, sire. She was beautiful, full of life, always smiling. The King met her at a great ball to celebrate his victory at Calais. She was about nineteen, and as she was dancing, her garter slipped off and fell on the floor.'

'Oh, yes, I've heard that story,' Wulfstan broke in. 'Didn't the King pick it up and tie it around his own leg?'

'Yes, and when the people laughed, he said, "Shame on him who thinks ill of it!" – which was taken up to be the motto of the Order of the Garter which the King set up at that time, *Honi soit qui mal y pense!* But the Countess had caught the eye of another man there, Sir Thomas Holland, and there was talk about them – how true it was I don't know, but Sir Thomas actually went to Rome, to ask the Pope for an annulment of her marriage to Salisbury, because he said that she and he had been married in front of witnesses before she was married to Salisbury, though she could only have been a child. The Pope took his time making a decision, and by the time it was granted, the Earl had divorced her for . . . well, on account of Sir Thomas. So she and Sir Thomas were officially married, and on the death of her brother, he took the title of Earl of Kent, so once again she was the "Fair Maid of Kent". Now that he has sadly died, I don't know what will happen.'

Wulfstan listened eagerly, though made no comment, feeling fairly certain that the good Mistress Dibbert *did* know, or strongly suspected what the future held for the Black Prince, though to speculate openly would be deeply disrespectful to the memory of Sir Thomas. Even so, having sensed the Prince's incredulous happiness, he could have no doubt of his eventual intentions.

When the Prince returned he offered no account of his visit to Canterbury, but to all outward appearances he was a changed man. Bright of eye and quick of step, he interested himself in all aspects of life at the castle, supervising the household with firmness of purpose but with much good humour. Gone was his former sluggishness over the Christmas period, and his drinking was limited to two small beakers of wine after the evening meal. He spent some time in the guards' quarters and in the stables, keeping horses and dogs exercised and organizing boar-hunting parties when the weather permitted, and small-scale tournaments in the tiltyard to keep the men occupied. Comments were whispered among the staff, and speculations as to the change in the Prince's behaviour, but none spoke aloud: the court was still in mourning.

In February he was off to London again.

'My father is determined that peace with France must continue,' he said. 'He and I and my brothers have to appear before Parliament and hear every single member swear an oath to preserve the Treaty made with King John of France. No more invasions, no more spoiling and plundering – England is about to embark on an era of peace and prosperity!' His eyes sparkled as if anticipating a golden age that would change all their lives.

'Depend on it, Wulfstan, our royal master has got some lady in his sights,' murmured Ranulf Ormiston. 'He wouldn't be this excited over an oath-swearing in Parliament. Some youthful beauty has caught his eye, and an announcement will soon follow, mark my words!'

Wulfstan smiled and said nothing. He enjoyed Ormiston's company and the support he gave in controlling the likes of Guy Hamald, now in the Prince's bad books, whose open insolence had been replaced by malevolent sulking. It was also reassuring to leave the castle in the unofficial charge of Ormiston while the Prince was away, such as when Wulfstan went on a two-night visit to Greneholt. Beulah's slim body was curving into womanhood, making her even more desirable, especially when she took his hand and smiled up at him adoringly. There were still two more years of betrothal before he could take Beulah as his bride in marriage, a fact which sorely tried his patience, though he knew that Sir William Horst would never agree to shortening the time.

When the Prince returned from Westminster, Wulfstan half expected him to make an announcement, but in April there was another occurrence which plunged the court into mourning again. The Duke of Lancaster, 'our beloved cousin' who had served the King in Normandy at the time of Poitiers five years earlier, died suddenly in a recurrence of the plague. The Prince joined the King and his brothers on a journey to Leicester where they knelt to pay homage at the bier where the great Duke lay in state, and on his return he told the household at the supper table that yet another journey was in the offing.

'For now, my friends, having done my duties, I shall be off to London to speak with the King and Queen and to start making preparations for a wedding!'

This was greeted with smiles and nods, with some relief that the news so long suppressed and speculated upon was now to be out in the open.

'What did I tell you?' murmured Ranulf in Wulfstan's ear.

'Yes, my noble knights, your Prince of Wales has at last found a Princess – the sweetest, loveliest, kindest lady in all the realm – the Fair Maid of Kent, for I would have no other!'

There was a brief gasp of surprise from some of the company, but being loyal members of the Prince's circle of male subordinates, they stood to cheer and congratulate him.

'God's bones, she must be as old as the hills, and her husband's hardly cold in his grave,' muttered Ormiston in surprise; but Wulfstan was not surprised at all.

The Prince's announcement was less happily received at court. The King was thunderstruck, remembering his own amorous inclinations towards the young Countess of Salisbury whose garter he had gallantly retrieved all those years ago. The Queen was disappointed at her son's choice, for although she had happy memories of Joan as her adopted daughter, the girl was now a twice-married woman with more than a breath of scandal attached to her name; her divorced first husband was still living, she was two years senior to the Prince and had three sons and two daughters clinging round her skirts. Of course the King's earlier infatuation with Joan was a hurtful memory to Queen Philippa, but she could see that the Prince would take no other bride, and was good-natured enough to forgive her husband's past foolishness. So preparations for a royal wedding went ahead.

Summer at Berkhamsted Castle was a time of special rejoicing. It was as if the Prince's happiness suffused the air they breathed, putting smiles on all faces, thankfulness in all hearts for the sunshine, the green leaves, the scent of flowers, and the calling of birds one to another as nests were built and eggs laid, the wonderful fecundity of the animal world.

All these thoughts passed through Wulfstan's mind as he rode to Greneholt Manor, for the signs of the awakening earth struck a chord deep in his heart; his eyes softened as he thought of his lovely Beulah, of holding her hand and, if opportunity offered, of kissing her eager lips; but oh, how he longed to take her in his arms, to worship her nakedness with his hands, to enter her body and become one flesh, man and wife . . .

Sitting with the family at table that evening, the talk turned inevitably to the Prince of Wales and his approaching wedding.

'It's as if the whole castle – the people, the servants, even the horses and dogs are sharing their master's happiness,' said Wulfstan, smiling. 'I have never seen him so . . . so on fire with love for his lady, called the Fair Maid of Kent.'

He paused, suddenly aware of a chilly silence around the table. He glanced at Beulah who smiled back at him, then at her parents and Mistress Craik who did not.

'The King and Queen take a very different view of his choice, so we hear,' said Sir William. 'It is regretful that this woman is far from being a virgin, a first requirement in a woman chosen to be bride to a royal Prince, and in due time to be Queen of England.'

Wulfstan felt his colour rising, not only for having incurred the displeasure of his future father-in-law, but in anger at the man's dismissal of a woman loved by the Prince since childhood. He wondered how the Horsts had obtained their information, and discovered that their source was a mendicant friar who had accepted their hospitality.

'We can only pray that the King and Queen will dissuade the Prince from taking such a lamentable step,' said Sir William. 'How can she have so blinded him?'

'Forgive me, sire, but I cannot agree that because the Prince's choice is a widow—' began Wulfstan, but Sir William broke in on his attempted defence of the Countess of Kent.

'Widow? She's no widow!' he said contemptuously. 'Her husband the Earl of Salisbury is still living, so her five unfortunate children are bastards. A fine example to give to the rest of the royal family – and the nation!'

Wulfstan simply could not sit and listen to this condemnation of the Countess, as if he agreed with it, for to do so would be unforgivably disloyal to the Prince. But this man was Beulah's father.

'Let God be their Judge, as he is ours, Sir William. I can assure you that nothing will dissuade the Prince from marrying the Countess of Kent.'

'In that case the King should send the pair of them into exile,' returned Sir William. 'And now we shall end this indecent conversation in front of the ladies. Beulah is pure and innocent, and I will not have her subjected to talk about an impious woman.'

A very awkward silence followed, in which neither Lady Judith nor Mistress Craik could suggest a more acceptable topic of conversation. Wulfstan burned inwardly with indignation at the old knight's judgemental attitude, and hoped that it would not prove typical of the country's response to the Prince's intentions.

As it turned out, Sir William's condemnation of the Black Prince's choice of a wife reflected opinion among the aristocracy, less so among the traders and militia. Queen Philippa was willing to accept the inevitable, but King Edward's sense of outrage made for a strained atmosphere at court that was not lost on the Prince; he was angry and offended at the cool reception given to the Countess of Kent, and made every effort to bring forward the wedding date as soon as was possible, though all kinds of legalistic objections were thrown in his way. First, the Archbishop of Canterbury who favoured the King, plainly told the Prince that because of Joan's divorce from Salisbury who was still living, the legitimacy of any children of her marriage to the Prince might be challenged; and then the Pope, when consulted, raised the question of consanguinity, she being first cousin to the Prince's father. As time passed, however, the Prince's resolve was seen to be unshakeable, and King, Archbishop and Pope found their objections swept aside. Seeing this, the Pope, who had no wish to quarrel with the heir to the throne, agreed to grant an annulment to Joan's marriage to Salisbury, if she and the Prince underwent a form of penance. A period of separation ensued, in which the Prince spent a week in a Benedictine monastery and the Countess in a Carmelite convent, where they submitted to long hours of prayer and fasting, and when it ended, emerged joyfully into each other's arms.

When the King unexpectedly bestowed on his son the title of Prince of Aquitaine, it was generally seen as a late mark of approval, though it was an honour with a price attached. As Prince and Princess of Aquitaine, the couple would be expected to make their home in Gascony, the scene of the Prince's greatest triumphs, where he would rule as a King, striking his own coinage and upholding the law under his personal seal of three silver ostrich feathers on a sable field. It would be an exile, such as Sir William Horst had hinted should happen, and would also put a good distance between the Countess, soon to be Princess of Wales, and her embarrassed father-in-law.

Rather to Wulfstan's initial surprise, the Prince accepted this honourable exile, not only with agreement but with enthusiasm.

'Depend upon it, Wulfstan, we shall make Bordeaux the most magnificent court in Europe, ruled over by the Prince and Princess of Aquitaine, the envy of all the rest!'

All of which put Sir Wulfstan Wynstede in a quandary.

As that summer passed, Wulfstan's visits to Greneholt Manor became more and more irksome. Any mention of the Prince's firm resolution was denounced as his blind obstinacy by Sir William, and the only way to avoid arguments was to say nothing at all on this all-important subject. Beulah's parents frowned on her unconcealed adoration of Wulfstan which showed in her bright eyes and the kisses she bestowed upon his hand when he kissed hers. Gladly would he have returned those kisses on her rosy lips if he only had the opportunity to do so. He began to dislike her father, and found it hard to be civil to him; to wait another two years for Beulah filled him with mounting frustration and anger, and he wondered if his patience would last so long. The Prince's absolute determination to marry the woman he loved, in the face of all objections, was an example he longed to follow, but he lacked the authority of his royal master, and to take Beulah away from the only home she knew in defiance of her parents would cause a rift that might never be healed. Wulfstan could not contemplate such an upheaval when the other option was to keep the betrothal vow and wait for two more years. But then came another possibility . . .

'You'll come with us, Wulfstan,' said the Prince as if there were no question of doing otherwise. 'My sweet Jeanette and I will be married before this year is out, and will set up court at Bordeaux, where I shall need you to continue as my scribe and treasurer, and you'll have a better life than you have here. Grant me two more years at least.'

Two more years. At first Wulfstan could not contemplate leaving England – and Beulah – for another two years, but on second thoughts it began to look like a solution to his problem. If he went to Bordeaux with the Prince's household, he would no longer have to endure Sir William's stubbornness, his insults against the Prince and his bride. He would not be constantly frustrated in his efforts to obtain one short minute of privacy with his love, the bliss of one brief kiss. Parting with her would be difficult, and her tears would accuse him of hardness of heart; but on his return when the two years were up, he could claim her as his lawful wife.

The Prince saw his hesitation, and spoke more bluntly. 'You'll never last another two years of swallowing insults from that old fool Horst, Wulfstan. It would be far better for you and the lady to dream of each other across the Narrow Sea, and if she loves you as she says she does, she'll wait, and the parting will prove your sincerity and hers. Tell old Horst that your Prince commands you to accompany him to France.'

Yes, thought Wulfstan, this could be the answer to his dilemma. He therefore told the Prince that he would do as he was commanded, privately deciding to say nothing at Greneholt of his impending departure until he knew the day of sailing.

Eventually a date was fixed for the wedding, the tenth of October, but the newly wedded couple would not sail for France until the next year.

'I have to show my father the King that we will not

immediately disappear,' the Prince said with a certain defiant humour. 'On the contrary, my bride and I will spend Christmas here at Berkhamsted, and invite my mother and father and half their precious court to enjoy our hospitality!'

There was time, thought Wulfstan, to visit Hyam St Ebba again. He was reluctant to do so, but his conscience reminded him of his family there, and his obligation to see them before he sailed for France, so on a clear September day he mounted Jewel and took the Winchester Road. He planned to stay three nights at Castle de Lusignan with his sister and brother-in-law, and from there ride over to Ebbasterne Hall to see his brother Sir Oswald and Lady Janet Wynstede; then on to Blagge House to see his orphaned niece and nephew, Katrine and Aelfric for whom he felt a special attachment, being Cecily's children. And he would also call on good Friar Valerian at the Abbey who had loved his sister Cecily and saved Wulfstan's life by ridding him of the hideous withered arm. Such were his intentions . . .

The first thing Wulfstan noticed about his sister Ethelreda was how much older she looked. Gone was the high-spirited little sister he knew, replaced by a care-laden woman with four children to bring up, an invalid husband and his two ageing parents who looked to her for their domestic comforts and the smooth running of the castle household. Lines had appeared around her eyes, and her pretty mouth drooped at the corners; nevertheless she was very pleased to see her brother.

'Dear Wulfstan, you are right welcome!' she cried, embracing him, and when he remarked upon her busy life and many commitments, she shrugged and gave a little sigh.

'The children are my greatest blessing, Wulfstan, and help me to carry out all my duties. Piers is eleven now, and such a comfort to Charles and me. He'll make a splendid heir to his father's title and the castle, I know it!'

Having talked with his nephew, Wulfstan was inclined to agree. Charles de Lusignan remained a thin, pale man resigned to lifelong invalidism. He seldom left the castle, and walked slowly with two sticks to assist his one leg. As his bodily strength had diminished, so his mind had become limited to the daily happenings at the castle; he did not want to remember wartime invasions and battles, and had little interest in Wulfstan's news of the Black Prince's marriage and subsequent banishment to Bordeaux with his wife. Ethelreda by contrast was eager to hear all the details of the Prince's 'fair maid of Kent', having heard something of the scandal surrounding the lady's name.

Count Robert de Lusignan was prematurely aged and troubled with gout in both feet which prevented him from walking very far. Lady Hélène had become a sad, white-haired old lady who forbade all talk of warfare. Having lost one fine son and seen the other crippled, she actually congratulated Wulfstan on his loss of an arm.

'It means you'll not take part in any further savagery and bloodshed,' she told him. 'The sooner you marry your lady Beulah and settle down to a peaceful country life, the better it will be for you. I have no time for your Black Prince, using our best men to kill the French and get killed in return.'

Ethelreda had further news for her brother. 'We have lost Friar Valerian,' she said sadly. 'He was ministering to the sick right up to the day he died. It was a lovely summer day, and he was called to the bedside of that horrid old man Jack Blagge. I've heard it said that at first he refused to go, because of the way Blagge had treated Cecily, but in the end he went, and Mistress Keepence says that the two men were closeted together for some time, and when the friar left, they were reconciled. Blagge died peacefully that night, and our dear Friar Valerian died also, sitting on a garden seat at twilight in his herb-garden. Of course we miss him, especially for the way he cared for us and our children in sickness. He was . . . why, Wulfstan, are you not well? You've gone as white as a sheet.'

For Wulfstan was deeply affected by the news. 'He saved my life when he cut away that dead arm,' he said, and she saw that tears had come to his eyes. 'He was a friend to all of our family, especially . . .' He could not continue, but turned his face away. Ethelreda laid her hand on his arm.

'Especially Cecily,' she whispered. 'She loved him, didn't she? Through both those marriages, and right to the end. I've never said it before, but I think I've always known it.'

'Yes, and he loved her in return. They're reunited now, so

we need not mourn them, Ethelreda. We should rejoice, even for our loss.'

At Ebbasterne Hall, Lady Janet Wynstede frowned and directed Wulfstan to go and look for Sir Oswald on the estate.

'He spends more time with that bailiff than with his own family,' she said resentfully. 'He takes the boys with him when they should be at their lessons with Brother Somebody from the Abbey, and I'm left here with Joanna and Lois. I don't wonder you're staying at the castle, instead of here with your own brother.'

'Lady Ethelreda is my sister,' he politely reminded her, knowing that she would not have welcomed him at the Hall. The twin girls curtseyed to their uncle, and seemed pleasant enough, good at embroidery and tapestry, so their mother said.

'I hear that Sir Charles has grown selfish and petulant,' said Lady Janet. 'I don't envy your sister married to that poor shadow of a man, and burdened with his old parents into the bargain! They say the old Count is laid up with the gout. Do you think he will make over the castle to his grandson Piers, with a proviso that his mother is allowed to stay on?'

'I can have no views on such a matter,' replied Wulfstan, repelled by her vulgar curiosity.

'Well, let's hope that *some* instructions are laid down before one or other of them goes to his Maker,' she said, and unable to think of a civil reply, Wulfstan went in search of his elder brother. He found Oswald and Dan in a corner of a harvested field with the three little Wynstede boys running around with their dogs. There were smiles and eager greetings, but not much approval of Wulfstan's plan to accompany the Black Prince to Bordeaux after the wedding.

'You'd be far better advised to marry the lady Beulah Horst and settle down over here in your native land,' said Oswald. 'Our country could be at war with France in another two years, and you – well, you could find yourself on the wrong side of the Narrow Sea, and no place to . . . er . . .'

Wulfstan knew that his brother was thinking about his lost arm which rendered him unable to fight as a soldier. And although Dan Widget believed that Wulfstan had every right to choose his own path through life, he was broadly in agreement

with his master. They commiserated with each other over the
death of Friar Valerian, while giving thanks for his peaceful end.

'I must visit my niece and nephew and good Mistress
Keepence next,' said Wulfstan. 'How have they fared since the
death of old Blagge?'

'We haven't heard much, except that the two children are
suddenly very wealthy from his legacy to them,' said Oswald,
'and we presume that Mistress Keepence is provided for. Lady
Wynstede said . . . er, I told my wife I think we should wait for
a while before stepping in, but you were always closer to Cecily's
sister-in-law than the rest of us, and she'll probably be glad to
have your opinion. Katrine and Aelfric are in their mid-teens
now, and the old man was looking around for a husband for the
girl. Kitty won't have to submit to *that* now that he's gone, but
there must be some thought given to her future. See what you
think, Wulfstan.'

As he approached Blagge House, Wulfstan was conscious of a
sense of freedom. The very air of the place seemed to be lightened, as if a burden of hostility had been lifted from it, and he
could now call upon Cecily's children without the tension of
former visits. Maud Keepence must have felt the same, for she
greeted him at the door with smiles and an outstretched hand.

'Welcome, Sir Wulfstan! Cecily's brother may now cross this
threshold without let or hindrance! Kitty, Aelfric, come and
speak to your uncle!'

As the young people approached, Wulfstan saw the resemblance to Cecily in both of their faces, and his heart swelled,
in spite of all his efforts to control his emotions. When Katrine
curtseyed to him, he held out his hand to raise her up, and
embraced her with his arm; as soon as he released her, he shook
hands with Aelfric, and then drew him close, together with
Katrine. Maud Keepence looked on, smiling with tears in her
eyes, and when the four of them sat down to talk, it was surpris-
ingly easy for them to come to an agreed arrangement.

'My father wanted Aelfric to go in for the Law, and there
is nothing but his youth to stop him going to London and
the Inns of Court to witness the course of justice from the
Bench,' she said, looking approvingly at the beardless boy who

nodded his agreement with his aunt. She then turned to Katrine, and tactfully omitting the question of early marriage, said that she would like her niece to be received into some noble house.

'Somewhere she could learn the arts of gracious living by experiencing life as lived at court, Wulfstan. She is already a competent needlewoman, and has a sweet singing voice. I wonder if you know of such a household? Somewhere she may be *seen,* rather than hidden away here.'

Wulfstan nodded. Finding a good husband was still paramount, he realized, but this should be a husband of Kitty's own choosing, or at least approved by her.

'These years of their childhood have been the happiest of my life,' Maud Keepence continued. 'But now with their grandfather gone, leaving them most of his money and property, it's time for me to think about their future. But it must be absolutely right for them.'

Wulfstan agreed, thankful that the brother and sister had such a wise guardian. They were both still very young. An idea came into his head.

'I could introduce Kitty to the court of Queen Philippa, and she would be able to advise as to where best she might be placed.'

'Oh, Wulfstan, bless you; it would be just what their mother would have wanted!' exclaimed Maud, and Kitty's eyes brightened in anticipation.

When Wulfstan spoke to Oswald about the matter, he said he would escort young Aelfric Blagge to London and one of the four Inns of Court to start training for the Law.

'But the boy's only fourteen, and next year will be soon enough for him,' he added. 'And Katrine is but fifteen. I suggest we leave them at home with their Aunt Maud until another year has passed.'

And so Wulfstan returned to Berkhamsted, satisfied that his reluctant duty visit had been of some real use to his family at Hyam St Ebba.

The royal wedding took place on a Sunday at Windsor Castle, and the Archbishop of Canterbury, having decided to overcome his scruples about the validity of the marriage, conducted the ceremony which included a Nuptial Mass in which the King and Queen took part, along with the Prince's three brothers. There was not the same exuberance as there had been at the May wedding of John of Gaunt to the Duchess of Lancaster five years previously, which had been accompanied by jousting tournaments, and much dancing and drinking. Nevertheless, the pride of the Prince and the beauty of the new royal Princess made an impression on all present, from the members of the court circle down to the townspeople who turned out to see the Fair Maid of Kent on her journey from Westminster to Windsor where the Black Prince awaited her.

Wulfstan cheered as loudly as any other man in the Prince's retinue, along with Sir Ranulf Ormiston; even Guy Hamald joined in, for it was not a day for harbouring grudges, at least not on the surface. In the King's retinue Wulfstan noticed André Demoins, and in the Queen's Lisette de l'Isle, a slim figure in green silk, with her abundant hair loose upon her shoulders, signifying virginity. He hastily looked away before she could notice him in lofty disdain. How happy he would be with Beulah at his side! The Prince had asked him to write invitations to the family at Greneholt Manor, but he had not delivered them, knowing that Sir William would consider himself insulted; he had composed a letter declining with regret because of an outbreak of fever at the Manor.

Berkhamsted Castle now had a gracious Princess and a bevy of ladies-in-waiting, along with the maidservants and semp-stresses she had brought with her. It made an enormous differ-ence. The Prince was in a constant good humour, generous with gifts and granting requests for a delay or even a cancel-lation of rents due from tenants. It was not difficult to find the reason for this largesse: Princess Joan was always willing to plead on behalf of household members, from courtiers and guards to maidservants and pot-boys, and the Prince could deny her nothing. 'If you can't move him, try her' was a joke based on fact, but it was not only her bargaining power that made her so popular.

'You were right, Wulfstan, she is as sweet as she is beautiful,' said Ranulf, adding with an appreciative grin, 'and where does she find all those pretty girls? Every one of them has eyes to melt the hardest heart – and what with their singing and their laughing, it's enough to drive a man crazy!'

The Princess's five children happily played around the great hall with a newly acquired litter of puppies, adding to the general gaiety; the grey stone aspect of the castle seemed transformed by the happiness within. At Christmas they entertained royal guests, for the King and Queen had accepted an invitation to spend the festive season with their son and his bride. Although at first there was a certain awkwardness in the presence of their hostess, the Fair Maid of Kent, the Prince's beloved Jeanette, her unaffected sweetness and the high regard in which she was held by the Prince's retinue caused them to suspend their objections over the festive season. Even so, Wulfstan keenly felt the absence of his own beloved, the lady Beulah, and when he rode over to Greneholt early in the New Year of 1362, he knew there would be trouble, for he had to tell her parents that he was going to France with the Prince and Princess of Wales for the remaining two years of his betrothal, and to bid farewell to Beulah until the summer of 1363.

In this he was not mistaken. Sir William expressed his disappointment and disgust in no uncertain terms, and said he doubted that he would ever see Wulfstan again, to which Wulfstan bowed and simply replied, 'I shall return, sire.'

More painful than her father's anger was Beulah's distress and her tearful promise to wait for him. To comfort her was difficult, for they were not allowed a minute alone; his farewell kiss on her hand and his reassurances of his love had to be made with her parents looking on, likewise his solemn declaration that he would return to claim her as his wife.

He had very mixed feelings as he mounted Jewel and rode back to Berkhamsted, thankful to be getting away from her bigoted parents, but full of regret for apparently abandoning his love and leaving her uncomforted.

Lord, make me worthy of her.

Fourteen

1362

If Berkhamsted had been transformed by the arrival of the Fair Maid of Kent, the court at Bordeaux surpassed it. The old archbishop's palace had been taken over by the new Prince and Princess of Aquitaine, and completely renovated. Its halls were hung with richly embroidered tapestries, and in the banqueting chamber great feasts were held, with veal and venison, sucking-pig and the traditional boar's head, severed from the animal as it roasted on a spit, and served with all manner of sweet and savoury accompaniments, notably the famed Bordeaux wine, used to steep duck and goose before roasting.

Wulfstan had his own servants, and aspiring scriveners to be taught how to read and write in English and French, so as to make his own work lighter. By day the court was entertained with jousting tournaments, archery contests, hunting deer and boar in the thick forest north of the river Garonne on which the city stood, and the popular sport of falconry. In the evenings there was music and dancing, and inevitably some flirting between the ladies and gentlemen of the court.

It was not only English nobles and courtiers who revelled in this earthly paradise. Many of the Gascon nobility had feared that the Prince's rule would be harsh, and expected to be heavily taxed, but their fears proved to be unfounded, for they were welcomed graciously by the Prince and his beautiful wife at the palace, and far from being taxed, they were showered with hospitality and gifts. After so many years of warfare, it was time to celebrate peace, to the relief of the whole nation.

Wulfstan enjoyed it all, and felt a certain pride at being on close terms with the Prince, and therefore a figure of some standing at this magnificent court. The Prince's boast that it would outshine all other European courts seemed to be coming true. Early on, Wulfstan made a discovery which caused him some irritation: André Demoins had somehow inveigled himself into the Prince's circle, and no doubt would be full of his own importance as a self-styled 'courier' of secret messages between the various European courts, including the Vatican, allegedly at risk to his own life and limb. Wulfstan made a mental note to keep well out of his way; the man's remark about 'old men's work' still rankled. However, unable to hunt or shoot arrows, his preference for outdoor sport was falconry, and it was at a gathering of hawking enthusiasts that he found himself in the company of Demoins again, who hailed him like a long-lost equal.

'Wulfstan, old friend, we meet again in fortunate circumstances, do we not? Our former comrades would envy us now! What opulence at the court of a banished Prince and Princess, eh?'

'Good morning, Demoins,' said Wulfstan shortly. 'I'd hardly use the term *banished*. The King is making good use of the Prince of Wales to preside over a period of peace after so much warfare.'

'Let's hope it will continue, then,' said Demoins sceptically. 'I wouldn't trust a Frenchman further than I could spit. Mark my words, there'll be local rebellions at all points of the compass.'

'Which is why we're here, to put down any uprising before it gets a foothold,' replied Wulfstan, turning away in the direction of the Princess and a group of her ladies. She smiled and beckoned to him.

'You're the brave young soldier who served my husband so well at the Battle of Poitiers, and lost an arm whilst helping to capture the French King John,' she said. 'My ladies have been talking about you, so come and show yourself to them!'

A wave of shyness came over Wulfstan who blushed like a schoolboy, but quickly recovering himself he bowed to the Princess and the eager young ladies who surrounded her. His eyes immediately fell upon one of them, auburn-haired and creamy complexioned; she had extraordinary green eyes with little flecks of gold – and his cheeks reddened even more, to his annoyance. He had no wish for involvement with Lisette de l'Isle, and withdrew his gaze, turning to the other ladies who were smiling and whispering to each other about his handsome features. He heard some praise his eyes, some his high forehead, his mouth and strong jaw; it was extremely disconcerting.

'Tell me, Sir Wulfstan, is there any lady here in the court at Bordeaux that you would like to meet and speak with?' asked the Princess in a teasing tone, only half serious, but willing to make an introduction for him if he so wished; she was known for her romantic schemes, always happy to smooth the course of true love between shy lovers.

Wulfstan shook his head awkwardly. He would like to have said that he was betrothed to the girl of his dreams, but he simply did not want to name his sweet, innocent Beulah in the company of these sophisticated females, nor listen to their comments about her.

'Or perhaps your heart is already engaged elsewhere?' asked the Princess with a knowing look at her ladies who tittered charmingly.

Wulfstan bowed again, as if to show that her guess was correct, and she smiled in good-natured understanding. 'Then we must not tempt you away from this lucky lady! Even so, I hope you will join in the dancing this evening, for you have a surer step than many a man with two arms!'

He bowed again, and said that he would be happy to dance with any of her kind ladies – and as he spoke, became aware that Lisette de l'Isle was openly staring at him. For a moment he met those greeny-gold eyes, then turned resolutely away.

'She's ravishing, isn't she?' said a voice at his side. It was André Demoins, still close at hand.

'She is indeed a gracious lady, and 'tis no wonder that our Prince chose her above all the others he might have had,' Wulfstan replied coolly.

'No, stupid, I didn't mean the Princess, though I grant you she is a gracious lady – no, I mean the lady Lisette de l'Isle, whose heart I intend to besiege this summer! She likes to pretend to play hard-to-get, but I can see through her tricks. Watch me, Wulfstan, I'll have her bedded before summer's end!'

His arrogance grated on Wulfstan. Even a haughty lady-in-waiting deserved to be spoken of with respect. He made no reply, but went to collect his falcon, Belle, to put her through her paces. Demoins' eyes narrowed as he looked at Wulfstan's retreating back.

Damned if our Sir Wulfstan Wynstede hasn't got his own eye on her, he thought, in which case he's heading for a very public humiliation. If he thinks his absent arm makes him irresistible, he can think again. Some chance!

As the days grew longer and warmer, the Princess turned her attention to the palace gardens. She had maintained a bountiful garden and orchard at her home in Kent, and was determined that her new home would boast one equally fine, one more jewel in the palace's crown. The Prince granted her every wish, allowing her to make what changes she wanted, and soon the rather nondescript acre within the palace's rear wall had become an ideal venue for pleasant walks, deep conversations and, inevitably, assignations of a romantic nature. The area had been laid out in the French style of formal squares and circles, but Joan said she wanted something to remind her of England. A wide central pathway, or *allée*, sloped downwards from the top end to the bottom, flanked by fruit bushes and partly covered by a pergola over which pink roses climbed. It ended with a tall, dense hedge of myrtle which curved round a shady arbour that the Princess had enlarged as a place to sit with her companions. Beyond the hedge the ground rose up to a grassy bank for those who preferred to sit in the full light and warmth of the sun, while beside and slightly below the arbour was a plot in which the Princess grew her favourite of all the summer flowers, the exquisite Madonna lilies – 'the Virgin's own', as she called them. Majestic purplish buds appeared for several days, and then one by one they unfolded their large white petals tipped with a faint pink blush, like angels' trumpets, the Princess said. Within each bloom the plentiful pollen, like gold dust, floated away on the still air or clung to the hairy honey bees that sucked the sweet nectar from the flowers' hearts; and by day and night the heady perfume drifted up and across the garden like some rare incense. Wulfstan inhaled the fragrance, closing his eyes and trying to picture Beulah in the garden at Greneholt Manor, but the scent of the lilies seemed to fill his head and strangely disturb his senses.

In such a setting the year drew towards midsummer. The Princess took half a dozen of her ladies down to the arbour one afternoon with their embroidery frames, to ply their needles and indulge in merry court gossip in the shade. They did not at first see Wulfstan seated on the bench behind the myrtle hedge, reading the *Roman de la Rose* in French; but the gentle rise and fall of their voices, which included that of Lisette de l'Isle, combined with the intoxicating scent of the lilies, caused his eyelids to droop, and he lost track of the allegorical love story; instead he tried to think of Beulah, and acknowledged to himself that she would never fit into the circle of this pleasure-loving court. He realized with some dismay how little he knew of her, the real girl under that pious demeanour, she who had always been taught by her parents what she should think and believe. In this exotic setting he could not visualize her face or remember her voice.

Footsteps were heard approaching the circle of ladies, and to Wulfstan's irritation he heard André Demoins greeting the Princess, all courtly charm. Wulfstan kept absolutely still, trying to close his ears and apply himself to the *Roman*.

'So much beauty is almost too much for one man to bear,' said Demoins, bowing low and addressing the Princess. 'Might I join you for a brief, privileged moment, Your Grace? I have been walking beside the Garonne, attempting to compose a poem in praise of your unmatchable court, but no words of mine can do you justice.'

'A poem? Oh, Monsieur Demoins, let us hear it!' begged the Princess with her delightful smile. 'Is it about any one of my ladies in particular?'

'I dare to say that it *may* be addressed to one of these fair damsels, Your Grace, and beg pardon for my presumption,' he replied, taking a piece of manuscript paper from inside his cloak. Suzanne d'Avour, a pretty, fair-haired girl of seventeen giggled, and glancing saucily at her companions, asked if the poem was addressed to her.

'I would not dare to name the lady, Mademoiselle, for fear of offending her,' he answered, 'and I hardly dare to repeat these unworthy lines, but—'

'Oh, say no more, André, but read us your poem and let

us be the judge of it!' The Princess's voice was just a trifle impatient, and Demoins began to read what he had written, a fulsome piece about a lover languishing for his true love; Wulfstan recognized several words and phrases lifted straight out of the *Song of Solomon,* and could not help listening. He wanted to move away, but dared not betray his presence.

At first there was silence among the ladies, and then one of them quietly rose and left the group; turning round the corner of the myrtle hedge, she came in sight of Wulfstan. He stared in surprise at her clinging turquoise-green gown and abundant red hair tumbling upon her white shoulders: Lisette de l'Isle. She walked towards him as he sat on the bank, and looked down at the book in his hands, bringing with her a wave of delicious fragrance – was it from the Madonna lilies?

'What book is that?' she demanded.

'An old French allegorical poem,' he said, looking up at her briefly and without smiling. He did not care to show any interest in her, even though she had apparently decided to condescend to him.

'Read me some lines of it,' she ordered.

He resented her imperious tone. 'I am no troubadour, Mademoiselle; I can't read or sing from the written page.' For a moment he looked straight into those green-gold eyes, and then said, 'You had better listen to Demoins for that sort of entertainment.'

He applied himself again to the story on the page, leaving her standing and looking down at the top of his head; then she moved away, not back to the Princess's circle listening to Demoins' poem, but by another path that led back to the palace.

Mixed emotions whirled in Wulfstan's head, and he could no longer concentrate his attention on the book. Then the thought came to him that the lady had shown a preference for him over Demoins, and for this he allowed himself a measure of mild satisfaction.

The minstrels' gallery was filled not only with resident musicians, but others the Prince had hired from further afield. They were practising for the evening's dancing, and Wulfstan sat listening to a very agreeable blend of stringed instruments like the lute and psaltery blending with the pipes and the long, curved trumpet of the sackbut. It was a warm summer evening, and Wulfstan sipped the red wine of Bordeaux as he listened, closing his eyes and trying to picture Beulah in the garden at Greneholt. The company were waiting for the Prince and Princess who liked to stroll lovingly hand-in-hand in the fragrant garden at close of day, and when they entered, the musicians struck up a lively jig, kept in time by a man beating the taut skin of a tabor with his hand.

'The music bids us all to dance!' cried the Princess. 'Everybody must stand up!'

The ladies and gentlemen needed no second bidding, but quickly formed a circle around the Fair Maid of Kent and her husband who hand-in-hand skipped round the inside of the circle in the opposite direction to the dancers – who then changed direction when the merry couple changed theirs. Obeying the Princess's command, Wulfstan finished his beaker of wine and joined the circle, the lady on his left putting her hand into his belt as they circled the hall, and as the pace increased amid shrieks of laughter, and the candles glowed, the wine he had drunk gave him a sense of weightlessness, of dancing on air. When the Prince lifted his wife up on his shoulders, twirling her round and round, it was the signal for the large circle to break into groups of four, linking their right hands together above their heads as they turned alternately left and right. Wulfstan found himself in a quartet with Lisette de l'Isle and André Demoins, with pretty Suzanne d'Avour, one of the Princess's ladies-in-waiting. When the royal couple began to dance hand-in-hand, the quartets broke into pairs and Wulfstan turned to Suzanne, only to find that his right hand was firmly linked with Lisette's left, while Demoins had hold of her right. He had no left hand to offer Suzanne, and at a nod from Lisette, she went to find another partner. Not all the dancers stayed in the hall, but disappeared into passages and dark corners of the castle for furtive kisses, and something of this nature must have been Demoins' intention.

'That fellow's still hanging on to you, Lisette,' he growled. 'Let him go!'

Wulfstan loosened his hold on her hand, only to find that the lady gripped it more tightly; he heard her sharp command to Demoins, 'Let me go, I tell you, or the Prince will hear of it!'

Wulfstan had a momentary glimpse of the man's furious face before Lisette began to pull him away from the dancers and out into a passage that led to the kitchen; his head was whirling after all the Bordeaux claret he had drunk, and he allowed himself to be led through to the Princess's garden. The intoxicating scent of lilies on the evening air roused forbidden sensations, and he seemed to be passing a series of hedges, then beneath a pergola and through it, following a rustling gown and a trail of perfume, and they at last reached the Princess's arbour, now in deepest shadow. Here she turned to him and offered her lips, snaking her arms around his neck. He could just see the glitter in her eyes, and desire awoke in him; he pressed her slender body against his hardness, and all self-control vanished. Breathing rapidly, he almost groaned with sheer, uncontrollable need, and felt himself sinking with her to the ground; it mattered not to him that the grass was already damp with the dew of night. She kissed his lips again, and he kissed her eyes, nose, forehead and neck, not gently but fiercely, and she drew away for a moment to pull up her costly gown and assist him to unbutton.

It was natural, it was simple, it was beyond description as beneath a sky full of stars, his member thrust into her. He had become a slave of his body as straightway his lifestream poured out; she responded at once, arching her back and moaning with a pleasure that seemed to link them with the garden, the lilies, the night sky. There were no words, only sighs and long-drawn-out breaths as the tempest subsided and they lay in each other's arms; his body was satiated, though his mind had not caught up with its heedless actions.

Slowly reality began to intrude. The air was chilly on their flesh, the grass was wet. From the palace the distant strains of music reached their ears. It was time to return to earth. She stood up, and held out a hand to him, inviting him to get up also; they rearranged their clothes, he drew her towards him for a last kiss, and then they went their separate ways, not back to the hall, but by winding passages and stairs, he to his bedchamber and she to hers.

He awoke in the early hours, needing to go to the close-stool. His head throbbed and there was a sour taste in his mouth from the red wine. His heart and mind began to ask questions: what had happened, what witch's spell had led him to lay with Lisette de l'Isle, a woman he did not even like?

The answer came with shameful simplicity. He had got drunk on too much Bordeaux claret, and had committed fornication while under the influence of it. That was all. He had betrayed his faithful Beulah. Again. He was utterly unworthy of her.

But what would happen now? Would Lisette de l'Isle now consider him to be her lover? Or would she revert to haughty disdain? How should he behave towards her when next they met? What would she say, if anything? He was not looking forward to the unavoidable encounter, and decided not to take any action, but leave her to indicate what direction they should take, what to show the rest of the world.

As it turned out, Princess Joan left them no choice. The next day she was full of smiles and congratulations to them both over the breakfast table. She had seen their abrupt departure from the dancing, and had assumed that they had gone to some private place of assignation, there to exchange kisses and lovers' sweet talk. She gently teased Lisette, causing a deep flush to spread over her lovely features, even to her neck.

'You're a very lucky young woman,' she said as her ladies smiled and tittered. 'Sir Wulfstan Wynstede has everything to recommend him – a knighthood for valour on the field of battle, a high position here at court and friendship with the Prince. He fulfils all the duties of scrivener and treasurer, without difficulty, and can mount and ride a horse, thanks to a strong right arm. And so handsome! Truly, he'll feel no lack of a left arm when he claims you for his own!'

The ladies simpered and exchanged knowing glances. Lisette lowered her head to hide her face, and Wulfstan, also blushing to the roots of his hair, tried to escape to a meeting of the falconers, but found himself restrained by the fair company who would not let him go. The Princess laughed and clapped her hands.

'And the best of it is, that tedious fellow André Demoins has suffered a *very* public put-down, which serves him right!' she said gaily. 'I know which man *I* would choose if I had not got the best husband – and lover – in the whole wide world!'

Her words were soon echoed around the palace, and it was no surprise when André Demoins discovered urgent messages to be passed between other European courts. He departed, smarting with humiliation and fury, and with no further words to anybody, much to the amusement of some of the men-servants who were tired of his imperious manner and liked to see him made a figure of fun.

But what of the lady? After enduring the Princess's affec-tionate teasing and the looks on the faces of the ladies, some amused, some frankly envious, Lisette now had to review her own situation. She had achieved her main objective, which was to humiliate Demoins, to ridicule his arrogant assumption that his advances would be welcomed. She had used Wulfstan as a means to achieving this end, but had not considered his own reaction to her fierce seduction when he had taken too much wine, nor had she expected to be overtaken by her own sudden surge of desire; she too had imbibed enough wine to override caution. Accustomed to rejecting the advances of unwanted admirers, she had taken no notice of Wulfstan up to now; in fact she had been quietly considering old Count d'Avour, the widowed father of Suzanne, who having intro-duced his daughter to the Princess to become a lady-in-waiting, had been invited to stay on at Bordeaux for a few weeks of high summer. He had noticed Lisette de l'Isle, but had no hopes of securing her hand, for being much older and inclined to put on weight, he feared to make a fool of himself.

'Aren't you being a little bashful, Wulfstan?' The Prince's eyes were twinkling. 'God's truth! You've made a conquest that many men must envy. We've all enjoyed the discomfiture of Demoins, but you'd better secure the lady Lisette without delay. She has other suitors out there, waiting to bed her!'

Wulfstan's confusion increased as he realized that the Prince – and presumably the Princess and their retinues – did not realize that he had already fully claimed the lady's honour.

'It is for Lisette – for the lady to acknowledge that . . . er
. . .' Once again he was blushing, and the Prince laughed out
loud. 'Christ a' mercy, boy, you're a cold fish! You'll lose her
for sure, she's not the sort to be trifled with. If you want her, say
so, tell her you love her and take her – or else some bolder
spirit will!'

Wulfstan could not let this misunderstanding continue. 'I'm
already betrothed, as well you know, my liege. I can't pay court
to . . . to the lady when my heart belongs to another.'

'What? That virtuous little creature at Greneholt who won't
marry you for years, and only does what her canting old father
tells her? Show some sense, Wulfstan, marry the beautiful de
l'Isle, and be assured of a lifetime in my service. Don't be a
fool!' There was a certain impatience in the Prince's voice as
well as amusement.

Wulfstan made no reply, so ashamed was he at his latest
betrayal of Beulah.

'Hah! I dare say when you go to claim her next midsummer,
she'll have taken the veil and be shut up in a convent, telling
her beads. I'm serious, Wulfstan, that pious type of girl just
isn't cut out to be the wife of a soldier and a courtier.'

Wulfstan winced at the thought of Beulah in a convent,
driven there by his treatment of her, but this time their betrothal
really was over. He could not marry her after what had happened
with another woman, *again*. And he would have to ask pardon
of Lisette de l'Isle as soon as the opportunity arose.

The problem was that he was never alone with her. She was
always with the ladies surrounding the Princess, in the dining
hall, at Mass in the palace chapel, or out walking in the garden.
If she saw him looking in her direction, she lowered her eyes
and turned away, but there was a notable change in her
demeanour; gone was the haughty disdain, the indifference
with which she had dismissed him formerly. It was replaced
by a questioning air of uncertainty, almost of shyness; was it
embarrassment at the wordless intimacy they had shared? And
at her urgent invitation? The conviction came to him that if
he were to follow the Prince's advice and propose marriage
to her, and if she accepted, they would be congratulated on
all sides; it would be a marriage approved by the Prince and

Princess; they would make their home near to the palace and settle in Bordeaux for life, raising a family of bilingual children in a land of peace and plenty. It was an inviting prospect if Lisette was willing. Old Sir William Horst would not be sorry to see the betrothal ended, and perhaps in the course of time a more deserving man than himself would pay court to Beulah and win her. And so he went to the Princess to ask to speak with Mademoiselle de l'Isle in private.

'Ah, most gladly, Sir Wulfstan,' she said with her usual good-will. 'I have reason to believe that the lady would welcome such a meeting. I'm sure she will have much to tell you, if you will but ask her. Just be at the gate to the orchard after the midday repast, and she will be there alone and waiting for you. I pray for you both to come back to us with happy news!'

And so Wulfstan came face to face again with the woman he had possessed two days previously. He bowed and took her proffered hand, raising it to his lips.

'Thank you for coming here, Mademoiselle,' he said.

She raised her eyes to meet his, and he saw again that look of uncertainty, of mixed emotions. 'The Princess said you wanted to speak with me, Sir Wulfstan.'

'Forgive me, Mademoiselle, I am here to beg your pardon,' he replied. 'I had no right to take advantage of you as I did, and I regret it. I . . . er . . . I beg your pardon,' he said again, and waited for her reply. There was a long pause before she replied.

'You have no need to beg pardon, Sir Wulfstan,' she said quietly. 'If you do, I shall have to do likewise.' And taking his hand lightly in hers she leaned over and kissed it. He drew a sharp intake of breath: the proud Mademoiselle de l'Isle had kissed his hand! He took her own right hand in his and pressed it to his lips, looking into her eyes, where he saw a question answered before it had been spoken. Enough had been said, and he drew her towards him. This, then, was to be his future instead of the marriage he would have had with Beulah, of whom he was now unworthy. If this beautiful woman was willing to take him as her husband, there was no earthly reason why he should not take her. Holding her within the circle of his arm, he kissed her lips and was assured of her response.

'The Princess will not be disappointed, Lisette,' he whispered.

But when they returned arm-in-arm to the Princess and her ladies, an urgent message awaited him.

'There is a visitor for you, Wulfstan,' she told him. 'He says his name is Captain Brack, and he's come all the way from England, across the Narrow Sea and the Bay of Biscay, and by his looks the news is not good. Shall I send for him at once, or will you see him in the Prince's counting-house?'

Astounded and dismayed, he took leave of Lisette, choosing to see the man alone, and a manservant led him into the presence of Captain Brack, a dark-browed man with a short black beard and the air of a soldier. He looked vaguely familiar to Wulfstan, who could not remember his name or where he had seen him.

'Greetings, Captain Brack, what's brought you here?'

'Good day to you, Sir Wulfstan,' replied the man. 'I come from the Castle de Lusignan in Hampshire, where I'm in Sir Charles's standing army.'

Wulfstan gasped. 'Castle de Lusignan?' he echoed. 'Then you must bring grave news indeed. Do you speak of Sir Charles? Is he . . . is he dead?'

''Tis not Sir Charles, nor his father, sire, but it's your own brother, Sir Oswald Wynstede. He went down to London last week on some errand or other, and on his return he fell from his horse and broke his neck.' The man crossed himself.

'Oh, my brother, my brother Oswald,' gasped Wulfstan. 'Tell me, Captain, who sent you here with this dire news – was it Lady Wynstede?'

'No, sire, not her. I was sent on this perilous journey by the young Lady de Lusignan. She asked me to tell you and bid you, nay, beg you to come home. Lady Wynstede is helpless with grief, and relies on the bailiff to run the estate, a man by the name of Widget. He came to see my Lady Ethelreda, and she sent me on this caper. And the sooner we get back the better it'll be, seein' there's no man to take Sir Oswald's place. Here's the letter my lady wrote for me to give to you.'

He handed over a folded sheet of parchment sealed with wax. Wulfstan broke the seal and opened a hastily scrawled letter from Ethelreda who had always been good with the alphabet and with numbers.

I call upon you Brother to take pity on the children left fatherless by Oswald's death. I beg you to come back with Captain Brack. Ethelreda.

Wulfstan reread the scrawl in dismay. What was he to do? Did he have any choice? With Oswald dead and his eldest son – what was the boy's name? – still a child, he was the obvious next of kin to cope with the changed circumstances. He made an effort to marshal his thoughts into some sort of order.

'I will have to do as the lady requests. I'll order meat and drink for you, Captain, and a bed for the night. As soon as you've rested and refreshed yourself and your horse, we shall set out together tomorrow.'

Great was the disappointment of the Princess on hearing the news, and the lady de l'Isle gave a cry of dismay. The Prince grimaced.

'It's a damnable nuisance, Wulfstan, and leaves me without my right hand, for Baldoc is slow and the two young scriveners are stupid. Get back as quickly as you can.'

Bidding farewell to the lady de l'Isle was not easy, for she too thought the haste was unnecessary. 'No sooner do you say you love me than you leave me,' she said reproachfully, tears in her green eyes. 'Is a brother's widow of more importance to you than your betrothed?'

He tried to explain that it was his duty to console and support his brother's family in their time of grief, and promised to return as soon as he possibly could, but she refused to listen, and in the end he had to kiss her cool cheek, bow and leave her unconvinced.

Wulfstan and Brack set off across country to the northern coast where they boarded a flat-bottomed cog about to sail for Southampton. The sun was hot, and Wulfstan could have wished for a more congenial companion. Brack complained about being ordered by a woman to travel so far on what seemed to him an unnecessary errand. All men must die at some time, he said, and their families had to go on living and making the best of things. Wulfstan let him rant on, too anxious and too weary to argue with such a grumbling bear of a man.

When the Castle de Lusignan came in sight, standing on its rocky height and bathed in late afternoon sunshine, Wulfstan's spirits lifted, and even more when he was met by his sister at the gate of the inner bailey; she had seen his approach, and now flung her arms around his neck.

'Dear Brother, how good of you to come!' she cried. 'You must stay here tonight, and go down to the Hall in the morning, after you've rested.'

'I think I should go this evening, Ethelreda,' he said. 'Enough time has been lost as it is, and I need to know exactly what I can do for my sister-in-law. Janet and I have always resented each other, and now I must show her that in trouble we can be friends.'

'I hope you succeed better than I have done,' she sighed. 'She just sits and weeps all day, and Mrs Benn has to take care of the children and keep an eye on the house servants.'

'Why did Oswald go to London?' Wulfstan asked.

'Why, to visit our nephew, young Aelfric Blagge,' she said. 'The boy's only fifteen, but he's enrolled at Lincoln's Inn, training for the Law. It's what his old grandfather Blagge wanted for him, and left him most of his capital to pay for it. Oswald just went to check he was happy and studying his books, not getting into bad company who'd spend his money for him, drinking and gambling. And then this happened – it's such a tragedy. Anyway, Wulfstan, go to see what you can do for them all, and may you have better luck than I've had.'

A pall of melancholy hung over the Hall, and Wulfstan was sorry for the children who would never again see their father. The twin girls, Joanna and Lois, were twelve years old, and tried to comfort their brothers; the eldest boy, Denys, was not yet ten, and the two younger brothers, Elmete and Cedric, were pathetic in their bewilderment. Lady Janet Wynstede seemed unable to attend to them without bursting into tears. She greeted Wulfstan without warmth, saying that Dan Widget had no business to call on Lady Ethelreda without consulting *her*, and that Ethelreda should have asked her permission before sending for Wulfstan.

'Widget's a good enough bailiff, though his duties are out

of doors with the grooms and farmhands,' she said. 'If you are needed anywhere, it is in my husband's counting-house, a place I've never needed to enter.'

'Then I shall do so today, Janet,' he replied, putting on a smile to reassure her. ''Tis fortunate that I am well experienced in such work.'

She shrugged. 'I never thought to see you again after you went off with all the nobility to Bordeaux. Oswald talked a lot about how you were a favourite of the Black Prince, his secretary and treasurer and heaven knows what else.'

'Yes, and I have come to carry out those same duties for you, Janet,' he told her, 'and to do what I can to make life easier for you and my nephews and nieces.'

'Denys will be his father's heir, but is but a child,' she said dully. 'Oswald left instructions in his will as to how the estate should be divided among the others after I've gone – and I could wish that day to be soon.' Her voice broke, and her eyes filled with tears again.

'Your children have need of you, Janet,' he said quietly, not knowing how best to comfort her, and sensing that she had not got over her former resentment of him. 'I will get to work straight away.'

The counting-house at Ebbasterne Hall was a chaotic muddle of bills, expense accounts and receipts; no single book had been kept to record the incomings and outgoings.

'I *told* Oswald time and again that he should have a treasurer in charge of money matters,' said Janet miserably. 'I've had to pay the servants their wages – Mrs Benn the cook, two kitchen maids, and the young nursemaid. And a washerwoman comes in every week. They take their wages readily enough, but need to be watched when they're supposed to be working.'

'Are all these servants likely to be kept on?' asked Wulfstan in a businesslike tone, not wanting to stir up her grief yet again.

'Well, yes, of course, if I can afford to pay them. And I hope *you* aren't expecting to be paid for sorting all this out. It's enough that you have bed and board while you're here.'

Chilled by her words, Wulfstan assured her that he had no

such expectations, and was willing to pay for his board if required.

'I need to be back in Bordeaux before the summer's end, so don't want to tarry here for any longer than is necessary,' he told her, 'so the quicker I can get through these papers and get the Hall's finances on a sound basis, the better it will be for us all.'

If only his duties had turned out to be as simple as that . . .

Fifteen

August was nearly over. Wulfstan sat in the room known as the master's counting-house, and leaned forward, putting his hand over his face; a great burden of doubt and uncertainty lay upon his shoulders, and nothing would lift it, nothing gave him release.

It was not the formidable task he had accomplished in ten weeks at Ebbasterne Hall, his childhood home, that now weighed upon him so heavily; that had been a challenge, and he had risen to it, to the eventual admiration of his sister-in-law, the family at Castle de Lusignan and his other sister-in-law Maud Keepence at Blagge House. Oswald had clearly taken a *laissez faire* attitude to the administration of the estate, easygoing towards the tenants and peasant farmers who farmed their own strips of land in the Great Field, adjacent to the manor's own fields of wheat and barley, the pasture for sheep and the edge of the forest where the pigs roamed and foraged. There were rents to be collected, and tithes to be paid to the Abbey; wool to be sold to the merchants who needed it ready for collection on specific dates; there were the stables for the horses who provided the only means of transport, the grooms and field labourers working under the supervision of bailiff Dan Widget, an excellent outdoor worker, but with scant knowledge of the alphabet.

Within doors he had gained the cooperation of Mrs Benn, a bustling woman with her own methods of housekeeping who watched the kitchen maids with a sharp eye and kept to a strict if somewhat unimaginative rota for cooking the daily fare; she also cared for the three little boys with the help of a nursery maid, Nell. Wulfstan was deeply touched when his nephew Denys, not yet ten years old, came to him with a solemn face, asking his Uncle Wulfstan to show him how to keep a book for recording the daily accounts of monies paid out and received. Wulfstan told him that he would learn these skills all in good time, and meanwhile his duty was to obey his sisters and help look after Elmete and Cedric who trailed around in sad bewilderment, looking for the father they had lost and the mother who spent much of the time closeted in her room. (But who *would* show the boy how to administer the estate, Wulfstan asked himself.)

There was now a much better understanding between himself and Lady Janet Wynstede. There had come a day when he had lost patience with her refusal to accept offers of help from her own sister Maud Keepence.

'My father Jack Blagge died a very rich man,' she had said resentfully, 'yet he left nothing to me and my children, though I'm as much his daughter as Maud – it all went to Cecily's children and enough to keep Mistress Keepence in comfort for the rest of her life. And if it hadn't been for that boy Aelfric, my Oswald would not have met with his death.'

'For shame, Janet, your mourning is selfish, and is no help to your children,' Wulfstan had answered quietly but firmly, not wishing to be unkind. 'What does it matter if your bad-tempered old father left most of his hoard to Cecily's children and the aunt who brought them up? God knows she put up with him for years, looked after him in his last days, and did all the duty of a daughter, as well as bringing up Katrine and Aelfric. And you can't blame Aelfric because Oswald fell off his horse after visiting the boy at Lincoln's Inn, a tragedy nobody caused. Come now, forget old grievances, make friends with Maud and accept her help. Let the children visit Blagge House and their aunt and cousin Katrine.'

He had expected an angry protest, even dismissal for his plain speaking, but to his surprise Janet had bowed her head.

'Your words are harsh, Wulfstan, spoken to a sorrowing widow, but in fact I'm grateful for all the help you've given me. I will go to see Maud and take the children.'

From then on the atmosphere had lightened, and the children became happier. Ethelreda too came to visit the Hall, bringing Sofia and little Robert with her. This was about the time that Wulfstan began to think seriously about his future. He was long overdue to return to Bordeaux, where Lisette de l'Isle awaited him. *And he did not love her.* These weeks of absence had made him face this fact, and something else: he had begun to enjoy his position at Ebbasterne Hall, the service he was giving to his brother's family, the sense of homecoming after the easy life at Bordeaux with its daily round of pleasures. He preferred England, especially the hundred of Hyam St Ebba, the home he had thought never to visit again. Could he stay here and continue to assist his sister-in-law? Could he desert the Black Prince who had so honoured him, and leave the woman to whom he was betrothed? In fact he had no serious scruples about Lisette, for she was the kind of woman who would always have admirers. She would never fit in with a rural English scene.

And Beulah would never fit in with the sophistication of the court at Bordeaux.

Now Wulfstan faced the truth. He had been betrothed to Beulah Horst before his promise to Lisette, and Beulah had never known about his fall from grace with Miril, or the passionate scene in the Princess's garden. She – and her dominating parents – need never know. Sweet, patient Beulah, he knew now that he still loved her. He had not told Janet or Ethelreda about Lisette, and with a joyful flash of realization, he saw that it need not be too late for him to change direction. In less than a year's time he could return to Greneholt and at last claim Beulah as his wife. The blessed surge of relief sent him down on his knees to give thanks for restoring his destiny, so nearly thrown away, but saved in time.

And then had come Janet's offer.

'There is something I have been meaning to ask you, Wulfstan, and I will put it to you now. You have been a good brother-in-law to me, and filled Oswald's place as master of the house. I had nobody to turn to, and now I have to thank bailiff Widget and sister-in-law Ethelreda for summoning you from your life at Bordeaux, to help me.'

Wulfstan had at first feared that she was going to propose marriage to him, and listened in silence; she then asked him if he would like to take up a permanent position at the Hall on behalf of the heir, Denys, until the boy came of age.

'You will be claiming the hand of Beulah Horst next year, Wulfstan, if your betrothal vows hold good after all this time. I want to let you know that I would agree to her coming here as your wife, living as master and mistress of Ebbasterne Hall. Your children will be Wynstedes, as mine are, and they would grow up together under your guardianship. It will be another ten years before Denys is able to take over as the heir, and who knows what will have happened by then? Meanwhile I could ask our attorney to draw up a legal document setting forth the agreed arrangement. What do you say, Wulfstan? Would you be willing to accept such an arrangement?'

Her words had taken his breath away, and he paused before he answered. It would mean that he had a prestigious home to offer Beulah for the foreseeable future, a home and an estate which he would continue to rule, having proved his skill during these past weeks.

'Oswald would have approved, and your sister-in-law Keepence thinks it a good idea,' she went on. 'In fact, she has suggested that I go to live with her at Blagge House if you and your wife agree to take over as temporary owners of the Hall. And you would continue Oswald's duties as Justice of the Peace in Hyam St Ebba.'

Wulfstan had been silently frowning in deep thought, but now his brow cleared and he declared he would put the plan before Beulah and Sir William Horst for consideration.

'Blessings on you, sister Janet!' he said sincerely, taking her hand. 'You've helped me to make a decision. I'll let the Black Prince know that I shan't be returning to Bordeaux, because to speak truth, I have no wish to do so, for I choose to live in England as an Englishman. I will ride over to Greneholt and tell this news to Beulah and her parents. Oh, God's name be praised, and let them accept!'

And so it was settled. Wulfstan sat down to write to Queen Philippa, asking her to send word to the Black Prince, and then to the Princess Joan, asking her to break the news to Lisette de l'Isle and wish her happiness with a better husband than himself; and then he rode over to Greneholt, a much greater distance from Hyam St Ebba than from Berkhamsted, and greeted the Horst family with his news. Old Sir William gave him a cautious welcome, and questioned him closely about the status Beulah would enjoy as mistress of Ebbasterne Hall for the next decade. He made no offer to shorten the long betrothal, as Wulfstan had secretly hoped he might: there was still one year to go.

But Beulah's soft brown eyes had shone with love and happiness at the sight of her betrothed husband-to-be, and she clung to his arm, asking no questions about his life at the court at Bordeaux, as her father did, and filling Wulfstan's heart with renewed thankfulness for the love of such an adorable woman, as truthful as she was beautiful. In front of her father's stern frown he managed to kiss her cheek just once when he left Greneholt, and rode away happier than he had ever been in his life before. He rejoiced over his prospects of living with Beulah at Ebbasterne Hall as landowner in place of the nine-year-old heir; at some future date he would become adviser to Sir Denys Wynstede, and by then he might well be the father of a family. God had indeed been good, and blessed him far above his just desserts.

And then the blow had fallen, overthrowing all his thanksgiving at a stroke: the blow that reminded him of his sinful state, his lechery and heedless courting of disaster: and not only was he reminded of it, but he was commanded to make reparation for it, straightway.

There came a message from the Queen, sent by rider from Westminster. She had received word from her son the Prince by the special courier used by royalty and military leaders, that the Princess, the 'Fair Maid of Kent', demanded Wulfstan's instant return to Bordeaux, on pain of dismissal from the Prince's service, and stripping of his knighthood.

The lady de l'Isle was with child, three months into her time. Wulfstan was its father, and therefore urgently required to return and marry Lisette before any more time passed. He had no choice: this was his only honourable course of action, with no time to lose.

'Why, Wulfstan, what dire news is this? You look to have seen an avenging angel!' Janet was staring at him in real concern, for he had gone as white as a sheet and his hands trembled as he held the message. The messenger from Westminster stood beside his horse, awaiting a reply to take back to the Queen.

'Has tragedy struck at the Black Prince's court?' asked Janet. 'Tell me what's happened, in God's name!'

He did not reply but turned to the waiting rider and hoarsely muttered, 'Yes, tell the Queen I'll return as soon as I can set sail.' To Janet he added, 'God's punishment has come upon me, Sister, and I have to make amends.'

'Amends for what, Wulfstan? Wait, tell me—'

But he turned away and went to his bedchamber where he fell to his knees.

'O Christ, my Lord and Saviour, have pity on me, for I repent with all my heart.'

He was used to attending Mass and hearing the liturgy in Latin, though his thoughts often strayed, and he had got out of the way of praying privately. He added a *Hail Mary* for good measure. 'Holy Mary, Mother of God, pray for us – for *me*, the worst of sinners, now and at the hour of my death.'

It was of no use. As he begged for divine intervention, his duty stood starkly before him, like the avenging angel Janet had spoken of. His words sounded hollow in his ears, empty and unheard. He rose from his knees and returned to the entrance hall where he had left his sister-in-law; she beckoned him to the counting-house where they could talk privately. As he began to speak of his shame and misery, he broke down in tears, and Janet laid a hand on his shoulder; when she spoke her words were unexpectedly sympathetic.

'I can understand what a shock this is to you, Wulfstan, and you are right, you must face your duty by this Frenchwoman.' She sighed deeply. 'I have suffered the loss of a good husband, and compared to that, your misdemeanour doesn't seem so terrible. I shall miss you, and so will the children, but the sooner you can be on your way, the better.'

Wulfstan did not tarry. He did not want to face the shocked reactions of Ethelreda or Maud Keepence. Before he saddled Jewel, he had one more duty to perform, and he forced himself to do it. He wrote a letter to Sir William Horst, making a complete confession of his two moral lapses, accepting his disgrace and asking that Beulah be told that he had to marry a woman at Bordeaux for reasons of honour, so would never see Beulah again. This made a complete end to the betrothal, making it impossible to change his mind. Janet Wynstede promised to send the letter by special messenger, and added that if the day ever came when Wulfstan returned to England with his French wife, her offer to him still stood, with Lisette in place of Beulah. He thanked her, but could not foresee it ever happening.

As a man sows, so shall he reap. The words burned into Wulfstan's heart and mind as he rode down to Southampton and boarded a flat-bottomed ship carrying cargo. It was a miserable journey for Jewel, one more cause for self-blame, and he rode southward across country from Honfleur rather than sail round the Bay of Biscay, for the mare's sake.

He arrived at Bordeaux and the former archbishop's palace, now the renowned court of the Prince and Princess of Aquitaine, bathed in mellow September sunlight. It was evening, and the well-proportioned building was a fine example of France's many beautiful chateaux, yet Wulfstan's heart sank at the sight of it. Like some perversion of paradise, it offered an over-abundance of pleasure, an endless round of entertainment, of satisfactions that remained ever unsatisfying – banquets that satiated the appetite, Bordeaux wine to lead a man into temptation, as he knew only too well – this was more like purgatory. And for Wulfstan it was a prison.

The massive front entrance, guarded by two military sentinels, was surely not his way into the palace, and he turned to go round to the rear of the palace, a humbler entry where there would be stabling for Jewel; but one of the helmeted guards called out to him.

'Who comes hither? Answer at once!'

He hesitated, not knowing how to style himself. The other guard eyed him up and down, then nodded to the one who had challenged him.

'Sir Wulfstan? Wulfstan Wynstede?' he asked.

He inclined his head, and dismounted. After a few moments of consultation, they came over to him; one led Jewel away, and the other beckoned to him.

'Come this way, sire.'

Wulfstan followed him into the entrance hall and then along a stone-floored passage that led to a flight of stairs which he remembered, and then another long passage and more stairs that took them to the Princess's solarium where she sat with her ladies. Wulfstan's eyes swept over the group, fearing to see Lisette. She was not among them. The Princess rose, and Wulfstan bowed low to her.

'You may leave us,' she said to the guard and her ladies. They hurried out, some glancing back at Wulfstan, as if half afraid or half amused. She resumed her seat.

'Be seated, Sir Wulfstan,' she said, indicating a long stool upholstered in green brocade. 'Have you had a good journey?'

He bowed again before sitting down. 'Thank you, Your Grace, it was good enough.' (How could it be *good* when accompanied by such a calamity as this?)

'You have come promptly in answer to my message.'

'I've come to do your will, Your Grace.' He wished that she would come to the point, but she seemed reluctant to do so.

'You may remember one of my ladies, a pretty girl called Suzanne d'Avour?'

He cleared his throat. 'I believe I do, Your Grace, but it is not her that I have come to see, but Mademoiselle de l'Isle. She was the lady you mentioned to the Queen.'

'Yes, indeed, Sir Wulfstan, I was highly incensed at your treatment of her, and I blamed you for deserting her at such a time.'

He looked straight into her face, tired of this exchange which seemed to be getting nowhere. 'I did not know then that she was with child, Your Grace, but I have now come to marry her with all possible speed.'

'But perhaps not quite speedily enough, Sir Wulfstan. You have been forestalled.' Now she was clearly embarrassed. 'I'm sorry, but Mademoiselle de l'Isle is now the Countess d'Avour.'

He stared back at her in complete bewilderment, as she continued.

'The Count d'Avour is a courtly, honourable gentleman who brought his daughter Suzanne to be a lady-in-waiting. She is very young, and the Prince and I invited him to stay here for a few weeks so as to continue to see her, he being widowed with no family at home. He admits now that he was immediately taken by Mademoiselle de l'Isle, and therefore disappointed at hearing of her betrothal to you. Then you were called to your brother's home in England, and it was said that you had forsaken her. My husband the Prince told him that you had *not* forsaken her, and would return when you had finished your business at home. But then we received your letter saying that you would not be returning, and the Count told me of his own feelings towards the lady. I advised him to wait before declaring himself, to give her time to recover from your desertion. But then she became deeply distressed and confided in Suzanne that she was with child, and the girl went straight to her father the Count.'

She paused and looked at him to see how he was taking this news. He sat open-mouthed, hanging on her every word, scarcely able to take it in. The Princess made a little apologetic gesture with her hands, as if denying any responsibility for this turn of events, but Wulfstan waited with a pounding heart for her to continue.

'And as a consequence of receiving the news from Suzanne, the Count came to me to offer his protection to the . . . to Lisette. And . . . and they were married last week in the palace chapel, Wulfstan, just after I had summoned you to return. She has become his second wife, the Countess d'Avour. He already has a son who will inherit his title, and other grown-up children, so the child Lisette is carrying will not pose any problems of succession – and as her husband, the child will be looked upon as his, which he gladly accepts. I was too hasty in sending for you, Wulfstan, and I'm sorry. I simply could not believe that you would desert a woman who was expecting your child, and I was right, you have come at once. I'm sorry,' the Princess said again, and looked at him helplessly. 'You have had a great shock, I know. Shall I send for wine?'

'No, Your Grace, I have no need of wine,' he said, rising to his feet. Feeling slightly light-headed, he held out his hand to her.

'My thanks are due to you, Your Grace, and to the . . . the Count. I wish them every happiness, and hope the child will be safely born. I . . . I must return to England.'

When the Prince heard of Wulfstan's arrival, and of his interview with the Princess, he greeted him with laughter and ironic congratulations.

'God's bones, Wulfstan, you've found a worthy husband for *another* of your paramours! Now you can return to your virtuous little English maiden who's waited for you all this time. I'm exceedingly sorry to lose such a scrivener and keeper of the royal purse, but I wish you as happy as I am with my lovely Jeanette.' He lowered his voice and spoke in Wulfstan's ear. 'We're going to be the parents of an heir to the throne of England! If it's a boy he'll be second in line to the throne, and if it's a girl, well, there will be more, another chance of getting a boy!'

Wulfstan smiled and shook his mentor's hand, not having the heart to tell him that there would be no marriage to the virtuous little maiden. 'I'm needed at Ebbasterne Hall, my liege, and must return as soon as I can.'

'But you must stay overnight, to rest both yourself and that poor, patient mare,' said the Princess. 'You'll join us for supper in the hall this evening, won't you? Unless you would care to eat in private.'

'It might be best *not* to come into the hall,' said the Prince quietly, with a warning look towards his wife. Wulfstan saw it, and immediately chose to eat in the hall. He was not likely to speak to either the Count or the Countess d'Avour at table, but if he did so, he would wish them happiness in their marriage.

'Thank you, Your Grace, I shall be happy to attend you in the hall.'

In spite of his resolve to face the newly wedded couple with dignified goodwill, Wulfstan went supperless to bed that night. He chose to walk in the palace courtyard, where the rich aroma of roasting meat drifted out on the air, improving the appetites of the groups awaiting supper. Suddenly he was face-to-face with Lisette, the Countess d'Avour, and at once bowed respectfully to her.

'Good eve—' he began, but that was as far as he got, stopped in his tracks by the look of utter disdain on her handsome face, the venom in those green, gold-flecked eyes. She turned sharply away, and beckoned to her husband who was standing near and who hurried to her side. She whispered something in his ear, but the words he then used to Wulfstan were certainly not whispered.

'I never thought to see such a blackguard as *you*, taking your ease in this place again after your wicked treatment of the Countess d'Avour!' he shouted in French, advancing towards Wulfstan with his hand on his sword hilt. 'To lay your filthy hands on a virgin and force her to yield to your evil lust – you who are not fit to lick her feet, how *dare* you show your face again in this palace! You quitted it quickly enough when you left her in deep distress, and now to come crawling back, you swine, you slimy toad, you . . .'

Heads were turning in their direction as the Count roared his accusations. Wulfstan instinctively drew back from the man's fury, and was only saved from a hand-to-hand fight by the Countess clinging to her husband's arm and begging him to show mercy on this one-armed knight who had ill-used her. Grudgingly, the Count drew back, though he had not finished threatening the said knight.

'I shall tell the Prince of Aquitaine that his palace is too small to contain both you and me under its roof – and I'll be damned if I ever sit down at table with you!'

He turned to the Countess whose face was flushed, and her eyes closed as if to shut out the man she had accused of raping her.

'Have no fear, my darling,' said her husband. 'I shall go straightway to the Prince and let him choose whether we remain here and that wretch is kicked out, or you and I will quit the palace at break of day tomorrow.'

He paused for breath, and Wulfstan took the opportunity to say a few quiet words without losing his composure.

'You have no need to go to the Prince, sire. I will remove myself from your sight forthwith. Good evening.'

Whatever the Prince and Princess thought of the scene described to them by the onlookers, they took no action, but said goodbye to Wulfstan at break of day the next morning, wishing him well.

Lady Janet Wynstede's unreserved welcome on the return of her brother-in-law went some way towards warming the chill in his heart, as did the children's delight at seeing their Uncle Wulfstan again. He had clearly been missed, and not just for his administrative duties. Ethelreda and Maud were also pleased to see him, and perhaps just a little amused to hear that his rush to Bordeaux to save a lady's honour had not been quite swift enough, because an older, richer suitor had got there first. They tactfully avoided asking questions about the lady, though Janet made no secret of her gratitude towards the Frenchwoman who had taken another husband.

'It's her loss rather than yours, Wulfstan, and I know that it's come as a relief to you. That old Count's welcome to her!'

'I hope they'll be happy together,' he said with a sigh, inwardly thinking, *I hope that my child benefits from having a French Count as father*. He then had a serious conversation with Janet, asking her to explain to Ethelreda and Maud that he had cut himself off from Beulah.

'I've banished myself from Greneholt for ever, Janet, and will never see that sweet, loyal girl again. I've proved my unworthiness by betraying her twice over, and now must accept God's just punishment. I don't even regret confessing my wrongdoing, because it was right that she should know the truth. I pray that a better man than I will gain her as wife.'

His sister and two sisters-in-law evidently sympathized, because Beulah's name was never mentioned, though one afternoon he came upon the three of them deep in a discussion which ended as soon as he entered the room. How changed was Janet's attitude to her Wynstede and Blagge relations now, he thought. They had become firm friends, and Ethelreda and Janet shared their children with Maud who was now alone at Blagge House, Aelfric learning law in London, and Kitty at sixteen had been received into a nobleman's house as a lady's maid.

'It will give her an opportunity for a wider glimpse of the world,' Maud said fondly, though it was clear that she sadly missed them, Cecily's children she had lovingly brought up as her own.

Resuming the reins of management of Ebbasterne Hall,

Wulfstan realized more and more that he preferred England to France, and the satisfaction of being truly needed, particularly by the Wynstede children. He introduced Denys to the mysteries of accounting, how to keep a book of income and outgoings. Elmete and Cedric were gradually introduced to the alphabet in preparation for their tuition by one of the brothers at the Abbey. Maud taught Joanna and Lois the art of cookery, bread making and pastry for pies and tarts, and how to grow herbs in the vegetable patch of their garden. Wulfstan started Denys riding a pony, and actually persuaded Lady Janet to mount a horse again, and teach the girls to ride; having only one arm, it would be too risky for him to sit up in the saddle with a child in front of him. He discovered a deep satisfaction to be found in this service to his brother's family, and he sometimes wondered if Oswald was looking down from heaven upon his efforts. *This*, he thought, is what I can best do with my life: no more warfare, no shedding of blood in battle. And no complications with a wife like the pleasure-loving Countess d'Avour, though he often thought of the child in her womb, *his* child, as was Pieter Van Brunt. The fact that he could never have knowledge of the bastard children whose lives he had so carelessly created was a matter of sadness to him, though he would not allow himself one moment of self pity. His busy life was his shield against the loneliness and remorse that might otherwise have claimed him, and with these blessings he was resolved to be content.

And then came an afternoon in late October, when the leaves were whirling down in a keen east wind and the children were gathering wood for a bonfire; Wulfstan shivered in the counting-house, and did not hear the maidservant call to her mistress that there was a lady asking to see her.

'She's come in a farm cart, Lady, with a rough old villain sittin' up behind a great horse. She says she's come a fair way, but won't step inside without you sayin' so.'

Janet rose abruptly from her embroidery, her eyes suddenly bright and expectant.

'All right, Tibby, I'll see her straightway.' She hurried down to the entrance, clasping her hands together and murmuring, 'Let it be her – oh, Lord, let it be *her!*'

And as soon as she set eyes on the tremulous young woman, she knew her prayer was answered.

'Greetings and welcome, my dear!' she cried. 'I've never seen you before, but I think I know who you are. Is it . . . Are you Beulah? Beulah Horst?'

'Yes! And you must be Lady Wynstede!' The visitor climbed down from the cart and held out her arms. 'God bless you, Lady Wynstede,' she said, all nervousness gone. 'I *am* Beulah, and I came as soon as I got your letter.' And the two women held each other in tearful embrace for a moment.

'Come in, come in, Beulah. I'll send a man to take your driver to the kitchen and the horse to the stables. Oh, how glad I am to see you, and so will my sisters be! Let me take your cloak – and you must be hungry and cold after such a long journey, so come up to my retiring room where there's a fire, and Tibby will bring you some refreshment. Then I'll send her down to Blagge House to let my sister Maud know that you're here.'

In the counting-house Wulfstan heard the distant bustle, and wondered if he should show his face to whoever it was, out of courtesy to a visitor. He decided to leave it to Janet to send for him if he was needed.

But his love came to him uninvited and unannounced.

As soon as Janet told her that Wulfstan was at home, Beulah jumped up and asked to be taken to him forthwith; Janet led her to the counting-house, where she rushed to open the door, and went in ahead of Janet, who was about to knock discreetly.

And there he was, sitting at the table, quill in hand.

'Wulfstan! I give thanks for the sight of you again! Oh, Wulfstan, my only love . . .'

He rose from his seat and stared in disbelief, glancing at Janet to confirm that this was real, and not some wishful dream. This girl – no, this woman – was speaking words of love that he had never heard in the three years of their betrothal. His throat went dry and words failed him. He stretched out his arm, and she flung herself upon him, laughing and weeping at the same time. Janet looked on in amazement; she had always got the impression that Wulfstan's betrothed was a modest, innocent virgin who meekly obeyed her parents in all things, not a woman like this, so openly and unashamedly in love.

Wulfstan held Beulah encircled within his arm, and tears filled his eyes; his lips touched her hair as she buried her face against his chest. Janet nodded to her brother-in-law and quietly left the room, closing the door behind her, happily vindicated in her resolve to write to Beulah Horst, supported by Maud Keepence and Ethelreda de Lusignan. His last letter to Sir William Horst on the eve of his departure for Bordeaux had confessed his misdoings, ending their betrothal and setting her free. When he returned, Janet privately thought that Beulah had a right to know that the Frenchwoman had married another man. She had written to Beulah, a letter signed by herself and her sisters-in-law. And this was the wonderful result! Beulah embraced Maud who had been sent for from Blagge House, and a messenger was sent to Castle de Lusignan, where Ethelreda rejoiced for her brother.

When they had calmed down sufficiently to converse, Beulah assured Wulfstan of her forgiveness, and even expressed some concern for his two bastard children that he would never see. She told him how much she had resented the interminably long wait imposed by her father, enforcing their separation from year to year. She confessed how much she had longed for his visits to Greneholt, and how her father's restrictions had vexed her; his criticism of Wulfstan had only served to strengthen her love.

'And when we got your last sad letter of farewell, my father was greatly pleased, but I wept over your honest confession, dearest Wulfstan, and loved you for it. And somehow I knew that you still loved me.'

'Oh, dearest Beulah, I did, I did . . .'

'My mother tried to comfort me, but I told her and Father that I would never marry, because I'd loved you so long, and knew I'd never love another man. And I think that deep in my heart I knew that it wasn't the end for us.'

She lifted up her head and he looked into her wide brown eyes, so full of love. This *had* to be a dream: this sweet, forgiving girl loved him in spite of his unworthiness!

'Kiss me, Wulfstan.'

'Oh, my love. My only love.' They drew together, and after all the setbacks and obstacles they had encountered, their lips met in a long, long kiss, a kiss to drown in.

'I give thanks to God for you,' he said a little shakily. 'We'll be wedded as soon as Abbot Damian can marry us.'

'Dearest Wulfstan, nothing will ever part us again.'

But the day had not yet ended. It was after dark when they heard the sound of horses' hoofs in the courtyard, and a loud voice demanding that the door be opened.

'It'll be my father, Wulfstan,' Beulah said, 'and he's probably brought his bailiff with him, to take me away by force. He'll have discovered that the cart has gone, and the big shire horse – I got a groom to put him in the shafts, and paid a hungry beggar to drive for me.'

'Open at once!' came an angry shout from outside, and Wulfstan rose, indicating that the three women should leave the room.

'I'll deal with him, Janet; you take Beulah and Maud upstairs out of harm's way,' he said, but the new, emboldened Beulah refused to obey.

'No, dearest Wulfstan, it is *I* he has come to see, and I'll see him. Let him in.'

Wulfstan himself opened the door, because he feared that the old knight might be brandishing a sword. But Sir William brought only angry words and curses. He strode past Wulfstan and into the room where he addressed his daughter.

'Weak, foolish girl, to be led away from God and his church by this deceiver, as full of empty promises as the father of darkness himself!'

'No, Father, I am not deceived in Wulfstan,' Beulah replied quietly but with iron resolution. 'His repentance is real, and here I stay at his side. We are to be married.'

Taken aback by her attitude, so out of character from his usually obedient daughter, Sir William spoke in a softer tone, holding out his hand to her.

'Come, my poor child, come home with your father. I've promised your mother that I'd go after you and bring you back, even as the great Shepherd went out to find his little lost sheep and brought her back to the true fold.'

But Beulah shook her head, and Wulfstan encircled her within his arm.

'No, Father, don't ask me; I have fretted and pined for Sir Wynstede long enough, these three long years you have forced us to stay apart, subjecting him to all kinds of temptations. I was a girl when we were first betrothed, but now I'm a woman, no longer subject to your orders. No, don't try to take hold of me—'

Sir William was trying to grab at her dress, but she drew away, and Wulfstan placed himself between them. '*This* is my home now,' she said, 'here with my husband.'

Seeing that he was defeated, Sir William turned on Wulfstan, calling him a liar and a lecher, cursing him and threatening God's vengeance, until he had to pause for breath, and Wulfstan attempted to answer him honestly.

'I agree with you, sire, I'm not fit to tie Beulah's shoes, let alone marry her and beget children,' he said, feeling pity for this frantic, elderly man who had lost his beloved child. 'But I have learned from life's bitter experiences, and will never, never grieve her again, as God above sees and hears me.'

Sir William looked stricken to the heart, and Beulah gently detached herself from the shelter of Wulfstan's arm. She stepped forward to look her father straight in the eyes.

'God bless you, Father, and my dear mother. I shall pray for you day and night, for I don't love you any less, but you must allow me to choose my husband.'

But he was not yet ready for forgiveness.

'Stop!' he interrupted. 'I shall pray for *you* day and night, girl, to save your soul from Hell, and may this devil's spawn get his just punishment in the same accursed place!'

Forced to leave his daughter at Ebbasterne Hall, he turned on his heel, and rode away into the night with his bailiff. Beulah returned to nestle in the circle of Wulfstan's arm. He held her closely against him, scarcely able to believe this change in Beulah, and feared that he might still wake up and find it had all been a dream whilst asleep in the counting-house; but when Janet and Maud rejoined them and eagerly started to make plans for their wedding, he began to understand the truth of this beautiful woman's love, and to rejoice that the long years of separation were over. Now they were free to look ahead to a shared life with no dark secrets to hide; he was forgiven by God and by Beulah, and from this day onward he would be faithful to her.

Sixteen

1367

'It's a little girl, Wulfstan,' said Mistress Keepence with quiet sympathy, knowing that he had been hoping and praying for a son; Beulah had suffered four miscarriages in five years, but had carried this child almost to full term.

'Thank God it's over,' he said with feeling, for the cries of pain he had heard from the bedchamber had been torture to him. 'And how is it with Beulah?'

'She's very tired and needs to rest, but you can come in and speak to her just for a minute,' said Maud. 'And see the baby.'

Beulah's face was pale as she lay with her eyes closed, but as soon as she heard his voice she opened them and held out her hand; he took it in his own and raised it to his lips.

'I'm sorry, dearest Wulfstan. The wise-woman said it was bound to be a boy.'

'Hush, my love. We'll love her just as much as a boy. Let's call her Judith for her grandmother Horst.'

'Oh, how kind of you, Wulfstan! We must let my mother and father know.'

'Of course. I'll send a message off tomorrow,' he said with a smile, though he felt no goodwill towards her father who had maintained the rift ever since her marriage, and had prevented his wife from visiting them.

'She's such a pretty little thing, my mother will want to see her granddaughter.'

'She's welcome to do so at any time,' he said, and the baby let out a lusty howl. Wulfstan turned and looked at her as she lay in Maud Keepence's arms, wrapped in a bloodstained towel. He was reminded of a squirming, red-faced, squealing piglet.

'Yes, my love, she's beautiful,' he said, and leaned over to kiss Beulah's forehead.

When the news was received at Greneholt Manor, Lady Judith burst into tears.

'A granddaughter, William, and named after me! Beulah's a mother at last, what joy! We must go to see her, William, we *must*, this cruel separation has gone on long enough!'

'Calm yourself, Judith,' said her husband drily. 'I see no reason to grovel to that man. He'd probably think we'd come to mock because it isn't a son.'

'How can you say such a thing, William! I'm tired of bearing a grudge all this time, and I want to see Beulah and the baby – and the baby's father. I shall ride my own horse to Hyam St Ebba, and you can provide me with a groom for the journey.'

'And suppose I don't?'

'Then shame on you, William, and I'll go without the protection of a groom. I want to see my granddaughter, and I *will* do so, whatever you say.'

Sir William was taken aback by this defiance from his usually obedient wife, and felt much as he had done when his daughter had stood up to him like this, five years ago.

'You'll be making a fool of yourself, then. Be sensible, for heaven's sake.'

'Then let me be a fool and enjoy my foolishness, whatever you say.'

For the second time in his life, Sir William was defeated by a woman's rebellion, and it shook his faith in his own authority. Racked by rheumatism in his joints, and a stone pressing painfully and embarrassingly on his bladder, he had reason enough not to go on a long and hazardous journey; even so, Judith's determination touched something in his heart.

Suddenly he capitulated and told his wife that he would arrange a mount for her and provide a strong groom to protect her from danger.

'Thank you, William – but won't *you* escort me? It would be such happiness to be all together, and give thanks for this great blessing.'

He grunted and shook his head. 'I'm tired,' he muttered, and they both heard the sound of mortality in the words.

Beulah made a good recovery and fed her baby without difficulty. When her mother entered the room, she stopped and stared at the beautiful real-life picture of a mother and child.

'God bless you, my daughter and granddaughter,' she said, and it was a moment to remember; both of them wept for joy.

That evening Lady Judith spoke at length with her son-in-law, and learned the family news. Wulfstan and Beulah lived happily as master and mistress of Ebbasterne Hall, pending the day when his nephew, young Sir Denys Wynstede, now nearly fifteen, would take over the reins of management.

'Beulah and I have been asked if we'll stay on here then, and advise him for the first year or two,' Wulfstan told his mother-in-law. 'Lady Janet Wynstede and Mistress Keepence at Blagge House are great friends and share the Wynstede children, now growing up. One of the twin girls, Joanna, is married and has a child they both dote on. My sister Lady Ethelreda de Lusignan is widowed and has lost both her in-laws, so her eldest son, Count Piers, looks to her as the lady of the house until he marries. She too is a close friend of my sister-in-law. It's a little confusing, isn't it, with the three families, Wynstede, de Lusignan and Blagge?'

Compared to her own increasingly lonely life, the friendliness between the three families sounded enviable, and Judith inwardly resolved to keep in touch with Ebbasterne Hall, and no longer submit to her husband's blind prejudice.

On her return to Greneholt Manor, her husband admitted that he had missed her, but there was no change in his own stance. He saw and noted her bright eyes and the smiles that so often lit up her face, and could almost have envied her, but he was a stubborn man, never ready to admit to being wrong in his judgements.

Seventeen

'No, sweetheart, don't go too close to the pond, you'll get all muddy!' And drown if you fall into it with nobody by, Wulfstan added silently. The dainty little four-year-old girl turned back and ran towards him. He put his arm around her, and lifted her up. She seemed as light as a feather, he thought; a puff of wind might blow her away, heaven save her.

It was good to walk around the estate now that spring had come again, but dangers lurked at every step for the little girl, from stinging nettles to rabbit holes to trip over. He set her down but held her hand firmly as they approached the great field where tenants farmed their own strips, now neatly planted with root crops and onions, with the occasional currant bush and gooseberry. Wulfstan encouraged his tenants to grow more than they needed, and paid generously for the surplus produce, either to use at the Hall, or sell at the Wednesday market, a new venture that he had begun in Hyam St Ebba, and proving profitable to sellers and buyers. Little Judith trotted along at his side, and he looked down at her fondly. She was especially precious to her parents, for there had been no further living children born to them. Oswald's brood were growing up, but still looked to him as to a father; Sir Denys at nineteen showed every sign of being a generous, fair-minded landowner, liked by his tenants and their families. Beulah visited their homes when a birth took place, though she avoided infections that might be brought home to little Judith. Lois, now twenty-one, undertook this duty, as did Mistress Keepence; Lady Janet Wynstede was plagued with women's trouble, heavy bleeding which left her pale and tired, thankful to have her duties taken over by her sisters-in-law.

'Look. Dada, look!' cried Judith, pointing back to the Hall. 'There's an old man!'

Wulfstan turned round to see whether the man was a genuine

messenger or a beggar, and unable to decide, he went to meet him. Judith had said 'old', and as they drew nearer Wulfstan saw grizzled grey hair and a beard. The stranger also had a limp, and had lost an eye, all too typical of a returning soldier; close to, he was scarcely older than Wulfstan. And he seemed vaguely familiar, though not immediately recognizable. His long woollen cote-hardie had worn thin.

'Good day to you, stranger, and what is your business?' asked Wulfstan, at which the man stared back at him with something like reproach.

'You've done well for yourself, Wulfstan! Will you turn away an old friend?'

On hearing his voice, Wulfstan smiled and let go Judith's hand so as to grasp that of Sir Ranulf Ormiston. 'How could I not know you? Come in, come in – Judith, go to fetch mama. Step inside, let me fetch you some wine – and meet my wife; she'll order a chamber to be made ready for you to stay with us. Oh, this is splendid, Ranulf, you must tell me all your news – have you come from the Black Prince?'

Ormiston was clearly touched by the warmth of this welcome, and bowed to Beulah when she appeared to greet her husband's friend.

'I feared you might turn me away as a beggar,' he confessed to them. 'Knighthood doesn't always confer wealth and prestige, nor does it guarantee hospitality. Yes, Wulfstan, I *have* come from the Black Prince, and won't be going back, for he is sadly changed.' He took a seat, and sipped from a beaker of barley wine. 'So you're master of Ebbasterne Hall now?'

'No, my friend, only holding it in trust for my eldest nephew, now Sir Denys Wynstede, until he comes of age. My days of fighting and killing my fellow men are over, thanks be to God.'

'But what of your own estate, then?'

Wulfstan smiled. 'I have no estate, as a younger brother, but am invited to remain here as a lifelong guest, myself and Beulah and our little one.'

'No other children?'

'No, only our little daughter, but my nephews and nieces have become like my own. But what of you? Where did you get *your* wounds?'

'In Spain, mostly. The French declared war on Spain for commercial reasons, and our gracious Prince could never avoid a scrap, and joined King Charles of France to march over the Pyrenees. There was a bloody battle at Najera, and I survived it, only just. A lot of good men didn't. The Prince was struck down with a wasting disease, and hasn't recovered – none of his physicians can cure it, and when his son Edward died at six years old, he seemed to lose all pity and mercy.' Ranulf frowned, and shook his head slightly, as if trying to dispel a memory. 'Two years ago he assumed the title of King of Aquitaine, though it wasn't his to take, and he wasn't in control to make wise decisions. We were all weary of fighting, and wanted to get home to have some peace, but he forced us to stay, on peril of beheading, and those of us with no fortune . . .' He spread out his hands and shrugged.

'Good God, Ranulf, you make me glad indeed that I lost an arm. Did *you* find him difficult to deal with?'

'I've never known such a change in a man. The only person able to calm him was the Princess, and sometimes he'd listen to her, otherwise we all went in fear of his temper. And then came Limoges. That was last year, but the memory lingers on like a bad smell.'

'I heard something about a whole town being wiped out,' said Wulfstan. 'Was that Limoges? Don't they make pottery there?'

'They *did*,' said Ranulf heavily. 'The Black Prince's army was camped all round the walls, and the Prince sent an order to the Bishop of Limoges, demanding to be acknowledged as their king and to hand over the town to him. The Bishop refused, so the Prince stormed the walls and sent in his men with instructions to kill every man, woman and child, three thousand souls in a day. The streets ran with blood, I saw it for myself.' Ranulf hid his face in his hands. 'Then the Prince became so weakened by his illness, he had to hand over the rule of Aquitaine to his brother the Duke of Lancaster, him they call John o' Gaunt, and return to England. He went straight to his castle at Berkhamsted and took to his bed. They say that he raves like a madman, and the disease has reduced him to skin and bone. What an end to a great man. He'll die before his father, so won't ever be king.' Ranulf's expression was bleak.

Wulfstan found it hard to take in this changed picture of the Prince he had so loved, and served with pride. He reflected once again on the folly and wickedness of war.

'What of the Princess?' he enquired.

'Ah, poor woman, she has suffered for his sins. Former so-called friends have disappeared since they left the court at Bordeaux, and the loss of little Prince Edward must have broken her heart. She has another son, Richard, he must be four years old now, and if he lives he will become king – but the irony is that the Princess was asked to be godmother to the son of old Count d'Avour. The Count is as proud as a peacock that he's sired such a fine boy, as handsome and strong as any father could wish, and quick at his lessons. They've named him Louis, he must be about nine, born to the Count's young wife when they left Bordeaux for the Count's home on the river Avour. Mind you, there were those who said that the boy was born many weeks before his time, and yet was big and healthy, the inference being that the Count had taken her earlier, hence the need for a hasty wedding. Or else –' Ranulf grinned – 'or else some noble knight had got in there first.'

'Forgive me, Ranulf, your belly must be empty and here am I keeping you talking,' said Wulfstan, getting up. 'Let's see what our kitchen can yield, and then you'll want to rest.'

In the counting-house, Wulfstan sat and pondered on what he had learned. So his son was called Louis, and was handsome and clever, but belonged to the Count d'Avour who had denounced Wulfstan roundly; this was his punishment, he thought, as were his memories of the baby Pieter Van Brunt, belonging to a proud father who knew himself to be a eunuch, and also knew that Wulfstan was Pieter's father. And he had forbidden Wulfstan to see the boy, even on the day of his birth. He sighed deeply: two fine sons, the result of his own misdemeanours, never to be seen and acknowledged by him. And his own dear wife had given birth to one little daughter, and suffered much by repeatedly miscarrying; the one son she had carried almost to the full time had been born dead. Truly, he was justly punished, and he prayed for the grace to accept what he deserved, and to give thanks for the delicate little girl whom they both adored, and pray for her preservation. Poor Ranulf, he thought, he had fared worse in his service to the Black Prince, now upon his deathbed after committing such atrocious war crimes.

He was partly consoled by Oswald's children, and had trained Denys well to be master of Ebbasterne Hall. His other niece and nephew, Cecily's children by her first husband, had also done well; Aelfric Blagge was a well-regarded lawyer based in London, and Katrine, now Mistress Percy, was married to the son of a nobleman and had borne him a son. As for his own future, he expected to assist Denys for perhaps a year or two, but could see no further ahead. One day he might be able to purchase a house in Hyam St Ebba, sufficient for the needs of a couple with one child. It would be a sad change for Beulah, he thought, used as she was to the manor house in which she had been brought up, and then Ebbasterne Hall. He knew that her love and loyalty would surmount any lowering of their social standing, and compared to poor Ranulf Ormiston, he considered himself a very fortunate man.

Master Aelfric Blagge, attorney-at-law, was mystified by the summons to Greneholt in distant Hertfordshire; it was a long journey up from London, and he would need an overnight stay at an inn for his sake and his horse's, which would add to his client's fee. Now in his mid-twenties, he had acquired a growing reputation for winning unpromising lawsuits for honest clients, and rejecting others, however lucrative, if he was unsure of the client's integrity. But to be asked to journey so far simply to draw up a settlement of inheritance seemed unnecessary, but he supposed the client must have his reasons.

At Greneholt Manor he was welcomed by Lady Horst, a tired-looking, ageing woman who offered him bed and board for the night, supplied him with refreshment and then led him to the bedchamber where Sir William Horst lay, his skin parchment-pale, his eyes hollowed. Aelfric realized that this was to be a deathbed bequeathal, and accepted a chair to sit by the bed; Lady Horst sat on the other side, holding her husband's hand.

'Master Blagge the lawyer is here, William,' she said gently, and the old man gave a grunt of acknowledgement. His words came as a surprise.

'You're Master Aelfric Blagge, and have you got parents?' Aelfric replied that both his parents were dead.

'But your mother had brothers?' the old man continued in a weak, querulous voice.

'Yes, sire, my uncle Oswald is dead, but my uncle Wulfstan lives at his seat, Ebbasterne Hall in Hyam St Ebba in the county of Hampshire.'

'Ah!' The half-closed eyes opened and a spark of interest showed. 'And this Wulfstan, does he have a wife?'

'Yes, sire, and she is my aunt by marriage,' replied Aelfric, wondering where this was leading, and how this sick old man knew so much about his family. Lady Horst gave a little gasp, and stroked her husband's hand.

'And what will happen when Ebbasterne Hall is given over to its rightful owner?'

Aelfric was beginning to be irritated by this inquisition. 'I really do not know, sire, and the ownership is no concern of mine.'

'Well said, Master Blagge,' came the unexpected reply. 'It is a concern of *mine*, however, and now we may proceed to business.' Sir William hoisted himself higher up on the bolster, helped by his wife. 'Have you pen and legal paper? Are you ready to take down my instructions?'

'I am, sire.'

'I am the sole owner of Greneholt Manor and the estate. I have sons who have grown up and are well settled in life, who have not bothered me unduly by visiting their mother and father. They will receive half of my capital between them, and certain jewellery, chalices and gold plate, which Lady Horst knows about, and can give you details; I'll leave it to her.'

'Yes, William, I will see that they receive whatever you think is due to them,' said Lady Horst, glancing at Aelfric who nodded and smiled in response.

'Not until after I've gone, mind.'

'No, William.' Her voice shook, and after a pause for breath, he continued.

'Everything else, the manor and its estate, together with the tenants and their families, is bequeathed to my daughter, Lady Beulah Wynstede and her issue.'

The air in the room suddenly seemed to crackle as if a flash of lightning had struck: in a moment Aelfric understood all that had mystified him. Lady Horst looked across the bed at Aelfric and smiled, though there were tears in her eyes. 'Thanks be to God,' she whispered. Sir William continued speaking, though his voice was weak.

'Beulah and her issue, mind. I believe there is but one sickly daughter who will inherit from her mother if she survives, but she could be supplanted by a brother.'

'And her husband, my uncle Sir Wulfstan Wynstede, sire?'

'He will live with his wife here, with all the privileges of ownership, to care for the estate and its tenants as I have done. Her issue will be his issue also.'

'Very good, sire.' There was silence in the room for a minute, then Aelfric spoke again. 'You have made your wishes known, Sir William, and I will draw up a legal document for you to sign. But first I must ask you – is there anything else to add to the settlement?'

There was a long silence, and Aelfric was about to leave the room and commence his official duties without further enquiries; Lady Horst gazed wordlessly at her husband's face, and he closed his eyes, as if trying to blot out her unspoken plea. But he suddenly raised his head from the bolster and in a stronger voice gave vent to all that had been suppressed in his heart.

'It's high time that old transgressions be forgotten and forgiven, Master Blagge, and I forgive my daughter for choosing to marry that man against my wishes,' he burst out. 'I forgive her, and wish that . . . oh, God be merciful, let Beulah forgive *me*. Let her forgive *me!*' Tears came to his sunken eyes, and Lady Judith rose and laid her hand upon his forehead.

'Ssh, ssh, William, don't worry, it's not too late to tell Beulah you love her,' she said quietly, with a glance at Aelfric. Sir William looked from one to the other in rising agitation as he repeated, 'I want her to forgive me, Judith. I've been cruel to her and unkind, and I want her to forgive me, my daughter

. . . oh, let her forgive me, I shan't be here much longer, but let her forgive me, please, please . . .' He tried to sit up, and as Judith attempted to soothe him, Aelfric Blagge sat down again beside the bed, took hold of Sir William's other hand and spoke soothingly, with reassurance and authority.

'Your daughter will know that you ask her forgiveness. Listen: when I leave this house, I will go straight to Hyam St Ebba, and see Beulah, and tell her that you love her, and let her know about the settlement that you have asked me to draw up. I promise most solemnly, as God above sees and knows all our hearts, I will tell her, and she will know, and so will her husband Wulfstan.'

A sense of calm descended upon the room, and Sir William lay back on the bolster, consoled by the lawyer's words. His wife kissed his forehead, and looked at Aelfric with all the gratitude that she felt in her heart. He nodded, smiled and left them.

Somehow Beulah knew that Sir Ranulf Ormiston's visit had affected Wulfstan deeply, and not just by bringing back memories of war and its degrading influence on men, the suffering of the innocent and the tragic waste of it all. She understood that her husband had been reminded of the two sons he had fathered, and would never meet. She said nothing during Ormiston's visit, but on the afternoon when he left them, she sat beside Wulfstan on an old wooden bench at the edge of the grassy slope leading down to the great field, with little Judith close by, playing with a frisky new puppy. Beulah always sat on her husband's right side, so that he could put his arm around her, as he did now.

'Poor old Ranulf,' he said. 'I think he envies me, and what man wouldn't?' He kissed her cheek. 'I've done better than he has, living here with you in my childhood home. And we have our pretty little Judith; I would not exchange her for all the boys in the world.'

'Yes, we've been happy indeed, dearest Wulfstan,' she said. 'You have paved the way for Denys to take the reins of Ebbasterne Hall, and be a credit to it and to you.'

'We shall probably still be here in another five years, for I

shall go on assisting him with the bookwork,' he said. 'And
poor Lady Janet will be happy for you to go on being the lady
of the house, as she can now do so little.'

'That will be until Denys finds a wife, Wulfstan,' she said
softly. 'Ethelreda told me that he has visited Castle de Lusignan
to seek out young Sofia; she has grown into a beautiful girl,
and she's been well trained by her mother in the domestic
arts.'

'Really? I didn't know that,' said Wulfstan, frowning. 'Denys
is only nineteen.'

'And Sofia is seventeen, quite old enough to bear children,'
replied Beulah. Wulfstan held her closely against him.

'If that happens, then Sofia would be glad of your guidance,
my love.'

'Not for long, Wulfstan, for she will be the true lady of the
house, with no need for a substitute.'

He tightened his hold on her. 'My own sweet Beulah, I
will purchase a house for us in Hyam St Ebba, somewhere big
enough for a man, wife and child to live in comfortably and
close to our relations.' He stopped himself from saying the next
words that came into his head: *poor relations.* 'Oh, Beulah my
love, I could wish for a better future for you.'

She smiled, and laid her head upon his shoulder. 'There
could be no better future than to be with you, dearest husband,
and little Judith . . . and perhaps another. Let us pray for a
happier outcome this time.'

'*Beulah!* Are you saying – are you sure – can it be . . .'

'Time will tell, Wulfstan. I have gone past the time when
I usually miscarried, and I feel strong and well. We may need
a house for four.' She kissed him, and he tried to respond
lovingly, but his heart sank as he contemplated an increasingly
uncertain future. What provision could he make for another
child? – and suppose it were a son at last, what inheritance
could there be for him? Long gone were the days when Sir
Wulfstan Wynstede was Keeper of the Purse to the generous
Black Prince.

'Mama, Mama! Dada!' called a little voice as Judith ran up
to them. 'There's a man, a man on a horse, and he's coming
to see us!'

Now what, thought Wulfstan, another old soldier? A messenger from the castle? Ah, no, this was someone he had known for much of his life, Cecily's son Aelfric, his nephew, the lawyer. He rose from the bench.

'Greetings, Aelfric! Have you brought news from London?'

The rider dismounted, laughing at Wulfstan's serious face, and holding out his hand.

'Truly I bring news, Uncle, but not from London. And it's for my aunt Beulah!'